FIC
ESTILL

Estill, Katie.

Dahlia's gone.

DAHLIA'S GONE

ALSO BY KATIE ESTILL

Evening Would Find Me

DAHLIA'S GONE

A Novel

KATIE ESTILL

ST. MARTIN'S PRESS ⚬ NEW YORK

This is a work of fiction. All of the characters, organizations, and events portrayed in this novel are either products of the author's imagination or are used fictitiously.

www.stmartins.com

Design by Maggie Goodman

Title-page photo © 2006 by Neal Singleton for OPENPHOTO.NET CC: Public Domain

ISBN-13: 978-0-312-35835-8
ISBN-10: 0-312-35835-0

First Edition: January 2007

10 9 8 7 6 5 4 3 2 1

To Daniel

*Of what can we be certain
except this—that we are
fertilized by mysterious cirumstances?*

—ANTOINE DE SAINT-EXUPÉRY

DAHLIA'S GONE

I

A PROMISE CAN change a life. Even a small, casual promise extended without much thought or contemplation.

Sand Williams kneels beside her garden plot, weeding between the rows of romaine and mustard greens. Overhead a breeze blows through the palm-shaped leaves of a sycamore with its great trunk like an Appaloosa. The lawn behind the cabin slopes gently down to the Seven Point River winding through the hill country. Bright coins of light dance on the water, but the limestone bluff on the other side is cast in cool shade and dampened by a trickling seep. A wild jackrabbit keeps Sand company, sitting just out of reach and nibbling at the abundant weeds in the yard. Now and again she speaks to the rabbit, "Hello, sweet one, my little cabbage head. . . ."

Then a human voice startles them; the rabbit takes flight into the brush. "Hallo there!"

Sand looks up to see Norah Everston ambling across the yard, and a crease forms between her dark brows. Norah wears a big straw sunhat, which she has clamped to her head with one hand as she walks. The Everstons are Sand and Frank's closest neighbors, which means Norah, her husband, and their kids live a quarter of a mile upriver.

"I can't believe the damage those rabbits have done to my asparagus! Get rid of them," she calls cheerfully. Norah is forty-one, plump and fair, with light sandy hair she rolls at night into bouncy curls. "They'll tear your garden apart!"

Sand pulls off her gloves, gives a shake to her auburn hair. She is lean and tall with small round breasts.

"Don't poison your yard, Norah. The rabbits will have plenty to eat; they'll leave your garden alone."

What is it about Norah, anyway? She's a decent enough neighbor, a good neighbor. No loud music or boom boxes blasting from the vehicles her teenage kids drive by the cabin several times a day. No long-suffering dogs chained to the house, howling and barking until exposure kills them off. The next property could easily be a rusted-out trailer with a meth lab inside or a family of burglars. She doesn't know what it is about Norah. She stands up and goes to get them something cold to drink.

Sand was a correspondent for fifteen years, then worked for the World Health Organization reporting on famine and other disasters, some of them natural. One day in a small village in Kosovo, she was photographing conditions at a makeshift Red Cross hospital and walked down to the village well for a drink. There was a man crouched over the well, watching threads of blue dye swirl in the public drinking water. He was an American named Frank Mason, and he was conducting trace-dye experiments to figure out where the sewage was entering the water supply. Frank became her husband. For years they lived abroad, but something inside of her changed and she just couldn't keep covering misery she could do nothing about. Her mind doesn't work the way it used to, and she can't shut out her feelings anymore. Which is why they moved back here, just to slow down for a while. All she wants to do is putter in a garden, hear her own thoughts. Talk to rabbits. Talk to birds. Maybe this is what they mean by perimenopause.

Inside, Sand leans over the kitchen sink and splashes her face with water and then does the back of her neck. The afternoon sunlight glistens over the Seven Point River, so bright, it almost burns. A graceful blue heron flies downstream, and for a moment Sand stares at a boulder and the river rippling around that massive obstacle.

Sand Williams was born in nearby Greenville, the county seat. After high school her first goal in life was to put the Ozarks behind her. She spent most of her adult years stuffing as much distance as possible between herself and her place of origin. But when her father was dying, she returned on a small commuter plane flying out of St. Louis. The pilot flew toward the sun at dusk, and she saw once again all the rivers snaking gold through the blue highlands, the dragon-shaped lakes, even humble farm ponds glistening like molten gold. A lost place so beautiful, it stole her heart away.

The thought of her father makes her eyes fill with tears, so she splashes her face again. She inherited "the hunting cabin" from her dad. When she asked Frank if he wanted to move to an Ozark cabin, he only asked if it had running water. Frank was used to living in tents when required, but he drew a line between hauling your water and drawing it from a pump or spigot. Compared with the way they had often lived, the river cabin is luxurious: a cathedral ceiling in the living room, cedar beams, French windows, smooth pine floors, a native stone fireplace her father built himself. It was a "hunting cabin" only in the way a comfortable family names these things. Most of the locals would declare it a fine house.

"It's got running water," she'd said, and Frank didn't hesitate about moving to the Ozarks. Wherever there was karst in the world, limestone topography marked by caves and underground streams, Frank would eventually show up. So they moved into her father's river cabin eight months ago, and Sand remembers that within the first twenty-four hours, Norah came knocking at their door with some kind of Jell-O salad and a big welcome to the neighborhood. True, there was a point to the welcome. They were being checked out.

———

NORAH SIPS HER glass of iced hibiscus tea with only the slightest wrinkling of her nose. She's trying to get along. "Well, I'll get right to the point, the way you do, the way you hit the nail on the head. Lyman and I are going to visit his aunt in Myrtle Beach, and we're leaving the kids behind. Dahlia has her job, and Timothy has all of his activities at school and at church. So I was wondering if you'd check up on them."

"Check up on them?"

"It's not too much to ask, is it? I mean, since you're right next door."

She does detect a certain feeling of doubt, but when she and Frank went to New York, they left the key to the cabin with the Everstons, who looked after things. Still, watching an empty house is different from watching over teenagers on their own.

"Hmm, I don't know. What if they have a party or something?"

"Oh, they're not the type to have parties," Norah says with a little laugh. "They're good kids."

"I know they're good kids. But the one time my dad left me in the house, he came back to find a swimming pool in the living room."

"Sand, don't take offense, but our children aren't like you."

"How long will you be gone?"

"Two weeks."

"That's a long time."

"I don't mean every day. Just once in a while. You know."

"Uh-huh. Yeah. Well, I guess so."

"You promise?"

"Okay."

Norah smiles at Sand indulgently, then looks down and studies the patchy grass. "You know, if you just got out here and sprayed some Roundup on all these weeds, you'd have this lawn problem licked in no time at all."

And that just sets her off. She doesn't even really like Norah, and as soon as she promises to do her a favor, Norah feels free to criticize her lawn.

Squatting on a hickory stump, Sand reaches down between her open knees to yank a dandelion out of the ground, then wag the sharp-toothed leaves at Norah Everston. "This'll clean your blood." She plucks a narrow plantain leaf from among the blades of grass. "Rub plantain on a bee sting, pain and swelling go away." She wonders what it is about Norah that drives her to extremes. Here she is, yanking out a tangled wad of chickweed and stuffing it into her mouth.

"See? It's good," she says, chewing the tiny heart-shaped leaves. "There's nothing wrong with it. You can eat off my lawn!"

———

"THAT'S A MISTAKE . . ." Frank calls to Sand from the shower. He lathers his head and orange clay runs down his neck and chest in soapy rivulets.

"What do you mean?"

"Well, they're bound to do something, aren't they, now?" He turns his face up to the pulsing massage showerhead that her father installed. The glass of the shower door reveals an impression of his lean body. Frank has been in a cave, and even after removing his shoes at the front door, he tracked clay footprints all the way to the shower stall. "I mean they're adolescents, suddenly on their own."

Sand flips down the toilet seat and sits. "I pointed that out. I said I wouldn't be responsible if they had a party or something."

"Of course you'll be responsible. That's the point, isn't it? If a string of cars goes by our place on Saturday night, it'll be up to you to find out what's going on over there. Did you tell her about the time you flooded your father's living room?"

"I did."

"And?"

"She said her children aren't like me."

"But she wants you looking after them. That Norah . . ." Frank says, shaking his head. "She likes to play it both ways, doesn't she?"

"I didn't know what to do. I mean, they watch our place when we're away."

"Look, it's no skin off my teeth if you want to baby-sit two teenagers living alone in a house together."

"What the hell is that supposed to mean?"

Frank slides the shower door open, then reaches for a towel. "I remember what it's like to be sixteen with a dick. Personally, I wouldn't leave them alone."

"You have a dirty mind."

He buries his face into the thick folds of a towel. "Don't forget, that's one of the things you like about me."

"They're brother and sister."

"No, they're not. Their parents are married, that's all. And you really have no idea how Dahlia and Timothy feel about that."

———

THE DAY THAT changes her life begins in a slow, luxurious way. Sand awakens to the sound of mourning doves and remembers her father once said, "I hate those mourning doves!" She wonders how anyone could dislike, let alone hate, the soft cooing of doves, despise their slim, ringed necks or the cap of delicate, iridescent blue they wear on the back of their heads. Frank once said, "It's because your father hunted them. You can't shoot a bunch of birds you love."

Sunlight pours across the bed. The air smells of wet limestone, with the ethereal sweetness of mock orange and Japanese honeysuckle. Frank is snoring and she idly rubs his back. Her hand moves over his hip and down between his legs. She cups his loose balls and holds them to his body, warming them, a small gesture Frank loves. He snorts softly, then his breath falls quiet and the skin of his sack prickles, tightens around those eggs. A catbird lands on the windowsill and peers at Sand through the screen.

"And when shall we take our pleasure, if not now?"

She feels a kind of benediction in the catbird's gaze. This morning Frank is driving to Wellington to help assess the damage of the city's collapsed sewage lagoon. He'll be gone three days to a week. He'll pour blue dye into the lagoon, then begin to check the area's wells and streams. He sighs, rolls over to show her his sleep-creased face—the shadow of beard along his jaw, his golden brown eyes with flecks of jade, the thick chocolate-brown eyelashes and dark eyebrows. He leans to Sand and plucks her lips between his own, their breath stale, sweet-sour.

When Sand's mother was a girl, she loved the poetry of Alfred Lord Tennyson. Once she told Sand, "There's a line from Tennyson that goes: 'If I had a daughter, I would name her Water.'" Her mother looked down at her hands quietly folded in her lap. "But when it came time, I couldn't do it. And so I named you Sand."

LATE AFTERNOON SHE is sitting in Merlee's Café in the village of Darian. Outside, the rain pours down the windows in a silver sheath. It's almost as dark as night. Sand blots her dripping hair with paper napkins from the chrome dispenser on the countertop. Her almond-shaped dark eyes and high cheekbones suggest the possibility that her Celtic ancestors once mingled with the Osage tribe. The windows light up with a flash of lightning, followed by brief silence, then an uproarious crack.

"Yikes," Merlee says, and her hand, pushing a damp rag over the Formica, suddenly halts. "That was close." They look up at the old pressed-tin ceiling. The hanging lights flicker twice, a third time, then blink out. "Oh, fine." Merlee reaches behind the counter with an expert hand, then fires up a cigarette, which is strictly forbidden inside her own café, but when the electricity breaks down, so do all the rules.

"Daddy? Daddy, you okay back there?" Merlee sucks down the smoke gratefully and calls to her aging father, who is chopping vegetables in the tiny kitchen for the next day's lunch. "Put down the knife, Daddy. Don't cut anything in the dark—"

"Merlee? The lights went off in the kitchen!"

"Daddy, they're all off. All the lights're off! We just got hit by lightning."

Merlee leads her father from the kitchen, holding him by the elbow and steering him to a stool down the counter from Sand. Merlee is a small, wiry person with a hard, leathery face and pale blue eyes. "Looks like you won't be goin' home tonight," she says.

"What do you mean?"

"Well, the river. Keeps up like this, you won't be able to cross Old Faros Bridge."

"You know where I live?"

Merlee nods. "You're Harry Williams's daughter. He used to come in here a lot. Every Tuesday afternoon for lunch, and then later on Thursdays for coffee and pie. His favorite pie was, uh . . ."

"Banana cream."

"That's right. That's when he was driving to the Greenville hospital for his treatments, you know. I liked Harry. He always had a joke, always had a smile for the ladies."

"Yes." Sand cups her hands around the coffee mug and relishes the meager warmth. "That sounds like him."

"Harry went young," Merlee says, glancing at her father, who is wizened and white-haired, hunched over the countertop, his gnarled hands a little shaky as he reaches for the sugar dispenser and pours a stream of white crystals into his coffee. "Relatively speaking, he went young. But he aged that last year. Every time Harry came in, he seemed older than the time before."

The thought of her father's last months humbles Sand. She doesn't think she can take much more of Merlee's talk. "I've got to get home," she says, pushing her cup away.

"You're fixin' to drive in this?"

"As soon as it lets up a bit, I'll make a run for it." Without the droning of the window air conditioner, the café stinks of old grease, burnt meatloaf, and Merlee's cigarettes.

"Bridge'll be underwater."

But Sand is pricked by a mood of restlessness and wants to leave this talk of her father behind. His driving all alone to Greenville for chemotherapy . . . this woman knows more about his last days than she does.

"I'll make it."

Merlee wags her cigarette. "Crossin' a bridge in high water ain't about you. There's plenty of dead people who thought they could get over a bridge when the river was running across. They can't believe two inches of water can sweep a truck from a bridge. You were born here, so you should know. You been gone a long time, and maybe you forgot. We had a young mother, just two years ago. Drivin' home with her baby. Both of them drowned. You can't fool with a river. It's a whole lot bigger than you."

"If it's over the bridge, I won't go."

" 'Nother twenty minutes, it'll crest the bridge."

"How can you know?"

"I live here. All the time."

Is that it? The implied criticism that she left Weleda County and went away . . . and moved back only after her father died. It's true that no one from here asks her what her life was like away from here. They're all like the mother who never inquires about the lives of her grown children, shows no interest whatsoever in their accomplishments, but goes on and on about trinkets and chairs and cups she bought at garage sales, the mysterious arrangement of her pictures on the wall, as if she's slowly revealing to them remnants of the Holy Grail. In her presence her children become small once again, uncertain they're real to her, surely not as real as the trinkets she has found. And once the children are as small as cups, she picks them up and places them in her pockets for safekeeping. The mysterious smile of Mona Lisa on her face.

"I'm out of here."

"Look at the water pourin' off the gutters."

"I'll go slow. Once I'm over the bridge, I'll wait till it lets up."

Merlee shakes her head slowly as she flips out another Marlboro and flames her lighter to its end. She inhales deeply and blows the smoke in Sand Williams's face. "Suit yourself."

Sand flings open the screen door, then the storm commands her full attention. Water sluices along the sidewalk gutters, up to her ankles. She's soaked by the time she slides into the driver's seat of her Audi, has to shake the water from her hands, push back her limp, wet hair. She cannot explain why she feels this sudden need to get home, but it's an emotion that just takes hold of her.

On the drive home she starts worrying about the kids next door. Her wipers furiously scrape the windshield, affording brief glimpses of the asphalt road, the canopy of trees overhead. The first time she called to check on the kids, nobody was home. That was Tuesday, just before dinner. Dahlia, eighteen, tall and blond, works the night shift at the hospital, earning money to go to college somewhere far away. Later that night in bed Sand was awakened by the rumbling of Timothy's truck on the gravel lane. She rolled over to read the red digits on the clock—1:15 A.M. Norah would have a fit. What on earth would Timothy be up to at this time of night? When she first met Timothy, she saw a big, handsome young man, the kind old-timers used to call a "strapping young man." Then she spoke to him, and his slowness became evident. Sand and Frank occasionally hire Timothy to help chop firewood, clear brush, and haul rocks, and he's quite capable of these tasks, takes pride in his accomplishments. He isn't retarded, Norah says, but he is slow, a little different, and is enrolled in a special class at school.

The next time Sand telephoned it was late afternoon, and Dahlia answered the phone. The girl seemed distracted. Sand understood she was having an argument with her stepbrother. "Say, how are things going over there? Everything okay?"

In the background Timothy barked some retort, and Dahlia broke their conversation to cover the receiver with her hand and muffle her reply.

"God, he's an ass. He won't clean up his dishes."

"Uh-huh."

"I wish I lived by myself!"

"Have you heard from your parents? How's Myrtle Beach?"

"From what I've heard, it's still there."

A few days later Sand pedaled her father's old fat-tired bicycle over to the Everstons'. Dahlia was down on the riverbank, sunbathing topless. All she had on was a yellow thong bottom that Sand was sure Dahlia would never have worn in front of Norah, whose own sense of bathing wear ran toward black one-pieces with a thigh-flattering skirt.

"Heads up!" she called to give warning.

Dahlia's golden hair had new blond highlights. She gleamed in the sunlight. Her long limbs were oiled and shimmering like pearl. She raised her head and blinked. She'd been napping and regarded Sand with slow, sleepy eyes. "Hi."

"You were sound asleep!"

"Yeah, I got off work a couple of hours ago."

She felt that Dahlia was vulnerable, lying there almost naked and drowsy on the banks of a navigable river. With no one else around. This is the heart of the Bible Belt, where some judges still think a rape victim is at fault for wearing a tight skirt. Sand knows about those things, because she grew up here.

"Honey, someone could sneak up on you. I wish it wasn't like that, but it is."

Sand gazed up to the house almost guiltily. The wide-planked porch Lyman built, the baskets of flowers Norah hung. "Is Timothy around?"

"He's in school."

"Oh, right." Relieved, she sat down on the bank beside Dahlia. Pale swatches of Dahlia's flesh revealed that the thong was a new acquisition, and Sand wondered where you could even buy a thong around here. Wal-Mart? JCPenney?

"I'm pretty sure your mother wouldn't approve of this."

"Oh, I wouldn't do this if my mother were around. I'm doing

it because she's not. Praise Jesus, I'm alone! Even Saint Timothy is sitting at his desk in his special class. So I'm taking my opportunity. I'm letting my skin breathe." Dahlia raised herself up on her elbows, then rolled over onto her back. "So, now I'm not alone. You're watching over me."

"Is it that obvious?"

"Mom—Norah—said you're going to make sure we follow all the rules."

"Rules? What rules? She didn't tell me about any rules."

Dahlia raised her pinkie finger. "Number one: Make sure we go to church on Sundays and Wednesday evenings."

"Oh, I'm not getting into that."

"Don't blame you. It's a running family argument. You could say we're split down the middle over Mom's church. Norah and Saint Timothy are going to heaven. Dad and I are going to hell. They feel terribly sorry for us. Last week she was standing at the stove, frying bacon. 'Dahlia, this is what it's like to burn in hell— it's a pain beyond belief and it never ends.' You should have seen her chewing that bacon, so satisfied with herself."

"What are the other rules?"

"You're going to drop by to make sure I keep a clean house."

Sand picked up a flat rock and skipped it across the bright face of the water. "Your mother has been to my house. She should know better than to think I'm going to be the housekeeping patrol."

Dahlia laughed. Her laughter trailed off into silence, a silence that was not silent at all but filled by the chatter of birds and the river rippling over stones. Later Sand will think: *There were too many things I never asked her, like why she went on the night shift at the hospital.* Sand closed her eyes. The sun ran orange behind her eyelids, and when she opened them, the sky was piercingly blue. Across the river a limestone bluff towered, and her gaze rose to a small cedar tree, high up, growing from the rocks.

Dahlia sat up on her towel. She stood and walked into the river. She looked down at baby trout nosing curiously about her toes. Then she plunged into the smoother, deeper water in the middle and let out a shriek of joy, the cold spring-fed water an exhilarating shock. Sand watched her float downstream a ways. When Dahlia pulled herself to shore, she grabbed hold of the branch of a maple tree. Sand saw the way she twisted herself around to look up at the sky through the window of a single maple leaf; felt her own breath catch, for she had sometimes looked at the world this way: the sun illuminating the veins in the leaf, the cells all connected like flesh.

———

HER HEADLIGHTS POKE through the rain and the dark. The road is narrow and winding, and it's slow going in the storm. When she reaches the river, water is cresting the cement panels of the bridge. The thinnest sheath of water appears to be flowing languidly over the top of Old Faros Bridge. It looks peaceful, serene, the way the water takes the bridge. She figures there's an inch or so of water running over the bridge. She remembers playing chicken when she was an adolescent—the elation, the illusory sense that she was in control of her life when she ran a bridge in high water. Once, on a dare, an older boy named Charlie Nash drove Sand across a flooded bridge. He'd had her life in his hands, and that's how it had always seemed with her father—as if he held her life in his palm—and part of that was thrilling, that testing to see if she was still alive, for it always felt as if a swift change in his mood could obliterate her very being.

She's done it before, and she's still alive. And something deep inside of her says, Go. Now. Sand lowers her window. Just in case she is washed over, there'll be a hole to swim out.

Her heart thumps as she pulls onto the bridge. Within seconds her whole world becomes a roar of surging water, and she knows she's just done something really stupid. By the time she reaches the middle of the Seven Point River, the bridge is gone. To every appearance she is driving on water.

"Holy shit!"

She recognizes that stab of panic behind the ribs. She can still feel the cement panels beneath her wheels, but the grip of the tires is loosening. She clutches the steering wheel and aims for the two gravel ruts rising on the far bank of the swollen river. At any moment the water's force will lift her tires from the bridge. Once in the torrent, the water would overpower, hurl her to the backseat. *I'll have to hold my breath until the car fills up, hope I can swim out.*

With each swipe of the windshield wipers: *You fool! You idiot!* Sweating, jaw grinding, she presses her foot down on the accelerator. Her wheels plow water. At some point she stops breathing, as if the slightest movement of her breath will cause the vehicle to be swept away. *If I can hold my breath,* she thinks, *I'm still in control; I'll make it to the other side.* The entire passage is only a minute or two, but the seconds seem to elongate, drip over the physical cup of reality into something like a falling dream.

The Audi leaps onto the bank with the clutch of gravel under the wheels. Sand pulls onto the road, rams the car into park. *You idiot!* She hears her daddy yelling: *How the hell did you manage to stay alive in China or Africa? You almost got yourself killed at home!*

She twists around and peers out the back window. The bridge has disappeared. No sign of a bridge at all.

She sits there panting for several minutes, trying to calm herself. She's just done something that's expected of "outsiders," and she suddenly wonders what Frank is doing. If it's raining like this in Wellington, he might have to start the dye tests all over again.

"I almost made you a widower," she whispers in the car. Then another voice rises from beyond the resonance of all the daily static, the guilt and memories, the fluctuating self-esteem. *Yes, you did, and now it's time to go home.*

She closes her window and slops back a wet lank of hair from her eyes. In a storm in Kosovo, in the village where she met Frank, the rivers flooded, and when it was over, there were starving dogs perched in the limbs of trees. Cows sleeping on roofs. A drowned child was found wedged between the wheels of a bicycle. What she recognized as clear and imminent danger in another land is somehow less obvious in a place she has so thoroughly domesticated in her own mind.

When she reaches the cabin, she pulls into the drive and sees in her headlight beams the river pouring swiftly over the grass, swirling around the trunk of the sycamore, a good ten feet above its normal boundaries. Tree limbs and debris bob wildly. Sand remembers the kids next door.

What if Dahlia left for work? What if she tried to make the bridge? Has the thunder frightened Timothy? The electricity's probably down. She imagines him sitting alone in the dark, wondering where his sister is, wondering why everyone has left him on his own.

———

THE EVERSTON HOUSE is dark, which always makes a place seem empty. Lyman Everston is a carpenter and he built the place himself. It's a modern log home with lots of windows that gape darkly, like hollows in the earth. Timothy's pickup truck and Dahlia's Ford Taurus are parked beside the house. So Dahlia didn't attempt the drive. Sand climbs the porch steps, gets out of the rain. Dahlia's flip-flops are set neatly beside the mat. Sand knocks, and when no one answers she cups her hands around her face and tries to peer through the watery oval of glass on the salvaged antique door.

"Hello! It's me—Sand!"

She can make out the rectangular block of a plaid sofa. Something white at one end. A pair of large athletic shoes dangling over the sofa's arm. Sand calls again and gets no response, so she tries the door. As is often the case in the country, the door is unlocked, and she walks in. She feels for the wall switch beside the door and flips it up and down to no avail.

"Timothy. Timothy, is that you?"

When Timothy fails to answer, Sand crosses the living room, leans over the sofa back, and finds him lying there, asleep. "Timothy, wake up." She jostles his shoulder, feels his muscles tighten beneath her hand.

"Ugh." He rubs his eyes.

"Timothy, it's me—Sand—from next door."

"Mrs. Mason?"

She doesn't go by the name Mason, that's Frank's name, but she doesn't correct the boy. She only wants him to understand who she is.

"Yes. From next door."

Timothy bolts up, then lazily scratches his head. "Mrs. Mason, what are you doing here?"

"I'm checking up. Are you all right?"

"I was asleep."

"Well, that's a feat."

"What?" Timothy peers up at her in alarm. "No, ma'am. My feet weren't on the couch. Not touching the couch. I didn't dirty the couch."

"Hey, that's okay. How long have you been asleep?"

"I dunno. It's dark."

"It's dark, all right. The lights are off. You must sleep like a rock. There's been a nasty storm. The river's up. I just came over to make sure everyone's okay. Where's Dahlia?"

"She should be at work."

Sand shakes her head. "No, her car's outside."

Timothy's gaze shifts to the coffee table, and he frowns. "I dunno where she is. Maybe she's asleep."

"Doesn't Dahlia get up at five for work?"

"Usually. Usually she gets up at five o'clock."

"Well, did she?"

"I don't know. I was asleep. I got home from school, and a little while afterwards I fell asleep—right here on the couch."

"Well, then I guess we better check on her. Lead me to her room."

"Okay. Okay." Timothy stands and towers over her. He shifts his weight fretfully from side to side. "Mrs. Mason, my feet weren't on the couch."

"Oh, Timothy, I don't care."

"Mom would. Mom would care. We're not allowed to put our feet on the couch. I wouldn't want you to tell Mom I put my feet on the couch, because I didn't. I didn't do that."

"Timothy, I couldn't care less. I'm not going to tell your mother your feet were on the couch."

"Okay. 'Cause that's the truth."

"Fine. I just want to make sure you're both all right and not afraid."

"Okay," he says. "Okay."

Sand follows him through the dark house. Timothy knocks on his sister's door. "Dahlia?" He leans to the wood and crosses his arms over his broad chest. "Get up! Mrs. Mason is here from next door."

His voice is met by silence, the beating of rain on the house roof.

"She must be asleep," he says.

"Dahlia?"

Sand raps her knuckles on the door. Nothing but the sound of rain. "Dahlia, wake up. . . ."

She feels strange, as if the molecules of herself are shrinking back from her skin into some deeper core, as if protection lies there. She places her hand on the knob and turns, and the door swings open, loose on the hinge. She makes out the lumps of furniture in the room, then the shadowy outline of Dahlia lying on her bed, the mirror, the dresser, the window. There's something wrong about the window. A wet gust blows the curtain into the room. Sand sees the broken glass. The rain-soaked curtain. She turns to the bed.

"Dahlia?"

For a moment she and Timothy just hang there in the dark, unable to move closer to the bed. Now she can see the faint gleam of

Dahlia's hair, her arms folded over her breasts, a white sheet covering her chest. She hears Timothy breathing, a harsh sound like a horse in stable.

"Stay here, Timothy."

"What's wrong?"

"I don't know."

Her closed eyes, her stillness. The whiteness of that sheet in the dark, and the way it's smoothed over her. How everything in that room has the stillness of a mausoleum. Dahlia's hands crossed upon her breast. The remote expression on her face. Sand feels her own body sway as she reaches for Dahlia's wrist, her fingertips absorbing the coolness of Dahlia's flesh, the strange slack quality it has. She searches for a pulse, first at the wrist. Then at her throat.

But Dahlia's throat is as lifeless as her wrist. Sand's breath comes hard and fast. She feels dizzy and wonders if she might pass out. Dahlia's skin is cool. *This isn't possible; this isn't right.* Sand's fingers trace along Dahlia's neck, feel a queer rupture of flesh. Her fingers draw back from a small puncture wound on the girl's throat.

"Maybe there's something wrong with her." Timothy has not left the spot where Sand told him to stay. Her gaze rakes over him, a long shadow standing there in the gloom as he stares at his stepsister. "Maybe she's dead."

Sand reaches for the headboard, then stops herself, steps back, clutches her arms to her chest so she won't touch anything. Timothy comes forward in the dark, and she is momentarily overwhelmed by her own terror. She can hardly explain what she feels—*this isn't happening.* This can't be happening.

"Timothy . . ." Her voice comes out harsh.

"Yes?"

"Do you, do you have a phone that isn't cordless, a regular phone with a cord?"

"Umm . . ." Timothy's eyes narrow as he thinks her question through. "Yeah. In the kitchen."

"Go back to the living room and sit down on the couch."

"What is it?"

"She's cold."

"I'll get a blanket, then."

"No. Just do what I say. Wait for me."

"All right."

Alone, Sand stares down at Dahlia. Her slim hands peek out from the long sleeves of cotton pajamas. Sand replaces Dahlia's hands the way she found them and covers them with her own, wanting to impart some warmth back into the girl. She thinks of Dahlia driving by the cabin, elbow sticking out the window, a flash of flaxen hair, a single finger raised to say hello. *I was supposed to look after you.*

She sees Dahlia floating downstream on the river just a few days ago, reaching up to catch an overhanging branch, and staring as though at God through the focus of a single leaf. "I'd like to go to school up in Chicago," she confided to Sand. "If I don't make it as an architect, well, I could become a nurse."

Sand claps a hand to her mouth, feels a rising wave of nausea, and has to run to the bathroom, vomit into the toilet bowl. She starts to flush and stops, drops the lid down instead. Darkness makes it worse. She stumbles around in the kitchen until she finds the phone.

"I need to speak to Tom Gravette. This is an emergency."

"Sheriff's on patrol."

"Put me through. This is Sand Williams out past Old Faros Bridge. I'm reporting a homicide."

The dispatcher's voice breaks, "Good Lord. Where are you now?"

"The Everston place on County Road 5683. The daughter is dead."

"What's the phone number there?"

Sand lowers the phone. "Timothy, do you know your phone number?"

In the dark she can see his rigid profile, his fingers knotted in his lap, body tense, waiting, as he sits, as directed, on the sofa.

"Yes."

"What is it?"

He tells Sand. The dispatcher says, "I'll get the sheriff. Stay on the line."

Sand is on a first-name basis with Sheriff Tom Gravette because her father ran the town newspaper. Sand has known Tom Gravette since she was a kid and he was a deputy. After college she'd always called him "Tom." No doubt Tom Gravette and her dad had shared a few bottles over the years, and probably a number of confidences, secrets that never make it into a newspaper that always reports a woman's age and address in the crime column for a parking infraction or a failure to yield.

"Sand?" Tom's voice crackles over the line. "What the hell's goin' on?"

"Dahlia Everston is dead. She's been killed."

"What? How's that?"

"Tom, everything's dark. I think I saw a stab wound on her neck. She's cold."

"Don't touch anything! Have you touched anything?"

"No—yes—"

"What?"

"I touched her. I took her pulse—no pulse—there's no pulse."

"Are you alone?"

"No. Her brother is here."

"He found the body?"

"No, we did. At the same time."

"Listen to me, Sand. I'm over by Harrison's Mill. Damn bridge is impassable."

She feels her knees sinking. "Oh. Yeah. Sure." She leans over the kitchen counter. Before her lies a plate of homemade cookies. By the smell of them, chocolate chip, and the sweetness of them makes her stomach flip.

"Are you listening to me? I'll have to come the back way. Through Rayburn County. It'll take an hour. Can you handle it?"

What difference does it make if she can't handle it? "Yes, sir."

"Callahan's on your side of the bridge. Expect her in twenty, thirty minutes. She's the closest deputy. You okay?"

"Okay."

"You know what to do. Secure the scene!"

"Yes, sir."

She hears the sound of her own voice, and once again she's her father's little girl.

2

OBJECTS SEEM TO swell out of the darkness and take hold of her attention. A needlepoint on the wall that Norah has stitched. The small rectangle of the *TV Guide* that Timothy taps with his fingernails. He sits as if the least noise will cause him to bolt and stares at the dark square of the TV screen. Sand sinks into an easy chair, leans forward, and takes a deep breath.

"Timothy, do you understand what has happened here?"

"I don't know. You mean with Dahlia?"

"Yes."

"There's something wrong with her."

"Yes. There is. She's not alive anymore. She's dead."

"She is?" His brow furls. He looks down, links his hands around one knee. "I thought maybe she was."

He's quiet after that. Sand sees him frowning in the dark. Her own understanding is overwhelmed by shock; tears fill her eyes. "A deputy will be here soon. We just have to wait."

"All right. I'm going to pray now," he says.

Then he knots his large fingers together and bends his forehead to his joined fists. Sand watches his lips move as he says his prayers. The rain comes steadily.

———

WHEN SAND WAS ten years old, her father took her to a murder scene. Harold Williams II had been a war correspondent in Korea, and when he returned to Greenville to take over the family newspaper, the only thing missing in his life was a son. But Sand's mother suffered complications in childbirth, and after Sand was born it became clear that the only son Harold Williams would ever have was Sand. So he began to train her as he would have a son. The first "toy" that caught his full approval was a Brownie camera she requested for her sixth birthday. Four years later she was on her second camera, a little Nikon with a flash. The week before Christmas, the year Sand was ten, her father got a call shortly after suppertime. The big house on Mellon Avenue smelled of fresh pine boughs, oranges, and cinnamon. The living room sat in hushed darkness except for the twinkling colored lights on the Christmas tree. When her father hung up the phone, he stared at Sand, then finally said, "Want to go for a ride? Take the camera."

"Where are you taking her?" her mother asked as she untangled metal tinsel hanging over her arm.

"Newspaper business. Time she started cutting her teeth."

Her father's truck smelled of sun-worn, cracked leather, spilled bourbon, and the Cuban cigars he obtained through a mysterious and extralegal process that had something to do with a reporter in Canada. It was a cold night and a hard snow had fallen. Her mother shouted down the drive, "Take her mittens!"

"Oh, hang it, Pauline! She's not a *sissy,* she's a girl!"

At the age of ten Sand knew that mittens got in the way of taking photographs.

Her father drove recklessly in any weather, and the snow on the unplowed country roads caused him to skid and swerve. Halfway there Sand remembered to snap on her seat belt. He pulled out a silver flask he kept stashed in the glove compartment and began to prepare her for the murder scene. "If you can't take it in this business, Sand, you'll never make it. Don't show emotion. Don't show fear."

Bourbon. Maker's Mark. He wiped his mouth with the back of his hand. His eyes had that glittery excitement they got whenever he was on his way to something terrible. By the time they arrived at a small, worn-out cabin on the edge of the county, he was half drunk, but it was always hard to tell with her father, because, as with everything, Harry Williams didn't let it show. Or maybe he was such a practiced drinker, this level of drunkenness was evident only in the carefulness of his stride, the acuteness of his stare. It never occurred to him to ask if she wanted to make it in his business. The generational ascension to the helm of the family-owned small-town newspaper was unquestioned in his mind, like the tides. He had followed in his father's noble footsteps, and Sand would follow in his. All they had to do was get over this one obstacle of her being a girl, and Sand's father, who considered himself a progressive in his day, didn't feel that hurdle was insurmountable.

Two deputies' cars were parked on the shoulder of the road before a mean little cabin. Her father pulled up behind the sheriff's vehicle. "All right. This is your first murder," he said. "What are you going to do?"

"Keep my mouth shut and my eyes open."

"That's right. Watch everything. You want to say something? Stick your eye to the lens and take a photograph. We'll discuss it *later*. You don't cry. You don't show fear. And remember, what did I tell you about wild dogs?"

The lesson of the wild dogs had many applications in life.

Sand saw her breath in the frozen air. "Don't let them know you're scared. Stand still. Talk to them in a commanding, even voice. Don't ever run, or they'll attack." If, following all these precautions, she was still beset by the pack, she was to roll on the ground, protect her face and innards. Find a rock. Bash them in the head.

"That's right, kiddo. There's the key to the whole world!" He took the last swallow of bourbon, then flung the empty flask down to the floorboards by her feet. The cab of the truck stank of Maker's Mark. "You want them to respect you? Never let them know you want to shit your pants. Let's go!"

The cabin was made of hewn logs. Dim squares of yellow light spilled from the windows. In those days the sheriff was Bank Cruder, who had the reputation of throwing people through plate-glass windows "when they needed it." Sand's father knocked for admittance, and the sheriff let them in. The cabin had no electricity, only a gas lantern, which fascinated Sand and maybe explained why three minutes passed before she understood that the man seated in a rocker was missing an apple-size chunk of his skull. The cabin wall behind him was splattered with his brains. She turned to a scarred wooden table where an old man in bib overalls sat. His name was Orlin. He had called the sheriff's office. His folded hands were resting on the table, his eyes oddly vacant. He had come to visit his friend, John Day, and found him unfortunately dead.

One of the deputies pointed to the outline of footprints leading through the snow to a pond in the backyard, so the men decided to search for the murder weapon beneath some broken ice.

"You stay here," her father said. "Stay at the table with Orlin. Just don't look over there," he said, meaning the corpse. "You'll be fine."

Was Tom Gravette among them? No. He worked for the city then, and this was a county jurisdiction. Sand figured the men were shocked by the murder and wanted to go out back to drink and smoke, and her presence would shame them into an uneasy temperance. So she turned her attention to Orlin, a haggard-faced man with a bald crown and long thin wisps of dirty gray hair that fell past his shoulder blades. Orlin made for bad company. At first he refused to look at her, but once he did he would not break his pitiless gaze. After what seemed a very long time, Orlin snapped his fingers and said, "Things change. Like that!"

"They did for him," Sand said, nodding toward the man sitting in the rocker.

Orlin nodded thoughtfully. "They changed right quick for John Day."

Do children understand these things? She knew she wanted the men to return. To squelch her fear, she raised her camera and took his photograph.

"Hey, what're you doin' there, vixen?"

"You called the sheriff. I'm taking your photograph."

He went quiet after that for about a quarter of an hour. Lamplight flickered over his craggy face. Once he wagged his finger at Sand and asked if she listened to the devil like John Day. This turn in the conversation made it impossible to sit down. So she stood and prowled about the main room of the cabin, taking pictures of Orlin, the table, the lamp, even poor John Day came into her viewfinder. The crater in the dead man's skull. The angle of his teeth, for his head had fallen back and his lips held a grimace of pain. She felt a mounting anxiety, so she took photographs of everything that frightened her. The next day her father published the one of Orlin on the front page of the newspaper. Some of the others were considered too graphic for print.

That night was the start of her career.

She heard men yelling from behind the cabin and looked out the window. They were all running back from the pond, the whole group of them, screaming and gesturing with raised hands.

"Get out! Get out!" Her father wildly motioned for Sand to run.

She opened the back door, but before she could step out, Sheriff Bank thrust her aside. She landed on the cabin floor with a splinter in her left thigh that didn't work itself out until she left home for college. The other deputies stepped over her in the crush. Her father grabbed her up like a sack of flour. Next thing, Bank Cruder had Orlin bent over, his mouth smashed to the table, lips warped into a semblance of protest.

"Goddamn it, Orlin, you threw your shotgun in the pond! Your damn initials are on the stock."

Later that night, when they got back into the truck to leave, her father said in his laconic way, "You did good, kiddo."

3

ON THE DAY of Dahlia's murder, Patti Callahan is sleeping in. She dreams of a large, boxy house she can never afford on her deputy's salary. Room after spacious room, every floor softly carpeted like a cloud beneath her bare feet. In this house there's a place for every desire in her life. On the third floor she discovers a ballroom for dancing. Even in sleep she's worried about paying high utility bills, but she wants the house. She calls her mother and says, "This is the house I was always meant to have."

Patti is the only female deputy in Weleda County. If a girl is molested or a woman assaulted, whenever the men in the department encounter "a woman thing," Patti is the deputy to call. The night before Dahlia is killed, Patti was awakened at two A.M. by the ringing telephone.

"Patti?"

Patti rubbed her eyes, glanced at the clock—another night of sleep lost. "Yeah?"

Deputy Welles had made a routine traffic stop.

Woman weaving down the road with a baby in the backseat. He claimed he saw drugs in plain view.

"I asked her if she had other drugs in the car, and she said yes."

"Uh-huh."

"Well, she just came out with it, and told me where the drugs are. So put on your raincoat, Patti, and find you some foot-long plastic gloves. Get down to the station right away, 'cause we got one for you!"

Patti stepped into the utility room they used for interrogations and slammed the door shut. Standing with feet apart, arms crossed in front of her chest, she faced a very tired woman. Patti's body was shaped like a barrel and conveyed authority. She was packed into her brown uniform so snugly, it looked like it hurt. She had a beautiful face with a porcelain complexion easily given to a rosy blush whenever her emotions flared, but in her uniform with a holstered pistol bulging at her hip, softness was not a quality that Patti Callahan conveyed.

"Take it out," she said. "Right now. Every bit of it."

The prisoner pulled down her underpants and reached up between her legs. Patti watched the woman remove from her vagina two syringes and needles, a cosmetics case filled with packets of methamphetamine and other unidentified drugs, even lipstick and paper money. All this done with the boredom of a woman hunting through a large and messy purse.

"You have a baby?" Patti said. "You live like this, and you have a twelve-month-old baby?"

When she got home about five, she sat on her front porch for an hour just to compose herself, for the female prisoner had shaken her. Patti lives in "town," a hamlet really, in a bungalow on a small patch of yard she has turned into flower beds. She sat on her porch sofa in the company of her cat and thanked God she lived in town. She'd had it with "the country life." At night you could hear the coyotes yipping in the hills. Quiet? You've got to be kidding. Out in the country she'd found herself living under the path of air force jets that trained over the area and broke the sound barrier several times a day. Then there was the fighting cock the last renters had left in a cage under the carport. Patti fed the rooster and let it peck around in the grass, but one night coyotes acquainted themselves with the fighting cock, and the next day she found its forlorn head in the yard, strewn feathers everywhere. The final straw was the afternoon she looked up from reading *Better Homes and Gardens* to find a Limousin bull at the window, observing her every move, his hot breath clouding the glass pane. Somehow a ton of bull had climbed onto her porch. Now what? How do you get a bull off the front porch? She was sure he'd break his leg on the steps, and then what would she do? She called her neighbor and said, "Jack, one of your Limousin bulls has wandered onto my front porch."

"Well, what's he doin' there?"

"Right now he's starin' at me through the window. Come and get him."

Country life? You can have it, Patti thought. In the middle of the night it's always quiet in town. She calmed herself by petting Noodles, her cat, and sniffing a few sprigs of lavender she plucked from her garden path.

The next morning she feels groggy from lack of sleep. She has the day off, so she putters about the house, doing laundry, dusting, mopping the hardwood floors. In the afternoon she takes a nap and awakens to the first cracks of lightning in the sky. She stands on the porch, calling for Noodles, but he must have taken shelter elsewhere. The wind comes up, and there's a brief pelting of hail, followed by pounding rain. Patti is fixing supper when the lights go off and she is thankful she has a gas stove. She lights a candle. She sets a place for herself at the kitchen table, and just as she is about to sit down, she gets the call. The body of an eighteen-year-old girl has been found. Probable homicide. Patti is the only deputy who has a direct route, with no river crossings or floodplains between her house and the Everstons'.

She grabs her rain slicker, blows out the candle, and opens the kitchen door. A bedraggled Noodles whips between her legs into the safety of the house. He finds her pork chop on a plate and drags the meat across the floor to a protected cubbyhole between the cupboards and the fridge, and there, over the course of the night, chews it down to the bone.

Patti Callahan is the first deputy to arrive.

———

THE SHORT RUN to the porch leaves her soaked to the skin. She aims her flashlight beam through the oval glass of the door, sweeps the room, then sees two figures sitting in the dark.

"Deputy Callahan!" she calls as she opens the door, and the woman says, "Thank God." Her flashlight beam picks up Sand Williams's face, the short tousled auburn hair, the high cheekbones and dark eyes squinting against the light. Williams is enviably tall and slender, and in the dark, Patti thinks, she could be my age.

A sternness enters Patti's voice, a reminder to the witnesses that she is not on anyone's side. "Are you alone?"

"Except for Dahlia, yes."

"Where is she?"

"In her bedroom. Lying in bed."

"And you and the boy found her?"

"Yes. This is her brother, Timothy."

"Hello, Timothy."

"Hello." The boy glances at Patti warily, then bows his head and folds his big hands together.

"What are you doing, Timothy?"

"I'm trying to pray."

"All right. You stay on the couch and pray. And you," Patti says, her flashlight beam gesturing to Sand, "show me where the victim is."

———

"HOLD THE LIGHT steady," Patti says. She unbuttons Dahlia's pajama shirt, with its childish pattern of romping puppies. At the sight of Dahlia's pale breasts and naked abdomen, the flashlight wobbles in Sand Williams's hand.

Dahlia Everston has been stabbed over and over, and Patti feels herself reeling. "Can you hold the light steady or not?"

"If I can stop shaking, I can! My God . . ."

Deputy Callahan notices her own hands have also lost their steadiness and asks more gently, "Are you going to be sick?"

"I'm not sure."

"If you're going to be sick, don't do it in here, okay?"

"I thought it would be safe here."

"Why did you think that?" Patti stares grimly at what had recently been a beautiful young woman. "You were born here. It's a violent place. You're Harry's kid."

"So?"

"You've seen things."

"But this is my neighbor! This was a live girl just a few hours ago."

"And how do you know that? How do you know she was alive a few hours ago?"

"I don't," Sand says in a hushed voice. "I don't know why I feel that. I mean there's no reason for her not to be alive."

"All right, I'm fucked up, too. Let's move on," Patti says. "Go see what he's doing in there."

Sand Williams feels her way through the darkness to the living room. Patti Callahan counts the stab wounds automatically—seventeen, maybe twenty-some cuts. "Sweet Jesus," she says to herself. She takes hold of Dahlia's cold, stiffening wrist, turns her hand upward, and looks for blood and tissue under the fingernails.

Sand Williams returns and says, "He's just sitting there."

Patti says, "There's no blood."

The two women exchange a glance, then look down at Dahlia, whose eyes are closed as if in sleep.

"We'd better get a rape kit," Patti says. Her heart flutters inside her ribs. "She's been stabbed over and over, and there's no *blood*.

Come on, help me turn her over. This can't be right. Where's the blood?"

How heavy she feels. How cold. How absent. Patti is still shocked by the heaviness of a dead body, as if the soul is a life force opposing gravity.

"What's wrong with him, anyway?"

"He's slightly retarded. We're not supposed to use that word."

Callahan examines the bedding and slowly shakes her head. It's clean. No blood anywhere. She points the flashlight to the victim's slender back and ticks off the details aloud. "No lividity. There's not even any sign of blood pooling *inside*. She's been washed. Even her nails are clean. At least to the naked eye."

"She was *washed?*"

"She wasn't wearing these pj's when she was stabbed. She's been moved and cleaned. Then dressed in the pajamas. Whatever she had on is a bloody mess and full of holes. Unless she was naked at the time. Where's the blood? It's like she's been drained."

"Oh," Sand moans, "who could have done this?"

———

PATTI IS ABOUT to question Timothy when the electricity returns. The TV screen abruptly blooms with colored images; voices and canned laughter explode into the living room. "Goddamn!" Sand Williams shouts, and claps her hands against her ears. Timothy blinks slowly at the light. He examines a miniature living room on the television screen, then turns and stares at Sand.

"What did you say?"

"The sound frightened me."

"Mrs. Mason, you should never take our Lord's name in vain. People go to hell for that."

Then to Patti's amazement, the boy starts watching TV. He seems to know they require his attention, but he's clearly torn. His head swivels to the wide screen, as if something has shifted inside his brain. In the face of a sitcom he knows and loves, this miserable house where his sister lies dead is slipping from his mind. As Timothy watches TV his mouth slackens, then hangs loose until the tip of his tongue gently rests against his lower lip. An absorbed look comes over his face, for apparently he knows these characters and the way their lives turn into funny lines. Patti stands there silently observing, feet spread, arms locked in front of her chest. Then she strides swiftly across the room and punches the power button. The thunderous TV world folds into a silent, blank square, and some emotion she can't quite name flits over Timothy's face.

"Son, where'd you say your parents are?"

So Patti goes to the kitchen and makes the call that destroys two parents' lives. The aunt in Myrtle Beach answers the phone, for Dahlia's parents have gone out to a movie. They will be laughing for a little while longer before they hear the news. On the phone the old aunt becomes hysterical, and Patti is trying to talk her down when she notices a plate of chocolate chip cookies on the countertop.

She tells the aunt to call her pastor or another relative, then hangs up and finds the baking pan, still lying in the sink. Tilting the pan beneath the kitchen light Patti counts twenty-four perfectly round, greasy impressions, then counts the cookies on the plate. She pulls the trash bin from beneath the sink. The torn cardboard cylinder for the ready-made dough lies at the top of the heap. She takes her tweezers from her pocket, carefully lifts the cylinder and bags it as evidence.

"Who did the baking, Timothy?"

"I did. I know how to do that. I made them for a snack when I got home from school."

"How many did you eat?"

The boy's eyes flicker thoughtfully as he contemplates her, his wide-set eyes failing to reveal anything. "I did laundry. Then I fell asleep. I forgot to eat them."

"You went to bed?"

"On the couch."

"With the TV blasting away?"

"It doesn't bother me," he says. "Listen, I'm real hungry. Can I have those cookies? I made them an' all. Really, they're mine."

"Oh, I'm sorry, Timothy. They're evidence."

"Evidence of what?"

"Everything here is evidence, just because it's here. Where your sister was killed. I don't know what it means."

"But I didn't eat supper!"

"Why not?"

" 'Cause I fell asleep! I told you that."

Finally Sheriff Gravette arrives. Tom Gravette is lean and wiry, with thinning hair cropped short, his face deeply lined but softening with age, like a sorrowful basset hound. The sheriff regards Sand Williams with something like embarrassment. Patti knows Tom ordered flowers to be sent by the department for Harry's funeral, but somehow the florist screwed up, the flowers did not arrive in time, and Tom was furious. She is sure he feels he should have dropped by to see Sand in person—and now this. He brusquely motions to Patti to walk him through the murder scene.

"What do we got here?" His smoky breath blooms in her face.

"Multiple stab wounds. No lividity. No sign of blood. Tom, there's no blood anywhere. And look at the way she's laid out."

"Very careful-like."

"Yeah. She was dressed after she was killed. I unbuttoned her."

"Where are the parents?"

"Myrtle Beach."

"And the boy?"

"He's been in the house the whole time. Said he heard nothing. Slept through it all. On the sofa. Williams awakened him when she came to check on the kids. All the doors were unlocked, but the window's broken over here."

"Hmmm. What do you think?"

"Well, there's somethin' wrong about it, isn't there? The boy, he's retarded an' all, but there's something else wrong. Nothin' here makes sense."

"Cover her breasts an' bring him in."

"IS THIS HOW you found her, son?" the sheriff says.

The boy nods blankly, then his gaze slides to the broken window. "He must've came in through the window there."

"Who do you think did this, Timothy?"

"I guess a burglar did."

Patti notices a subtle shift in the sheriff's face, the slight narrowing of his eyes suggesting a spike of interest. "Why would you say that?"

" 'Cause he took some stuff."

"He did? What did he take?"

"I don't know. I think some jewelry."

"What jewelry is that, son?"

"Her stuff. I'm not sure what all. A necklace she wears with a purple stone. She wears it all the time. She never takes it off, ever."

"And it's not here now."

"Well, she's not wearin' it."

"No, no she's not. What else is gone?"

"Usually she wears her opal ring."

Gravette sends Timothy back to the living room, then has Sand Williams brought in for interrogation. "Did you see anything out of the ordinary today?" Williams emits a strangled breath, then tries to compose herself.

"You mean strange cars, that sort of thing? No. No. But I was gone most of the day."

"Where?"

"Greenville."

"What'd you do in Greenville?"

"I went to the doctor's."

"You okay, Sand?"

"Yes. I'm okay," she says with a trace of annoyance. "I went to lunch. I went to Wal-Mart. I made the rounds."

"Where'd you eat?"

"The Lime Tree."

"Any good? I hear it's good."

"Yeah. It's good. I had the potato leek soup and eggplant Parmesan. You know what this sounds like, Tom?"

"It's called protocol. You're gonna have to make a statement. That's the procedure we fall back on. Can you go over to your house with Patti and get your camera?"

Sand pales. "You want me to photograph?"

"I already called Riley Gant seven times and he don't answer his phone. In weather like this, who am I gonna get out here?"

Sand crosses her arms tightly in front of herself. "So you want me to photograph the scene while you're checking me out."

"You got any problem with that?"

Sand just stares at him.

Finally she says in a whispered voice, "I was supposed to look after her, Tom."

Patti drives Sand to the cabin in her department-issued Crown Victoria. They ride in awkward silence down the road, Patti's headlights pinwheeling through dark trees. The rain comes steadily, but the storm has spent itself. Her wheels splash through deep ruts on the gravel lane, the car's flank scraping branches bowed low from the storm. The police band radio comes on, announcing more distant emergencies: an old man's soaked and frightened cat stranded high in a tree, a domestic disturbance. Patti breaks the silence.

"The Everstons—they're not from here, are they?"

"No. They're 'foreigners.' He's from Colorado, I think; she's from Kansas. I believe they met down here."

"Do they get along?"

"Of course they do. As far as I know, they do."

Patti says quietly, "We went to school together, you and I."

"We did?"

"Yeah, when you were a senior, but you wouldn't remember me. I was in first grade."

"Right." Sand turns to stare out the passenger window.

"So why'd you come back?"

"I got tired. I thought it would be simpler here. And for a while it was."

"I've always lived here. Never been further than Kansas City. Never even flown on a plane."

"Never?"

"Once. I took off before the plane did. I don't think that counts."

"You going to be like these old women who never leave the island where they were born?"

"Only if I can."

"Never leave, or get old?"

"Here we are," Patti says as she pulls into Harry Williams's drive. She parks close to the lane, for the gravel is cluttered with broken tree limbs and debris. "Nice place."

"My father liked nice things."

As they step inside, Patti takes a breath as if she may smell him yet, his faint odor of sandalwood aftershave, his mouth scented by cigar smoke and frequently bourbon. Harold Williams II. *Harry.* Sand turns on the light. Patti is shocked by the cabin's dishevelment. Harry had a woman who came to clean once a week and always used an orange scent in the vacuum cleaner. *Jesus, the place is going downhill.* The faint odor of unwashed dishes drifts in from the kitchen. Patti finds herself swallowing hard.

Harry's daughter says, "Always been a slob. Even as a kid I only cleaned my room under threat of punishment. Guess I've led a nomadic life. By the time a place got dirty, I was moving on."

"Where's your camera?"

"In the bedroom. On the bureau."

Patti doesn't want to see Harry's bedroom and says huskily, "Go get it. I'll wait here."

She walks over to the fireplace, where his arrowhead collection remains on the mantel, just as he left it. You can still see Harry in the place, despite the untidiness. She remembers him leaning back in his blue leather chair when he was sick. His features seemed harsher, more stark. She didn't know how to comfort him and began to rub his feet. Harry closed his eyes and a blissful smile came over his lips. "A sense of touch," he said, "is the most important thing between two people."

"Why don't you tell her, Harry?"

Sand's footsteps sound in the hallway and Patti quickly swipes at her eyes. She turns, but the glistening of her tears is seen. Sand halts in her tracks.

"I knew your father," Patti says.

"Oh. In what way?"

"Not the way you think."

"Well," she says, holding out two cameras. "Which do you want, silver-based or digital?"

"Bring 'em both. We'll use the digital for backup." Patti sniffs and searches for a tissue in her hip pocket. "He had a woman came to clean. She probably could use the work if you wanted her."

——

THE HOUSE IS in perfect order. There is no sign of a struggle in the Everston home, no blood found anywhere. Dahlia's body testifies that a terrible battle ensued, but if it took place inside the house, the slaughter was followed by an exquisite cleaning job. The mattress beneath her body is damp, where someone scrubbed out stains. This is one of the details never released to the media. Dahlia bled on her bed, but the bloody sheets and whatever she was wearing when she was stabbed to death are gone. Even the evidence of cleaning has disappeared. Which is to say, nothing about the scene makes sense.

By midnight more deputies arrive to dust the place for fingerprints. Patti stands with Tom Gravette and Sand Williams out on the porch. Tom smokes a cigarette. The rain has ceased, but water drips from the eaves and the limbs of trees. Patti shivers in the damp. The swollen river roars in the dark.

"You want to see the brains of the department?" Tom says to Sand, waving the burning tip of his cigarette at Patti's head. "There's most of 'em, I know that." Patti sips a cup of coffee and gently blows the wafting steam. "So you're head investigator on this, Patti-cakes. First bright deputy on the scene. Plus, we got ourselves some kind of woman thing."

"A *woman thing*?" Sand says, bristling.

"Well, we got ourselves a dead woman here, now, don't we? And it's likely to be sexual. Nothing else makes sense. Looks like a break-in burglary, but no burglar I ever knew bothered to clean up. If they did, I'd hire one myself. And burglars don't kill, not in my experience. Now, a sex criminal might, but taking so much time to clean up after himself—that's a big risk."

In her other hand Patty holds a sticky pastry, for the deputies have brought provisions for a long night. She chews a mouthful of cinnamon bun, then brushes crusty white flecks of icing from her lips. "Where's her clothes? The bedding, the things used to clean up?"

Gravette stubs out his cigarette on the sole of his boot, then stuffs the butt into his trouser pocket. "Maybe he burned them, or he buried them. You tell me. How do you get rid of stuff fast?"

Patti stares out through the dark to the turbulent high water. She wedges another third of the bun into her mouth and chews thoughtfully.

"You walk out of the house. The river takes it away."

4

AT DAWN THE high water has begun to recede. Patti Callahan and Sheriff Tom Gravette are floating downstream through a thin layer of morning fog. Patti leans over the prow of the johnboat as they skim along the far side of the river. They are searching for evidence: a set of twin sheets, towels or rags used to clean up blood, knives, the missing jewelry, and whatever Dahlia was wearing when she was stabbed to death, for nothing had been found in the house or on the grounds. A nightgown maybe, since she slept during the day. Patti lifts her hand and calls, "Hold it!"

Gravette maneuvers the boat over to the spot; Deputy Callahan stirs the river with a long hooked pole until she snags something white. She flings it down sopping into the bottom of the johnboat: a disposable diaper.

As they glide along the riverbank, scanning tree roots and branches hanging over the water, they pick through a number of ragged T-shirts, some too obviously weathered to be what they're looking for. Three more diapers show up, along with a diaper lying on the bank that's full and crawling with maggots. Tom Gravette mutters, "People are filthy," and tosses it back.

They find several pairs of underpants: torn white and flowered briefs, three pairs of men's Jockey briefs, old gray-weathered flags with torn elastic bands dangling from tree branches, the gifts of high water. Tree pollen floats on the surface, and Patti has a sneezing fit. By hour two she has run out of Kleenex and is reduced to blotting her nose on the sleeve of her uniform. The landscape is dotted with blue plastic Wal-Mart bags snagged on limbs during the flood, and she muses philosophically over each kind of refuse. The bags are a sign of monopoly in rural areas.

"But why's there so much underwear?"

Gravette pushes back the brim of his cap and wipes sweat from his brow. "Why do you think? Kids out here foolin' around."

Their attention is caught by bright gleams of the occasional aluminum can or bottle nestled on the riverbed, which they don't bother to collect. They find shoes of various sizes, mostly tennis shoes. Where the river divides for a small island, a left loafer sits perched on a root knob. A mile down they find its mate.

Patti imagines that the boy, Timothy, had a sudden inspiration about what to do with the bloody sheets and clothes and rags. Where else could that much evidence have gone? Quit jumping to conclusions, she tells herself. What was it Tom always said? *Every time you make an assumption, you make an ass outta you an' me.* They have no evidence against the boy, and this bothers her, too, for it came out that Dahlia had been dating one of Patti's relatives. Tom suspects the boy, too, she's sure, because the sheriff had acted as if he were on the boy's side. Late last night, about four A.M. while the deputies continued to sift through the house, Patti and the sheriff sat down in the living room with Timothy Everston. "Let's go back to the missing jewelry," Patti said as she studied the boy. "Why do you think the killer took those particular pieces of jewelry?"

" 'Cause they were on her, I guess."

"But why would he take just those? You see what I mean?"

"No."

"Well, a burglar who comes through the window to rob and murder, why wouldn't he go through her jewelry box?"

"The rest of her stuff isn't worth anything."

"Uh-huh," Gravette said, nodding. "That makes sense, son. But after all the work of cleaning up—I mean, he had to be in your house a long time, so why didn't he walk into your parents' room and take your mother's jewelry?"

"He probably ran out of time and had to leave. How would I know?"

Gravette leaned forward and made a church steeple with his fingertips. "Tell me, what do you think he did with the cleaning things?"

Timothy stared at them, baffled, then shook his head. "I don't know what he did with them. I can't know the answer to that. How can I know that answer? Why are you asking me things I can't know?"

"You could take a guess. Use your imagination. We need some help on this, son. We got to find who did this to your sister."

"This is just like school, isn't it? When they ask me things. I'm always guessing, but it doesn't mean I know."

Patti said, "So let's go over things again. How did you find your sister?"

"I told you!"

"Well, tell us again."

"Why?" He leaned forward. "Aren't you listening?"

The sheriff opened his hands, placating. "Hey, don't get mad, Timothy. We're just doin' our job here. You're not mad at us, are you? When did you wake up from your nap?"

Timothy fumed. "When Mrs. Mason came into the house and woke me up."

"And what time do you think that was?"

Timothy rocked back and forth. "How would I know? I was asleep. Didn't you write it down? I'm trying to answer your questions." He hunched over and knit his hands together, his brow furled in anger or frustration. "I'm gonna be sick if I don't eat something!"

Half an hour later the parents arrived. At the sight of his mother, Timothy broke into tears. The mother, Norah, wailed on the verge of hysteria. Lyman, Dahlia's father, stood there woodenly, a dried-out husk, wordless, emptied of feeling. Patti had seen that faraway look on the faces of survivors at scenes of terrible accidents, as if their attention lay beyond the world they were in and part of them was still walking around like a ghost in a life that was utterly and forever beyond their reach. Now that his mother had returned, Timothy wept openly. Despite his hulking man-size body, he became a little boy in need of his mother's lap. Norah clutched her son's large blond head to her breast, then saw Sand Williams standing across the room, and cried out, "How? How could this have happened, Sand?"

Patti took hold of Sand's elbow and quickly steered her out the front door. "Go on home," Patti said. "Get some sleep. We'll be in touch."

Sand nodded, but at the sound of Norah's wail inside the house, her knees started to buckle and she grabbed hold of the porch rail as she unsteadily climbed down the stairs.

"Can you drive?"

"Yes."

"Then get out of here."

Patti looks up from the murky water of the Seven Point River. As the boat passes through Harry Williams's property, she sees Sand on the cabin deck. For a moment Sand looks a bit like Harry, the way she raises one hand to wave. She has her father's nose, his tall, thin carriage that eventually became slightly stooped. Patti gives Sand a long, slow nod of recognition, then returns her gaze to the river bottom. God, what a night. And going by Harry's cabin on top of everything.

"Timothy seem nervous to you?" Patti asks Gravette.

"Yep. It didn't look right to me. The boy acted more nervous than grieved."

"And he didn't start to cry until the parents arrived."

"I know. Hey, look—look over there, something pink. . . ."

Patti snags a rosy T-shirt into the boat, but shakes her head. "Looks kind of small."

"Hang on to it, though. These girls nowadays are wearin' toddler clothes."

They search three miles of river. Down one bank, then up the other side, down the middle and back once more. Patti thrashes the thick vegetation along the bank with her stick.

"Watch your hands," warns Gravette.

"I'm mad. I want to find something."

"You find yourself a cottonmouth, I don't even got a snake kit on me."

"I'm being careful."

"Reed got hisself bit by a copperhead last spring. Went down to the basement to get a cooler and the damn snake was curled up inside. Disturbed that demon after a long winter's sleep, so them fangs was full. They had to cut his arm from the wrist to armpit and put him on IV to drain him out at the hospital."

"I remember."

"Patti, look out, there, that's poison ivy."

They search downstream as far as the Crossing Over Bridge, a loose plank bridge with rope railings swaying high above the river. The Crossing Over Bridge is owned by Jarrett Maberly. From a distance the bridge looks like nothing more than twigs improbably crossing the sky between two limestone bluffs. Patti has walked the footbridge a couple of times to deliver a summons to Maberly. The bridge terrified her. Beneath the planks lay nothing more than a rope-and-wood-branch girding. The whole bridge swayed and jostled as she inched across, clinging to the rope railing, looking down to see distant splinters of river gleaming between the planks.

That morning the curved rope bridge emerges dreamily from the mist as white beams of sun cascade down through a green canopy of trees, and it seems to Patti they are indeed crossing over into the unknown. By the third turn of the johnboat, the sun has burned off the mist, and as they troll one more time beneath the bridge, Patti sees a flash in the water. An iridescent gleam of light catches her eye, and she thinks of Dahlia's missing opal ring. But no, it's just the bright rainbow flank of a river trout. About 10:30 A.M., their heads aching from hunger and the sun's glare off the water, Patti notices a mysterious scent beneath the Crossing Over Bridge, a hauntingly beautiful fragrance she can't place but somehow reminds her of being a child at her grandmother's house, the simple pleasure of sleeping in an old iron bed until early in the morning, when, as she remembers it, a certain mockingbird would come to the window and awaken her. Her first grasp of the day arrived with the smell of chicory coffee and oatmeal cooking in the kitchen below, and she realizes she felt perfectly at home in the country when she stayed at her grandmother's house. Perfectly at ease. With a swell of emotion, Patti rubs her bloodshot eyes, then immediately regrets touching her eyelids with the same fingers that are picking garbage. She rinses her hand in the river and splashes her face clean, and this memory of her grandmother with her wide baggy dresses and straw sunhat, her bunioned feet and knees the size of cauliflowers, is swept under the boat like the shadow of trees.

Patti does find a pair of Ray-Ban sunglasses perched on a massive gray rock in the middle of the stream and calls, "Dibs!" for them, revealing a childlike happiness with the find. She holds them to the sky and squints through the frames. "They're not even scratched! You know what shades like these cost? A hundred bucks or more." She tries them on, then leans over the prow and admires her reflection on the river, for she seems a changed person in sunglasses, sophisticated and worldly, with a touch of sensuality.

"What's the best thing you ever found in the river, Tom?"

Gravette pulls his cap bill lower to shade his eyes. "Once I found a watch. A lady's Rolex. Stainless steel. Sitting all by its lonesome on a gravel bar. Got it fixed for thirty bucks and gave it to my wife. She's still wearin' it. Not that she cares about time."

Patti's mood is buoyed by the salvaged sunglasses, but Gravette begins to complain. "How can we find nothin'? It couldn't all just disappear. Surely somethin' would have snagged."

"Yeah. Unless the river won't give it back, or we're wrong," Patti says, "and he didn't throw the stuff into the river."

"Don't you go actin' like we know who did it yet. We got a procedure."

"Okay. It could be an unknown perp, or someone else she knew. You think she was raped?"

"Twenty stabs? Lot of passion. Sounds sexual to me."

"Rape isn't—"

"You know what I mean."

"Dahlia's ex-boyfriend . . . he's a distant relation to me. A cousin of a cousin—something like that."

"I thought maybe he was."

"I'll go talk to him," Patti says.

5

SAND SEES THEIR johnboat moving downstream with Patti Callahan leaning precariously over the gunwale as she scowls at the river. They're searching for evidence, for nothing was found in the house or on the grounds. They must be exhausted, she thinks. Sand is so tired, her limbs are trembling, vibrating with weariness, and yet she knows she won't sleep. Too tired to sleep, an exhaustion so profound that when she tried lying on the sofa, the room swirled around her head as if she were drunk and couldn't find a stable place to sink into unconsciousness. She has to keep moving for a while.

Her father's empty bird feeders, their roofs bristling with long nails, dangle lethally from the limbs of a pine tree and sway with the breeze. Sand goes to the small metal trash can wired to the corner of the deck, pries off the lid and fills a plastic scoop with sunflower seeds. She steps down to the lawn and approaches one of the bird feeders her father built, lifts the spiked roof. Her father always complained about the nuisance of squirrels, how they would break into the feeders and make themselves gluttons on seed that he had bought for the birds.

"They're nothing more than rats with puffy tails!"

He had tried a number of designs to outwit the rodents, each feat of cunning engineering soon overcome by the industrous squirrels. He could not stand his lack of control over the situation, his charity to the songbirds foiled. Once in a mood of righteous indignation, he called Jarrett Maberly, a known pot grower from a family that once owned stills, and paid him to drive over and shoot all the squirrels in his yard, then take them home to his wife for stew.

Her father called her during the great squirrel hunt. It was after midnight in Kinshasa, where Sand was lying on a lumpy bed in a hotel where the hot water stopped after six P.M. But who wanted hot water, anyway? The night was sweltering and she slept nude, the sheets soaked when she was awakened, her body aching for water. Behind her father's voice Sand could hear the blasts of a shotgun firing.

"What the hell is going on?"

"I'm getting rid of those thieving squirrels!" It was dusk in Missouri, and he was seated on the deck, drinking dry martinis and marshaling his single trooper to destroy the enemy.

"You've hired an assassin?"

"Maberly—he's a good ol' stick. My father knew his father well."

"That goes without saying."

Sand leaned against the wall and ran a hand through her damp and tangled hair. Her family's need for intoxicants was as strong as the Maberly tradition of making them. During the Prohibition years Sand's young father had run errands for his dad, loping across the swaying rope bridge with an empty lidded tin that swung heavily on the way back.

"Over there," her father shouted, "over there, damn it!" and Sand pulled the phone away from her ear.

His voice crackled over the line. "So I got your number, kiddo—where the hell are you, anyway?"

"I'm in Kinshasa."

"The Congo?"

"Yes—two forty-three—that's where I am.

"Christ, that's no place to be. Jarrett—pile 'em up over there!"

"Dad, are you sure retirement is a good idea?"

"Best thing I ever did. Now I have time to take care of all the things I never had time to do when I was a workingman."

The sharp report of the gun disrupted their conversation. "Like killing all the squirrels in the neighborhood?"

"They steal the seed! I'm teaching them a lesson they won't forget."

"Dad, that shows great confidence in the size of their brains."

"So what are you doing in the Congo?"

"People are starving. Several million people. And I don't seem to be doing very much at all. I'm rather pointless, if you want to know. We've got birdseed coming in, but the army is diverting it. I'm just making a record of all the obstacles."

"You be careful—you hear me?"

Her father's tone threatened punishment should she fail to heed his words. Sand thought she simply couldn't deal with him, didn't want to tell him about the sea of distended bellies she'd seen. She pressed one hand over her eyes and rubbed, as if she could erase the blowflies, the dead bodies strewn along the road, lying where they dropped, frantic, bony arms fighting for the few provisions being unloaded from the back of a truck.

"Daddy, think about a part-time job. Or maybe volunteering at the school."

"Hell, retirement's the best thing I ever did."

But retirement didn't serve his health, for in three years her father was dead. In that remaining time he did, however, figure out how to foil the squirrels. When her father left this world, all the bird feeders in his yard were armed with nails. Any squirrel foolish enough to jump down onto a feeder would be instantly impaled. She is still unsettled by the sight of his bird feeders with their spiked roofs dangling lethally in the air. She's reminded of thick stucco walls, bristling with broken glass, to protect the houses of the wealthy in places like Latin America.

———

"I'M TRYING TO reach Frank Mason, my husband. I called his cell, but there's no answer." Sand twists the spiral phone cord around the tip of her index finger, the way she did as an adolescent talking to boys on the phone.

A voice drawls, "Well, no, no, don't suppose there'd be. I believe Frank's in a declivity. He won't have no reception long as he's down in Bell Valley. Now, when he drives back up the hill . . ."

She collapses onto the bed in hope that a horizontal position will encourage an hour or two of sleep. The mattress is a soft cushiony expanse, for she and Frank laid egg-crate foam over the hard bed her father had favored in life. Most of the time she does not think about the simple fact that she's sleeping in her father's bed. But this morning her body hunches into a fetal position, and she feels herself open to the knowledge that this is the bed he slept in, the bed where he died, and she weeps over the loss of him, as if this loss will entwine itself with every other loss she encounters in the present, and perhaps for a long time to come.

The murder of the girl next door is another entry into a world of personal loss, for it triggers her deep well of grief. When she photographed Dahlia's body, Sand remembered her father's last moments as he left the fragile shell of what he had been. Sand mistook his final breath for a continuance, and it was the hospice nurse who said, "He's gone." She did not throw out his bed; she found she couldn't part with it.

She lies in a swell of tears as if she might merge with the bed on which he'd lain and contact him once more. She read somewhere that after about a year of use a mattress is teeming with microscopic bugs that crawl off our own bodies. If we were consciously aware of this disgusting fact, we would be tossing out mattresses right and left, but on this forlorn morning she welcomes his bugs and feels no compunction about their bugs and his mingling, setting up living colonies beneath their dreams, creating an invisible empire of life that continues to thrive after one of the hosts departs from the world. Sand weeps and feels herself reeling on an inward spiral of descent.

When she hits bottom, she's jarred by what comes forth.

It is dark. She is sitting with Timothy Everston in the living room. Waiting for help. Waiting for the deputy. The presence of death like a cold void in the dark. His sister dead. The soft murmuring of his voice in righteous prayer. Sand feels split open and a child's body-memory spews up through the cracks. How can she explain to Frank, or anyone, that sitting in the dark house with Timothy, waiting for Callahan to arrive, she began to have feelings of that other time—the uncertainty and terror of a child abandoned by her father in a cabin with the bloody remains of a man. A child wondering: *Why has my father left me alone with the corpse?*

Lying in bed, she folds her knees and bows her head to them. When the father betrays, the body curls over to protect the unconsciously remembered attachment to the mother. She observed the fetal curl so many times in her travels. In hospitals and refugee camps. Babies, children, adults pushed beyond what they could psychologically endure all curled into a fetal pose. Whether seated upright and rocking obsessively over their navels or lying on a bed of dirt, instinctively, under duress, the body curls over the navel to protect the site of one's bond to the lost mother host.

That morning she sees vans with the logo of the regional TV station rumble by the cabin, en route to the Everstons' place. There go the vultures. With the smell of death in their beaks. At noon she reheats some minestrone soup and turns on the TV. Norah is on the screen, seated on the sofa where Timothy slept through the storm. Norah looks ravaged, wrung-out, fifteen years older than she was ten days ago, and yet there's a defiant rage in her grief that makes her eloquent, almost beautiful. Lyman sits beside Norah, with his long hair pulled back into a ponytail. He is silent, a shade of himself, a coalescence of vapors whose shape your hand might pass through.

"We live on the Seven Point River," Norah says in a shaky voice. "The authorities believe the intruder was from somewhere else. A drifter, probably. Our daughter worked nights at the Greenville hospital. The killer may have followed her home or been on the river and decided to target her. The evidence shows he broke our daughter's bedroom window and entered the house that way. So, if you've seen anyone suspicious in our area, please call. We need your information to find who did this to her."

The camera turns to the beautiful newscaster, a stylish redhead with sharp little glasses so fashionable this year. "Local law enforcement are searching for leads in the brutal slaying of young Dahlia Everston. Dahlia was stabbed late yesterday afternoon in her home while the parents were out of town visiting relatives."

"Please," Norah says. "We need your calls. Whoever did this to Dahlia is still out there. We're begging for your help. Any detail you might have could make the difference."

Sand holds a spoonful of soup over the bowl until that mouthful goes cold. Slowly she becomes aware of two things: her heart is beating faster at the sound of Norah's voice and she knows who killed Dahlia, who stabbed her body twenty times. Her spoon clatters against the bowl. She is next aware of a dull pounding at the front door. She crosses the living room to the noise of several fists banging on wood. Her figure behind the glass ignites a general clamor, a barrage of questions, demands.

"We just want to talk to you! Your perspective on the tragedy!" A flashbulb goes off in her face. The lovely newscaster screws her long finger into the doorbell. Sand locks the chain into place, then cracks the door. The door springs forward and strains against the brass chain.

"Sandra—Sandra Mason?"

The sheriff never calls her "Sandra" *or* "Mason." She is Sand Williams and everyone in these parts, who knows her family, knows Sand by the name she has always used. It's Norah who insists on changing her name to suit the impression she feels Sand should make on the world. Norah once helpfully suggested she go by

Sandra, because Sand is a silly name, and Mason, well, that's obvious. Mason is Frank's name. She should take her husband's name. That's why the boy called her Mrs. Mason.

"You're looking for Sandra Mason?"

"Yes, are you Sandra Mason?"

"No! There's no one here by that name."

Sand heaves her shoulder against the door and wrenches the dead-bolt lock. The front door shakes against the jamb as she turns on her heel and quickly retreats. Journalists, she knows, are ambitious enough to walk around the cabin, look into windows until they find her or the room that is curtained from their view.

She grabs two pillows from the bed and drags the heavy duvet. She finds sanctuary in the second bathroom and locks the door for good measure. Sand folds the duvet lengthwise inside the claw-foot tub, then climbs into the nest with her pillows. It's not the first time she's slept in a tub. Once in India she slept dry in a tub as several inches of dirty water flowed over the parquet floors of the Alhambra Hotel.

WATER HAS ALWAYS been involved in everything she's ever had to do with Frank. The hidden bond, the name her mother did not give her. When Sand met Frank in Kosovo, he asked her what she was doing, and she said, "Taking pictures of things that frighten me." Heavy storms had been forecast for the following days, and everyone worried that the riverside village would flood. "Like that old bridge over there. It's gonna go. And after that, how will we get supplies?"

The bridge collapsed the following day in the flood. Her eye to the lens had noticed the pilings giving way, and sandbags could not dissuade the river. Cholera became the next concern and how to secure more medicine, since truck convoys now had to come around from the south. As long as there was firewood, people could boil water to drink. But even firewood did not last. One night, after the hospital announced that antibiotics were running low, several of the foreign workers took refuge in a dry barn, for there were rumors of armed insurgents roaming the hills.

They didn't make wars, she thought; they cleaned up after them.

When Sand thinks of her first longing for Frank, she remembers the earthy scent of hay. She had not been with a lover in more than a year and wasn't looking for one. They bedded down in the barn that night, Frank lying beside her. For several hours she had noticed that whenever the two of them were physically close, the air between them seemed to coalesce into a moving current. They couldn't sleep. They began to whisper, soft and fervently, as if their two hearts were making a nest. She asked him how he had got into this sort of life, and he told her a story about a flight he once took out of Idlewild, back when he was in college. The plane just didn't take off. The cabin got hot, the air went stale, but the plane remained fixed to the tarmac, and no one would say why.

Finally the first-class curtain was flung back and Frank's uncle Walter emerged, two sheets to the wind. "Frankie," he shouted, surprised by the coincidence. "They tried to bump me! Can you believe they bumped me?"

Airlines were always over-booking, and Uncle Walter didn't consider himself a passenger who could be bumped. Incensed, he called the FAA and informed them how much of the GNP he made in a year; then another first-class flier met with disappointment, and Uncle Walter was drinking champagne.

In the barn Sand felt something scurry along her hip and hoped it was only a mouse. Frank said that's when he understood about the little club the wealthy had. He wasn't going to be in their club, and he didn't want to be.

"I think I like you, Frank. What are you, some trust-fund kid who took a different path?"

"Uncle Walter was my guardian."

"What do you mean?"

"My parents were killed in a car crash when I was eight. Uncle Walter was my guardian. I lived in boarding schools. Near Houston."

"That's terrible."

"It was, sort of."

Sand's mother had also died young, when Sand was twelve, and she told Frank she couldn't imagine losing both parents in a single day.

Frank whispered in her ear, "Being alive is a very fragile condition."

"It is," she said softly. And then they were in each other's arms, and a sort of fusion took place. Sand gave her mouth to him, and she soon lost any sense of where he began and she ended. She had never known the meaning of "swoon" before—the closest thing had maybe been an overindulgence in slivovitz and those few minutes of profound euphoria and physical pleasure before the room began to spin, but this wave of pleasure kept on going. She seemed to lose her solidity and sank into a warm, oozing puddle, and yet she remained, still grasping his body to hers.

She could hear the Swede snoring to her right and the French guys moving restlessly, but she couldn't have stopped kissing Frank for all the world. Finally the Aussie called out in the dark, "Hey, give us a break, would you?" And startled, they both gasped as they broke apart and lay panting in each other's arms.

Sand stared into the dark pools of Frank's eyes, amazed by her body's response to him. She was enchanted, she supposed. They lay with their faces close, inhaling each other's breath, falling into each other's eyes. Frank brushed some pieces of hay from Sand's damp cheek, then slipped his hand under her sweatshirt and covered her breast.

"I'll be very quiet."

"We'll never be quiet," she whispered hopelessly. But she had already surrendered herself and lay there immobilized, even as the others turned restlessly about.

"Don't do it. I'm not on birth control."

"I won't."

His fingers caressed her breast with soft, feathery strokes. "You're really not on the pill?"

"No—I wasn't expecting . . . to be with anyone."

"God, that's hot."

"It is?"

"Yeah."

The way they lived, traveling from place to place, sex was often a casual business. The French guys had a name for it: *le sex hygiene.* Sexual intercourse was like brushing your teeth or taking a needed shower—for hygienic purposes. For health. That she was unprepared for easy sex made him want her all the more. Frank stroked her breasts until her whole body was shot through with quivering. She felt the walls of her vagina cramp, flutter, then finally give in to their longing and pulse. They seemed like enamored witnesses to what was happening to them, how open she was to his touch, how exquisitely vulnerable.

Frank whispered, "We'll let them sleep now, if they can."

A sense of shame came over her then, a feeling that often plagued her although a lot of the time it didn't make sense. It was just life on the road. The intimacy of relative strangers. People who lived as they did—how many times did they catch one another crouched over a hole in the ground, pants around their knees, or naked, taking a field bath with a strung blanket and a bucket of water. And now Sand's fellow travelers in the barn knew she had just had an orgasm with the water guy. She rolled away and, put her spine to Frank, but he pulled her close and spooned.

"I just want to hold you," he whispered, and they fell asleep that way, two little orphans in the dark.

In the morning over campfire coffee, the Aussie laughed and said it was damn good thing she didn't have birth control. Sand was saved from a long ribbing, for the Brit got a radio message that the foreigners were to depart immediately. The WHO workers had to report back to a base camp to the east, while Frank was to head south. In fifteen minutes a Red Cross van arrived for them, and they hustled to the next village, where they said good-bye.

"What's going to happen now? When am I going to see you again?"

"Look," she said. "About last night . . ."

"Don't start that," he said. "I'm from Texas; you're from Missouri. It could be beautiful."

"I don't even know you."

"Quit thinking. Are you scared of falling in love?"

"You bet I am." Sand hopped back into the van. And that was the last she saw of him until India, when she walked into his tent. Once more water brought them together. She'd been sent to assess mysterious symptoms caused by a foreign chemical company's pollution of the water. Frank was monitoring the chemical spill into the local river. She recognized Frank Mason from a distance: something about his bearing caught her eye, then he turned and Sand saw his face just before he ducked into a tent where he kept his mobile laboratory. She shocked him when she walked in.

Frank dropped the glass vial in his hand and didn't even look at what had shattered against the crown of a rock bulging from the ground.

"Another disaster." Frank whispered, "I was hoping you'd show up."

Sand knew what she wanted then, and that time she didn't hesitate. It was as it was in the barn, that breathless joy. He sat them down on a camp stool in the stifling green light of the tent. "You're all I've thought about for the past three months. Are you on birth control?"

"No . . ."

"No?" he asked, anguished.

"No! I didn't know I'd be seeing you."

"Oh," he sighed in relief. "That's hot. . . ."

Two years later they got married in Colombia.

———

SHE MUST HAVE slept, for a knocking on the bathroom door awakens her, and she wonders how the reporters got into the house and if she can slide down the bathtub drain and make her escape from there.

"Sand?"

"Frankie—" What a relief. She clambers out of the tub, unlocks the door. Frank looks haggard, worried. "I see you got my message."

"It's on the radio. Is it true?"

"Yeah." Then she feels his strong arms around her back, lays her head on his shoulder, breathes in the acrid, musky smell of him.

"Are you all right?"

"In a manner of speaking, yes."

"What are you doing in here?"

"I was taking a nap. Hiding from reporters."

He squeezes her tight. "I saw cigarette butts on the front stoop, but I figured it was the cops. Have they searched our property?"

"Ours?" Sand shakes her head. Frank releases her. His face is pale and strangely emotionless, with a queer tightness about his eyes. He heads for the closet and rummages among the hanging clothes until he extracts her father's hunting rifle and a box of shells. Frank hunkers down on the bed and loads the rifle. Somehow she is surprised that he knows how to do these things.

"Frank, what are you doing?"

"Well, he's still out there, isn't he?"

Sand feels a certain sadness watching him. "We weren't even armed when we were over there. All over the world."

"Over there it wasn't our fight. Over there we had qualities that made it advantageous to keep us alive."

"Not everyone felt that way. . . ."

"Our neighbor was murdered! We're the next house downstream. He could be holed up on our land right now. Dreaming about the knives in our kitchen."

"I don't think that's what happened, Frank."

"I'm going to check the perimeter."

And so she lets him go, because whenever Frank is scared he gets extremely irritable. He tears through the closets, the pantry, even the clothes dryer and the crawl space under the house. Once he's convinced the house is clear, he moves outward in concentric circles from the cabin—thrusting the rifle into the myrtle bushes, clanging his way among the tools of the shed, even turning over the compost pile. There's no point in protesting; he won't rest until his search is complete. This is a man who, after an oceanic hour or so of making love, is frequently compelled to get up and check the house.

"Okay?"

Frank nods gruffly. "He isn't here."

"I think we'd better talk."

Sand brews them a pot of tea and tells Frank how she came upon the body of Dahlia Everston. As she sits at the kitchen table, she understands she's a deceptive and secretive person, just as her father was, for she doesn't mention driving over Old Faros Bridge in high water, how foolish she was, how close she came to being swept over and drowning herself. Nor does she mention what she was doing in town or why she went to the doctor's. Her story begins with the storm, the lights going out, driving over to the Everstons'. No one answering the door. The door unlocked, the boy asleep on the sofa. She does not tell about that other time, or how it was the sudden, unbidden memory of that other time when she was ten years old that caused her to see Timothy in a different way. She doesn't think it's fair to feel that way about Timothy because of that other time. Maybe she's just seeing the present through the lens of the past, but in the end Sand blurts out, "I think he did it. Killed her. Stabbed her twenty times—"

"Timothy? He couldn't have. Why do you think that?"

"Things—little things."

"Like what? What things?"

"How could he have slept through it, Frank? She was stabbed so many times!"

"I don't know." He rakes a hand back through his hair. "You said the TV was pretty loud."

"And there's something wrong about that, but I don't know what it is."

"Look, you're jumping to conclusions. What else?"

"The cookies. He baked cookies and didn't eat one."

"So?"

"Teenage boys. They're always hungry, remember that?"

Frank slowly shakes his head at her. "You've been up all night. You're not thinking straight."

"He wasn't wearing the shirt he wore to school that day. That night he was wearing a clean long-sleeved shirt. He said he came home and did laundry, Frank."

"So?"

"Dahlia complained that he wouldn't do chores around the house. A bone of contention."

"That's it?"

"No, no, that's not it. The place was made to look like a burglary, but only two pieces of her jewelry were stolen. That sounds personal. And the bedroom window. When I photographed the broken window, one of the deputies said to Tom Gravette, 'Looks like it was busted from the inside.' The inside, Frank."

"You said yourself, the front door was unlocked. He could have just walked in. Like you did. If the boy could sleep through bloody mayhem, he could sleep through someone walking through the house. It's a big leap, a big leap to think Timothy could do something like that."

"But now I'm thinking . . . why did Norah want me watching over them? What was she worried about?"

"Goddamn it. I wish you had stayed out of this. I told you not to get involved. I warned you!"

"Well, good for you! You win!" Sand leaps from the table and heads for a door to lock behind herself.

"Oh, fine! Great!" Frank raises his open arms. "Just get up and leave! Like you always do! Whenever we get to the crux of something, you're up and out the door!"

"I need to rest. I'm exhausted. Then I have to go over there, pay my respects to the family."

"How can you even think about going back to their house?"

"I have to. That's the code of honor. That's what a person does."

"I don't give a damn about the code of honor in the hills. These people aren't even from here!"

"But I am."

"Even here has changed since you lived here last. Now listen. If the boy did it, his parents are going to be looking for an alternative solution. Don't you get it? You're in a vulnerable position here. In fact, I think we should be hiring an attorney right now."

"What?"

"You had a relationship with the victim. You were at the scene. You found the body. That makes you a suspect. You had to get involved with these people, didn't you?" But he's talking more to himself than to her.

"They're our neighbors," she says feebly. "It's as simple as that."

"Nothing's going to be simple now."

"That's probably true. But no lawyers. People hear I've hired a lawyer, I'll be done for. Oh, Frank, hold me. I am falling apart. I've seen bad things before—I don't know—I just can't hold it together anymore. Can't pretend."

Frank stares at her then, shocked by her gaunt face, then nods slowly and draws her chair across the floor and pulls Sand onto his lap.

Cradled in his arms, she starts to cry. "I just don't have the nerves of steel I used to, baby. I think he killed his sister. I can't shut that feeling out."

Frank rubs her back with long, even strokes. "It's okay, honey. It's okay. Everything will be okay."

———

SHE HAS ALWAYS taken photographs of things that frightened her. Ever since her father left her in a cabin in the snow. Two years later her mother died of cancer, and Sand's first instinct was to take a photograph, because the camera lens had become a necessary buffer between her and reality. So she raised her camera and took aim at her mother's dead body lying in bed. It was the only time her father struck her, his backhand to her face.

What the hell are you doing?

And she had no words to answer him.

The loss of her mother made her father withdraw from Sand. Like any child, she thought she must be the cause of the rift. His grief was cold, and he criticized her even more than he used to. In time he didn't have to say anything. A sharp look, a quiver of disgust about his lips, she understood. His angry voice had moved into her head. He didn't have to rebuke her. She would do it for him. She watched him sink further into a bilious bourbon sea and felt she was somehow responsible for his ruin. By the time she went to college, she made a point of getting involved only with men she didn't really like. After graduation she fled from the prospect of returning home to work for her father at the newspaper. She went abroad, made a career, and eventually forgave herself for all the sins she had never committed.

When Sand returned home to live after her father's death, she put away her camera. She no longer wanted to photograph anything at all. She preferred just to sit and look at the world about her without having to capture anything. One night in the rain she is asked to do what she's always done. And once again Sand Williams discovers that, for her, the act of taking a photograph of something terrible will distance her from the pain.

So Dahlia lay before her, a body of cold flesh, pale and slightly blue. Sand had to force herself to see her young neighbor as a corpse to be observed, first dressed as Sand and the boy found her, then naked, exposed, and somehow vulnerable even in death. She was glad that Patti Callahan was there, and not just a couple of good old boys as she inwardly divided Dahlia's body into grids.

"How many?" Tom Gravette asked Patti Callahan.

"Nineteen."

"Shit. I got twenty-two—count 'em again."

Sand took a close-up of every wound, and there were so many, it was hard to keep them all straight. She leaned over Dahlia's hip, enlarging a ragged cut between the ribs. It occurred to her that an investigation would happen in this manner only in an outback rural place.

She looked up at them and said, "This one's different."

"How's that?" Tom snapped.

"It's serrated."

The sheriff and the deputy quietly stared at Sand, and she wondered what they were thinking. "It's the lens," she said. "It gives focus." When she was finished, she announced that two of the wounds were made with a different knife.

Tom Gravette whispered under his breath, "What's that mean?"

Callahan planted both hands on her sturdy hips. "Two perps."

"Or the killer went and got himself another knife. But why would he do that? Check all the damn knives in this house."

"Collect them?"

"Yeah. . . ." Tom scratched his head. "No, wait. Mothers usually know about the cutlery. Let the parents see if they're missing any knives."

Sand remembered a marvelous leap Dahlia once made as a forward on the girls' basketball team, almost flying, arm stretched toward the hoop. She looked away to compose herself. When she turned back, Gravette and Callahan were bending over Dahlia's body. Gravette had put on his reading glasses, his brow furled as he examined the serrated wound gaping on Dahlia's side.

"There's something else," Sand whispered, feeling hesitant, as if knowledge and observation were signs of guilt. "Did you see her neck? There are faint bruises on either side of her windpipe."

Tom muttered, "I'll be damned."

"So he choked her, too," Patti said.

Tom stood upright, stretched his back, then took off his eyeglasses and chewed at one of the tips. "Yep. I'd say this girl's been choked. But not when she died. Huh-uh, those bruises aren't fresh. They look like they were starting to heal."

What could it mean except that someone had been abusing

Dahlia? *Why didn't I see it the day I came over,* Sand wondered, *and Dahlia was sunbathing? How did I fail to see?*

Tom turned to her and crossed his arms in front of his chest. "Okay, Sand, tell me everything you know about this girl."

"She was smart. She worked nights at the hospital for college money. She had a boyfriend, but I haven't seen his car on the lane in—I don't know—maybe three or four months. Dahlia is Lyman's child, Timothy is Norah's."

"Did Dahlia and Timothy get along?"

Again Sand hesitated. "I don't know."

"But what is it you do know?"

"They were arguing when I called to check up on them a week ago. That's pretty normal, isn't it?"

"Yep. Anything unusual about Dahlia?"

"No." She sounded defensive, she heard it herself.

"That don't sound like you're sure. So what is it you aren't saying?"

Sand snapped on the lens cap, rewound the film, then extracted the canister. Tom held out his hand, and she passed the film canister to his outstretched palm. "I came over one morning. She was down on the riverbank, sunbathing topless. All she had on was one of those shoestring thongs."

"I noticed the tan lines. And Timothy?"

"He was in school."

"So . . . was Dahlia fast? Was she a loose girl?"

"No! I have no reason to think that."

"But you don't know."

"She was just happy to be alone, she was letting her skin breathe. Christ, Tom, don't blame the victim here."

"I ain't blaming nobody yet. But this is a girl who goes sunbathing naked. Somebody could have seen her. Decided to target her. Stalked her. Lay in wait."

"Yeah." Sand rubbed her aching head. "Yeah, I know. I thought about that. I told her it was risky. I tried to warn her. It's not something she would have done when her parents were home."

Patti interjected, "But the bruises on her neck—doesn't that mean it's someone she knew?"

"Could be. But don't start makin' any theories yet, Patti-cakes. Maybe she was strangled, maybe she walked into a fence. An' if somebody strangled her a week ago, that don't mean the same person finished her off. There's lotsa women get themselves hit by different men. It creates a pattern. A pattern of risk."

A pattern of risk, Sand thought, and remembered gunning Old Faros Bridge when the river was running across.

6

THE DAY OF the autopsy is gray, cool, sodden with misery. Norah is drinking coffee at the kitchen table and staring out the window at the early-morning rain. She sits there dull-eyed, wrapped in a wool afghan that she and Dahlia bought together at a flea market in Egypt Grove. Dahlia liked the bright pansy flowers against the soft black wool. Norah shudders. She keeps thinking Dahlia's in another room, reading or daydreaming. She waits for the ragged rumbling of her stepdaughter's Ford Taurus to pull into the drive. The house itself frightens her. When she walks through the living room, she thinks Dahlia's killer must have crossed the same wide pine-planked floor. It pains her to breathe the same air that he must have. The house that had been their comfort failed to protect them at all.

The rain pours from the roof in crystalline beads, and Norah is assailed by images. How long was Dahlia alive while it was happening? Quickly her mind veers from that thought. Is he a transient?

A sex criminal from out of state who was sent to live with relatives in the hills? Where is he now? At home in bed, or riding an empty train car into another state? Why Dahlia? Why pick her? Did he follow her home from work? He could have been watching her for days. He might have been canoeing and seen Dahlia on the back porch.

In the summertime, flotillas of drunken, boisterous canoeists came floating by their property. Norah always loved the view of the Seven Point River from their house, but she soon learned the river was also a window into the safety of their private world. A navigable river drew tourists from as far as St. Louis and Kansas City. Just last summer she told Lyman, "It bothers me . . . so many strangers coming down the river." A few times drunken men in canoes had whistled at Dahlia sunbathing in the backyard.

Norah pads down the hall to her son's room and stands outside his open door, the sound of his deep breathing an immense comfort to her. Too much has been taken away. She watches his large handsome figure, and for a moment she acknowledges her tremendous relief that her son is alive. For some reason, God took Lyman's child but spared her own. She feels guilty for the thought. She loved Dahlia, but there is at root a matter of blood, and she loves her own son more. Can God blame her for this secret, guilty relief that Timothy is alive?

Later Norah helps her husband out of bed and leads him to the bathroom as if he's an invalid, a very, very old man. In the bathroom Lyman sees Dahlia's pink robe hanging from a peg. He drops to the floor and begins to wail. Norah leads him to the kitchen table, where he sits, his fingers wrapped around a coffee cup, his gaze centering on the wood grain of the table, which seems to ripple in a moving current.

Norah and Lyman met down here in the hills. Lyman on a fishing trip, Norah visiting her now-deceased mother, who had retired to a house on a nearby lake. She and Timothy were shopping at Bart's One Stop. Timothy, ten years old, a string bean of a kid, ran down an aisle and into Lyman, who spoke good-naturedly to the boy. Then Norah and Lyman began a conversation that would change their lives. Norah was divorced, Lyman widowed. They both had a child, and what attracted her most to Lyman was the kindness in his eyes, the way he seemed to touch everything gently, even a two-by-four he was going to saw in half. Her first husband had not been so gentle. She and Lyman went to dinner that evening. Fifteen months later they were married lakeside behind her mother's house, and from then on they began dreaming of moving to that country place.

Norah glances up to see her son standing by the stove, a look of fear settling across his broad features, and her heart flies out to him. "Oh, Timothy, come here. . . ."

The three of them hold one another over the table in a hug they sometimes attempted when there had been four of them. "Thank God you're all right," Norah whispers. "You're all we have now."

Lyman says, "You—you didn't see anything?"

Tears spill from Timothy's eyes. "No." He shakes his head.

"Didn't hear anything?"

"Lyman, don't press him. He found her. He's been through enough."

Lyman sobs. "I'm not—I—just can't understand. She must have cried out. . . ."

———

NORAH CAN REMEMBER the last good day of her life. It's the day Dahlia was killed, the hours before her death. The afternoon she and Lyman walked on Myrtle Beach. Norah had not been to the ocean in many years. They brought along Lyman's old aunt, clutching her feeble arms as they crept slowly toward the sea. Norah and Aunt Emma tied scarves around their heads, and the bright silk triangles flapped in the wind. Aunt Emma, a former dressmaker, was wearing white gloves and black heels. When they stopped to rest and breathe the salt air, the pointy heels of her shoes sank into the hard-packed sand; the old woman began tilting backward. "I'm going over!" the aunt cried, arms flailing.

Norah gripped the frail figure, felt the birdlike bones in her arms. Then Lyman knelt on the sand and gallantly removed his aunt's shoes from her vein-gnarled feet. The sky was overcast with a stiff afternoon breeze. In the struggle, the aunt's scarf fell loose, and her thin white dandelion fluff of hair whipped back as if those feathery seeds might be torn from the stem and dispersed with the wind. The raucous calls of gulls ripped the air above their heads.

"I wish we had some breadcrumbs," Norah said. "I remember feeding the gulls at St. Petersburg when I was a girl. It was a day turning like this—windy, a gray sky. . . ."

At the shore's edge, they helped the aunt shuffle forward into the brine. A little sound of joy rattled in her throat as wavelets played with her long bony toes. "It's quite cold, isn't it?" she said to Norah, and Norah said, "Mmm."

The aunt leaned against Lyman and took a deep breath, filling her lungs. "Ah! The smell of the sea! There's nothing like it, is there?" And Lyman said, no, there wasn't, except maybe in the womb. Two spots of blood rose on Norah's cheeks.

"Lyman—please . . ."

"What?"

"Well, for heaven's sakes . . ."

"What?"

In the last three years of their marriage they had conversations like this, where one of them simply could not fathom the mind of the other.

"You don't have to turn the weather into something dirty."

"What are you talking about?"

"Never mind," Norah said. At least the aunt was forgetful, and his little joke probably slipped right by her, unawares.

Aunt Emma rubbed the smooth skin on the inside of Lyman's wrist and asked, "Have you any idea what a wonderful girl you are?" She reached up and patted Lyman's long graying mane of hair, pulled back into a ponytail.

"You see?" Norah said. "You see?"

Lyman laughed, unruffled; he was enjoying the day. "I'm Lyman. I'm a boy. I'm your nephew. I'm not Marie."

"Where is Marie?" The old woman asked, looking down the beach as if Lyman's sister had simply dropped behind. Marie was dead of breast cancer, but neither of them wished to go into that.

"She can't be here with us today," Lyman said, putting his arm around her. "You'll just have to put up with me, old girl."

"You're very kind," the old woman said. "I like you."

This mention of Lyman's long hair made Norah feel crabbed. When she had married Lyman, he cut his hair like a perfectly normal man. Then he started working with a construction crew of rough types and grew a beard. After much argument, he shaved his face clean. But after Norah started attending Pastor Allen's church, the more she spoke about her passion for spirit, the longer Lyman grew his hair. He refused to admit it, but the fact was that Lyman stopped cutting his hair after she and Timothy pledged their loyalty to church. When she pestered him about it, Lyman would say, "What's the problem? Jesus had long hair." This sort of adolescent rebellion was repellant in a middle-aged man.

Still, it had been so long since she'd been to the ocean, she wasn't going to let it ruin this day for her. Norah knelt down on the beach and took a pinch of sand, rolling the rough little grains between her thumb and fingers. She thought of her children then. Admitted for a few seconds what a relief it was to be away, a relief to shed their teenage whining, their constant needs—they were like these bits of grit, she thought, and she was constantly having to smooth things over, make a pearl of their discontent.

Rubbing sand between her fingertips, Norah thought of her neighbor, Sand—or Sandra, as she preferred—and wondered what kind of a job she was doing, taking care of their kids. Wasn't she like this rough grit? What a silly name! That woman can't take care of her own house, Norah thought irritably. But really, how hard is it to come by now and again, have a conversation with Dahlia and Timothy? Even she is capable of that.

"I hope Sandra is checking up on the kids."

But no one was listening to her.

The aunt said gaily, "I haven't felt so alive in I don't know how long. I feel quite young again—inside."

Lyman's old aunt reached down and patted the crown of Norah's head. "Someday when you're old, my dear, remember me and go to the sea. When you stand on the shore, it's like you're standing on the edge of eternity."

Now, when Norah remembers the ocean at Myrtle Beach, she thinks, at that point in the day, by all accounts, Dahlia was alive.

AS NORAH DRIVES around the town square she stares at Merlee's Café, where Dahlia ate breakfast on the last morning of her life. In the past Norah hardly noticed the place. The café with its dusty chintz curtains and front screen door hanging askew blended into the square's collection of dreary, small mercantile businesses, but today the place almost vibrates with an intensity that is more than the sunlight glinting from the whitewash of Merlee's humble café. A tear in one of the chintz curtains seems a hugely disturbing feature that fills Norah with unease.

Norah chauffeurs Lyman to the sheriff's department, because her husband is on medication and only vaguely remembers the way.

She helps Lyman out of the truck, then enters the sheriff's office in a state of agitation. Sheriff Gravette tells them what progress has been made. Their daughter died of multiple stab wounds, but they have not yet determined the location of death. It seems to Norah that whenever she meets the sheriff's gaze, he falters and looks away. There is evidence that Dahlia was choked, but possibly not at the time of death.

Norah feels like an empty hull under the rain of so many details. Then the sheriff is asking her about Dahlia's friends. Was Dahlia seeing anyone? Who did she bring home? Norah can't remember the last time Dahlia brought a friend home. "No one," she says. "Not since she graduated." This seems wrong to her now. What was Dahlia ashamed of, what was she hiding from them?

"Don't you think that's odd?"

"What? Oh, the night shift makes it hard to socialize."

Lyman says, "Sometimes she'd stay up an hour, and we'd fish down on the riverbank."

The sheriff nods, as if he knows what it means to fish on the riverbank with someone you love. "How long has she been working nights?" he asks, speaking of Dahlia in the present perfect tense, which comforts Norah and loosens her tongue.

She turns to Lyman. "Since the end of summer. Right?"

"Around the time she broke up with her boyfriend."

"No, it was before they broke up." She is certain of this. "Dahlia's night schedule was one of the issues. After she went on nights, they couldn't date as much as they used to."

The sheriff asks why she went on nights, and Lyman clears his throat. "I thought she didn't want to see him anymore. But she didn't come out and break it off."

"Why? Was she worried about some kind of confrontation?"

"That's just the way she is. She doesn't like to hurt anyone's feelings. After a month or so he got frustrated, I guess, and broke it off with her."

"And this boyfriend was Dwayne Parker?"

"Dwayne, yes. He lives out past Weaversville."

"I know where he lives," the sheriff says.

Norah thinks about Dwayne Parker now, tall and skinny with ropy arm muscles. Lyman regarded him a normal country boy, an avid deer hunter who had once shown them the heads of three bucks he had shot and mounted over his mother's fireplace. But those heads now take on a peculiar depravity in Norah's mind. What seemed quite ordinary then now hints at a penchant for violence, and she remembers Dwayne telling them how he had skinned a deer out of season for a big family barbecue.

Norah says, "There are a lot of knives at his house. Knives and guns."

"What about at your house?" the sheriff asks. "Are you missing any knives?"

Norah turns to Lyman, and they stare at each other blankly.

"Search the house and let me know. We're looking for a murder weapon. Chances are, the perpetrator was an opportunist who picked up a weapon inside the house."

Facts pour over her and drain away. Then she is raising her voice, demanding to know why they released a vagrant who'd been held for questioning. Sheriff Gravette asks Norah if she's all right. And she isn't all right. She feels dizzy, and her heart is thudding. When the sheriff helps her to a cot inside the single, empty jail cell, Norah loses her temper. "Oh, fine! Lie me down where her murderer slept!" But she does close her eyes, tries to burrow away from her panic.

Gravette says to Lyman, "I don't like the way she looks. I'm callin' Doc Griffin."

She flings back at him, "Is that your plan of attack? Just drug the family?"

"Norah, please," Lyman says, "they're doing everything they can."

"Ma'am, we're following all the leads. All of them."

"You can't tell me that vagrant didn't kill her! You don't know that."

Doc Griffin gives her a sedative, then Tom Gravette drives them home. Norah closes her eyes for most of the ride, feeling a slow burn of resentful fury toward the country sheriff. When she hears the pebbles of their gravel drive, she opens her eyes and her own house has taken on that hyperreal intensity, as if the whole house were trembling against the trees and sky.

"Let's go lie down," Lyman says.

NORAH DREAMS OF the green postage-stamp-size yard of her house in Garden City, Kansas. Her first husband is seated on the grass, blowing up a plastic wading pool. In her dream he casts a kind of umbra, a shadow, a sense of her misgivings, even then. She walks out the back door, carrying her golden son in her arms. She smells the wonderful scent of his baby skin and soft pale hair. The father of her child turns on the hose. Timothy pats the arching water spray. Then he climbs into the wading pool and plops down, and his diaper balloons. He crawls to the pool edge, grasps the softly inflated wall in his fat fists, hoists himself forward, and throws his chubby arms around her neck.

About two A.M. she reenters the world. At first Norah can't remember where she is, or her age, or which husband lies beside her. The cruel one or the gentle one. She acknowledges a passing notion of lending money to Dahlia so she can go to school in Chicago and become a nurse, then she feels herself break open, shatter like a piece of glass. For a while she lies there unable to move, unable to think, unable to put anything together. She stares at the ceiling, at a crack revealed in the white plaster like a crack in an eggshell. She listens to Lyman breathe. She gets up carefully.

———

THE HOUSE IS too quiet. Gone is the sound of her voice threading through the rooms. Norah steps through the moonlight and cannot stop herself. The door to Dahlia's bedroom is closed, and she is compelled to open it. Some part of her believes behind that door Dahlia is still alive, asleep perhaps, or reading late.

Norah walks into the empty room. So very quiet in this room. Not a sound but the quiet ticking of the bedside clock. She stares at the ceiling and walls, her stepdaughter's desk and chair. She feels a tremendous unease about the room and cannot explain why she is drawn to the bed. Before long she crosses the hardwood floor, lies down on the bedspread with her heart pounding. She cannot make herself leave. For a moment she panics, her body seizes up, and she just lies there with her heart thudding, her mind dazed, fallen into a trance of loss. She cannot tell Lyman what she feels about the room, for she is unable to explain it to herself.

She has to force herself to walk away. Close the door. Norah spends the rest of the night taking inventory of the household knives, starting with Lyman's tackle box. Her breath catches as she raises the aluminum lid, then her fingers slowly probe through barbed lures and down to the bottom of the tackle box where Lyman keeps his fillet knives. Norah takes them out and lays them on the kitchen table. How lethal and cunning they look. All three knives are there.

The kitchen knives are another story. She's never had reason to count the small paring knives. Is it possible they haven't run the dishwasher since they came home? Yes, possible. Covered dishes arrived. Green bean casseroles, Swedish meatballs, pies and breads, even disposable plates and forks. Country people understand that when someone dies, you need encouragement to eat. The parishioners from Norah's church arrived with plates of cookies, meatloaf and mashed potatoes, pots of spaghetti and soup. The locals seem ashamed that a young woman could be murdered in their hills.

They came with condolences, but eventually someone always asked about the rape test. Norah told them they were still waiting for the results from the state lab, but already she senses that people are starting to look at her differently. She felt it when she walked down the aisles of Meecham's Grocery. A strange distance loomed between her and everyone else. An unspoken something. It's one thing to have a dead daughter, another to have a raped daughter.

Norah remembers when the young Walbert girl was raped by that awful uncle of hers; parishioners stared at her family, even shunned them at church. People recoiled from the Walberts as if they carried a communicable disease. Eventually the Walberts moved away and everyone was relieved. People acted as though they had cast out something unclean from themselves. It was almost as if the girl carried her uncle's sin away when she and her family left town. Of course, everyone felt that if the uncle had done it, his behavior was deplorable, but the girl was the one who was talked about. What had she done to invite this sin against her? And who could be sure, after all, it was even rape, and not just an excuse she thought up afterward?

A wooden butcher-block knife holder sits on the counter. Two wide slots empty. Norah checks the dishwasher and finds one of the knives—the bread knife with a serrated blade for gripping hard crusts. The knife must have been washed while they were gone, for Norah would never put one of her prized Williams-Sonoma knives into the dishwasher. She returns the wood-handled bread knife to its appointed slot, then proceeds to search for the missing knife. Did one of the kids misplace it and shelve it among the cutlery?

Norah's heart clutches at the word *kids*. That word is over, that word no longer applies.

She looks out the kitchen window—moonlight on the river, silver rippling behind dark splotches of trees.

Something's happening between her and Lyman. They can't understand each other. She tried to explain to him her fears about the rape test, what the results would mean to them as a family. Lyman was sitting in his study, his face drawn and thin, dark circles beneath his almond-shaped green eyes, a three-day salt-and-pepper stubble on his cheeks. His long dirty hair hung loose, and he was staring at the empty, cold fireplace. At first he said nothing, then, "What the hell difference does it make?"

"Well, we just have to pray she didn't go through that, too."

"He stabbed her twenty times. . . ."

Her face reddened. "But at least, if he didn't sully her."

"If he raped her, then we'll have some evidence."

"You can't mean that."

"I do. You can't mean it was better she was stabbed to death than if he'd stuck his dick in her."

"I'm not saying that. I'm just saying—he killed her, anyway. At least, if he didn't rape her too—"

Lyman held his palms over his face. "I don't understand you. I haven't for a long time."

"Don't you remember what happened with the Walbert girl? Everyone talked about her, it was terrible! At least if she died chaste, Lyman—"

"Chaste? Chaste?" Lyman's eyes widened, and he stared at Norah as if he didn't recognize his wife. "We're talking about rape." Lyman leaned forward, grasping the leather chair arms, his knuckles going white. "What does 'chaste' have to do with it? Whatever that word means, it means choice. If she was raped, Norah, she didn't have a choice."

"It's the way people see things."

"No. No." He was adamant, his eyes flickered with rage. He turned away from her. "It's the way you see them. The way you and that church of yours sees them. Oh, I get it. You won't be as acceptable to your fellow parishioners if our daughter was raped. What kind of people does that make them?"

"It makes them normal, Lyman. People naturally fear a terrible thing like that."

"It makes me sick. You'll be the brunt of their gossip when you most need their support—and you're defending them for that!"

"A woman who is raped, Lyman, she's no longer chaste."

"What?"

"It's not her fault, but that's the way it is. That's what the Bible says."

Lyman shook his head in disgust. "We've never been the same since you joined that damn church."

Norah breathes to calm herself. Nothing changed in those moments. It was just a fight. They haven't ever agreed about her church, so this was nothing new. She must focus. She must see with her own eyes that all the knives that should be in the house are accounted for. She is not finished with her task, and she must finish what she began.

About four A.M. she knocks on Timothy's door, then steps inside his room. Timothy is lying on his belly. She turns on the bedside lamp and gently shakes her son awake.

"Timothy, I have to talk to you." A faint scent of his perspiration wafts upward, and it strikes her that he's starting to smell like a man. Her son lurches up, his sleepy face lined from the folds of his pillowcase.

"Wha— What is it? Didn't the alarm go off?"

"It's early yet. I'm taking inventory of all the knives in the house."

He's wearing a long-sleeved flannel pajama top and Jockey briefs, his face flushed and sweating. Norah reaches over and brushes his damp hair from his forehead. "Honey, aren't you hot in that flannel?"

Timothy rubs one eye and says, "I was cold when I went to bed. Maybe I'm comin' down with the flu."

"I have to check your knives."

He glances at the illuminated dial of his clock. "It's four o'clock."

"I know what time it is." She rubs his shoulder to reassure him. "It's important. Let's do it now."

"Okay. They're in my desk."

Timothy pads heavily across the room, his flannel pajama shirt stuck to a patch of sweat between his shoulder blades. He turns on the desk lamp and she opens the shallow center drawer. Three knives lie side by side where pens and ruler might rest. A Swiss Army pocket knife, a bone-handled hunting knife in a black leather case, and a cheaper blade with a compass built into the knife handle.

"Wasn't there another one?"

"No. Huh-uh."

A six-inch wooden crucifix lies on Timothy's desk, an artifact he carved himself a few months after he began youth study classes at church. As Norah regards her son's handmade cross, a lump lodges in her throat. Deep rough divots were hacked into the wood, sloppy work that escaped the blessing of sandpaper. Yet these flaws make his creation all the more beautiful to her because Timothy's love for the Lord is pure, and in God's eyes, Timothy's crucifix is as good as any Lyman could make as a master carpenter. Norah suddenly understands the difference gaping between herself and her husband. Lyman will judge a crucifix by the way it is made, while she and her son see only a perfect holy object, a symbol of their faith. Timothy's crucifix is as good as any crucifix, because it is a crucifix.

"What about the knife Gramma Jane gave you?"

Timothy yawns, then scratches his damp flaxen hair. "I lost it. Months ago. On a canoe trip. We dumped, and I lost the knife in the river."

"You didn't tell anyone."

"It was no big deal."

"But I thought you really liked that knife."

"I didn't want to say I'd gone and lost Gramma's knife—okay?"

"All right. I understand. But you should have told us, honey. There are at least two knives missing from the house. Maybe more, I don't know, but at least two are gone."

"This knife was lost months ago. That doesn't count, does it? If it was already gone, I mean."

"What about the other knife?"

"I don't know about the other one. You said it was gone."

"One of the Williams-Sonoma knives is missing from the block."

"Well, don't ask me. I don't keep track of stuff in the kitchen." Then he sighs heavily. "Mom, can I go to sleep now? I've got to get up in two hours."

"Sure, honey, but let's pray first." She takes his hand and they kneel on the floor, praying over the side of his bed. Timothy is a good boy who only needs his father's approval, an unconditional acceptance Lyman has never quite given her son. Norah wants to cleanse her soul of this bitterness she feels toward Lyman, for feeling any rancor toward her husband now is unacceptable to her. Norah asks her Lord for strength. *Father, it is your will that Dahlia has been taken from us. Do not let my husband come to resent our son simply because he survived.*

7

PATTI IS MANNING the phones when Gravette drags himself into the sheriff's office three days after the murder. She knows he hasn't been home or really slept since the slaying of Dahlia Everston, and he's starting to look like a tweaker.

"Are you on something?" she says.

"Just that herbal stuff they sell to truck drivers."

She herself is no lovely sight. A pink swatch of calamine lotion covers her right forearm and below one eye, which has puffed up against a poison ivy rash and looks terrible. She is pale, with dark circles under her eyes, and her vision blurs as she deciphers her own notes. "I think I've got a hundred tips logged in."

"Great. That should only take us six months to follow through."

"People are getting riled up. Did you see the editorial last night?"

"I don't need to read the paper to know that if I don't arrest every transient around, this'll be my last term."

"Reed and Brier picked up four more."

Patti was briefly married to Deputy Reed. She wonders if it was the promise of motherhood that had made him seem so attractive at first. She used to call him Bob; now she calls him Reed and can almost forget that she used to sleep with him.

Tom says, "Have them put an extra cot in cell number three."

"We can only hold eight at a time."

"Double up. And call Merlee's. Let her know we'll be servin' hospitality to every homeless bum and shiftless hitchhiker around. An' tell her to go easy on the meat. This ain't the Taj Mahal. She's gonna have to stretch the meals to fit our budget here."

"Okay, Tom."

"And tell her to quit waterin' the coffee, at least our pot. That last stuff she sent over looked like Lipton tea. You shouldn't see the lint on the bottom of your cup, dammit. How're we supposed to protect and serve if we ain't half awake?"

"I'll put her on notice."

"An' call my wife and tell her I hope to be home tonight."

"Call her yourself."

WHEN DEPUTY CALLAHAN traces Dahlia's movements on the last morning of her life, she goes to Merlee's Café and asks what the victim talked about. A low cloud of cigarette smoke hangs in the air a few inches above the heads of the customers. Since the murder cigarettes have moved back into the restaurant, and the breakfast crowd is larger than usual. Merlee stands slumped over the counter, smoking a Marlboro and dabbing her pale blue eyes with a tissue.

"What's to talk about? The kid worked nights. She'd just got off her shift. She was tired."

"Try to remember."

"Jesus, Patti. I still expect to see her walk in, ask for a glass of milk. I don't know. The weather, I guess. She said it felt like it was going to be hot that morning."

"What else?"

"I asked after her dad—he's a carpenter, and I sure need to get my screen door fixed. I'd barter it out, you know. But her parents were away, visiting some relative."

"She specifically mentioned her parents were gone?"

"She mentioned it. They'd been gone for more than a week. I keep thinking, it could have been my kid, you know what I mean? Could have been any one of us. You think Dahlia went for a swim in the river, and some California maniac got his hands on her?"

"It's Easter," Patti says. "Kind of early for a swim."

"If you're local, it is."

———

THE GRAVEL ROAD becomes increasingly potholed as Patti nears the home of her distant relatives, and the deep itch of her poison ivy rash assaults her equilibrium. Carla's boy went out with Dahlia Everston. Patti remembers when Carla and she both got divorced about the same time, and the two of them got drunk one night in a show of solidarity. After that, Carla tore through a bunch of ad-dled men, trying to forget her husband in every one-night stand. Patti spent most of her first weeks as a free woman down on her hands and knees, scrubbing the wooden floors of a country rental house with Murphy's oil soap until the hardwood dully shone. She wept and cursed as she scrubbed, her mood alternating between tremendous relief that she had left Deputy Bob Reed and regret that she lost two years of her life and that he knew too much about her now and would gossip with the other deputies.

Patti's honey-blond hair was piled on her head and held with a barrette; her large breasts hung close to the floor, and there was a pleasant looseness to her belly. In the living room lay unopened boxes stacked high around all the furniture: her life from the years of Bob Reed and before. While she polished the dining-room floor, Patti came to a decision about what to do with the past. *I can't deal with it now. I need every ounce of myself to deal with the present.* But where would she store all those cardboard boxes? The good dishes and crystalware. The albums of photographs, the childhood mittens and shoes, love letters, even the ones from high school that her husband never saw, the vague feelings of shame she had about the dresses that no longer fit but were saved in hope that one day she would lose weight again. All the skins she has outgrown. That little house had no room for the past, and neither did Patti Callahan. She poured the pail of dirty water down the kitchen sink, then started lugging boxes into the yard. How heavy the past is, she thought as she lumbered back and forth across the lawn. Sweat poured from her hairline, trickling down between her heavy breasts. She stacked the boxes of her past into a pyramid, several feet from a rough of tall Johnson grass, then doused the cardboard with gasoline, threw a match, and heard a tremendous roar. It was thrilling to watch her past go up in flames, the wild freedom of giving in to rage that ended in smoke and ash. Something like the thrill Carla was seeking as she grabbed a man at closing time, until a communicable disease brought her period of sexual license to an end. Carla noticed her son was losing weight and started cooking again.

"WE HAD RELATIONS. But not sexual."

Patti's distant cousin Dwayne Parker sits at the kitchen table, chewing on a toothpick he plucked from a holder shaped like a porcupine. He jiggles one of his legs, right foot hopping nervously.

"Why don't you explain that to me, Dwayne?" Patti leans back so her holster bulges from her hip in an attempt to intimidate her relative.

Carla stands in the doorway, arms crossed in defense. "Now, Patti, what are you messin' with my boy for? He tol' you he ain't even seen the girl in months and months. You ought to be ashamed, questioning one of your own family."

"Carla, would you leave us alone?"

Carla is her second or third cousin, Patti can't remember which, but interrogating anyone who shares a speck of her own blood is always considered at least rude. At worst, it is cause for bad blood to ensue, the kind of feud that could disrupt family reunions for years to come.

"I just want to hear what you're askin' my boy."

"No, you don't want to hear, Carla. Now, I'm askin' you nice to go sit on the porch. Take a load off your feet and give us some privacy."

"Well, I never." She puffs up with offense taken, then says, "You want coffee first?"

"No. I just want to ask Dwayne some questions."

Carla turns her skinny bum on them, marches through the main room and out the front, letting the screen door slam behind her.

"What happened to your face?" Dwayne says.

"Poison ivy." Patti pulls out a packet of cinnamon gum from the shirt pocket of her uniform and offers a stick to Dwayne. Dwayne shakes his head, so Patti unwraps one for herself and chews in silence for a minute or two. "Now, tell me what you mean by that. You had relations, but not sexual."

"We didn't have sex."

"Well, what did you have?"

Dwayne shrugs his lean shoulders and looks uncomfortable. "You know. We did oral."

"Dwayne, you know what the second word of 'oral' is? It's sex. Oral sex."

"Oh, no, I never fucked her once."

"You sure about that? 'Cause we're runnin' a rape test on the girl right now, so if you're lying about not having sexual intercourse with her—"

"No—never."

"That was the problem, huh?"

"Yeah, that was a problem. Wouldn't it be a problem for you?"

"Don't get fresh with me, Dwayne."

"We broke up—"

"So you went over and she was going to get what she deserved. But things got out of hand."

"I didn't fuck her!"

"Is that what we'll find? You just killed her, then."

"No! I didn't kill her. I didn't kill Dahlia—I haven't seen her since summertime."

"Uh-huh, so who are you having sex with?"

Dwayne sighs heavily. "Belinda Taylor. I broke up with Dahlia, and since then I've been with her."

"What were you doing last Wednesday—from noon to seven?"

"You mean the day—"

"Yeah. That day."

"I was at work."

"Seven to three?"

"Yeah."

"What'd you do after work?"

"I picked up Belinda from school."

"And?"

"We went for a drive."

"Where?"

"I don't know!"

"That's too bad."

"All right. I bought a six-pack at Bart's and we went to the river—and parked. You know, over by Two Springs."

"And what did you do at Two Springs?"

"What do you think? We fucked. Like we always do."

"You know what I think of alibis backed up by someone you're fucking? They're fucked. They're fucked-up alibis."

"Well, it's the truth."

SOMETIMES PATTI CALLAHAN dreams of babies. In her dreams she saves plump little cherubs from cradles set high in tree branches. She rescues babies hanging by tiny fingers from basketball hoops, from roof gutters, and from parents who should have passed a test and got a license before they went and started dropping kids, as though there was something noble about doing nothing at all. Cripes, she once told Bob Reed, people have to get a driver's license before they can take to the streets. But anybody can have a kid, just by being irresponsible. I mean, when they can't take care of themselves, let alone their kids, all we're doin' is reserving those children a cell in the Big House in Jeff City. "You're just jealous," Bob Reed said, and this observation had the nagging prick of truth.

Patti dreams of the baby whose mother keeps a cache of powdered drugs, needles, and money inside her vagina. In the dream Patti steals the baby from that sharp and lethal womb and is on the run, the smell of that baby's head so real to her that when she wakes up there are tears in her eyes.

IN THE AFTERNOON Patti Callahan climbs the steps to the front porch of the clapboard house where Dwayne Parker's new girlfriend lives. A large deep freezer sits on the porch, as the house cannot accommodate such a bulky appliance. Patti raises the lid and looks down among the bags of frozen peas, bagged quail, rabbit, the frosted carcass of a whole deer lying on the bottom. A dog barks inside the house, then the girl's mother comes to the door and steps out. "What are you doin' out here, snoopin' in my deep freeze?"

Patti is wearing the Ray-Ban sunglasses she found on the river to hide her poison ivy rash. "Better cook up that deer," she says. "It's takin' on freezer burn."

"You got a warrant on you, a warrant for snoopin' around?"

"Nah. Huh-uh. I'm not snooping, and I'm not so dumb as to snoop without the paperwork. It got hot this afternoon. I was just borrowing a little cool air."

"Well, Patti, I sure as heck don't work my tail off to cool the whole outdoors."

"You sound like my mother. Can I come in?"

Marjorie Taylor grunts, then with very reluctant hospitality opens the door farther. "What, may I ask, are you doin' here?"

"I just need to talk to Belinda. Is she home?"

Mrs. Taylor calls her daughter to the front room of the house. Belinda wears low-slung jeans and a green crop top that displays her pale, pudgy midriff. Patti's gaze falls to the girl's navel circled by a sunburst tattoo, the flesh pierced by a small gold ring. The girl plops herself down on a worn sofa and crosses her arms in front of her breasts.

"Marjorie?" Patti says. "Would you get me a glass of water? I'm just about parched today."

When Marjorie Taylor goes to the kitchen, Patti says to Belinda, "Tell me about your relationship with Dwayne Parker."

Belinda blanches. "He's my boyfriend. We go out."

"Are you having sex with him?"

"What? Why? Is he sick? What kind of a question is that?"

"I need to know before your mother comes back."

"Okay. All right." She glances nervously toward the kitchen door. "We are. We have sex."

"How often?"

"What?" She rakes her fingers back through her fine sandy hair. "What are you, weird? Okay, okay, three times a week. Whenever we can."

"What were you doing last Wednesday?"

"Mom!"

Marjorie steps back into the main room with Patti's glass of water. "What's going on, Patti?"

"I'm questioning Belinda about her whereabouts last Wednesday, and about Dwayne Parker."

"Dwayne? What's he done?"

"Why would you ask that?"

" 'Cause you're the law, and you're here."

"Before Dwayne and Belinda started dating, he was going out with Dahlia Everston."

"The dead girl?"

"The murdered girl, yes."

Marjorie hands her the glass of water, then sinks down on the sofa next to her daughter. "That's terrible."

"Well, so what? It doesn't mean anything," Belinda says. "I was with Dwayne that day. After school."

"Where'd you go?"

"I don't know."

Marjorie turns to her daughter. "You said you had band practice last Wednesday."

"I was with Dwayne. We went for a drive."

"A drive to where?"

"Somewhere on the river."

"What did you do on the river?"

"We parked."

"You what?"

"When's the last time you talked to Dwayne?"

"I don't know."

"How about today? Did you talk to him today?"

"No."

Marjorie Taylor turns to her daughter. "Don't you lie to me," she says, and backhands her daughter across the face. The casualness of the move shocks Patti, but before she can respond, Marjorie turns to her and says, "He called here an hour ago."

The girl rubs her reddened cheek but does not seem at all surprised by her mother's striking her.

Patti nods slowly. "That's what I call a screwed-up alibi."

———

IT'S AN OPEN casket at the funeral; Dahlia's wounds are concealed by a high-necked confirmation dress. Her pale cheeks are rouged, her dead stare mercifully hidden by closed eyelids. Patti recognizes the shade of lipstick on Dahlia's full mouth—"pink divinity"—one of the shades used by the mortuary for young girls and unmarried women. The whole funeral makes Patti ashamed of her roots, the traditional heritage of the highlands where she was born and reared, but then she'd never been much of a churchgoer. As Pastor Allen begins the eulogy, Patti feels a vague unease she cannot fully articulate. She thinks of the gurgling little fountain she keeps on her front porch and allows her imagination to drown out the pastor's words. It's another hill-country death sermon full of fire-and-brimstone eloquence. Halfway through, the minister points to Lyman and declares he'll never see his daughter again unless he repents right now. Then Lyman springs to his feet, shouting, "You bastard! You son of a bitch! Don't you dare use my daughter's funeral to threaten us!"

Norah and Timothy attempt to quiet him. "For God's sake, Lyman!"

"Dad, please, please—don't be blasphemous—"

Lyman has to be escorted from his own daughter's funeral, which, in his absence, proceeds to become a full-blown diatribe on the dangers of dying when your soul is impure. Norah trembles at the word *impure*. The minister observes that Lyman's soul is hanging by a thread. By the time it's over, everyone feels chastened and shaken and slightly nauseated. Sheriff Tom Gravette and Patti walk outside and stand on the curb so Tom can smoke a cigarette. "Our dad's got a temper on him."

Pollen is high on the air. Patti coughs and blows her nose. "He's also got an alibi."

"You goin' out to the internment?"

"Think I will."

At the cemetery Patti stands at a distance, on a knoll beneath a cedar tree, watching the mourners gather around the grave. Lyman has recovered himself enough to rejoin the others, but his wife keeps glancing at him nervously, as if he might fly apart. When the coffin is finally lowered into the hole, Lyman sinks to his knees and Timothy catches him as he falls. Patti thinks the boy is handsome in his dark suit. He seems stunned when his father collapses against him and wails.

8

FOR SAND, THE funeral brings it all back. Why she left this place, why she doesn't go to church. Norah's pastor is one of those fiery orators who regards death as an opportunity to flail a congregation for their sins.

His God is all-powerful, and you can not hide from Him, you worm. Squirm before His scorching gaze. Your fate is in His hands. He will find you out. He will crush you if He wants.

Sand lowers her head and presses her cool hands to her eyes, thinking: *It's not my love He wants so much as my fear. My submission to His will.*

For He is a jealous God.

How could I forget? Sand thinks. They'd been teaching her ever since she was a little girl. When she wore white anklets and patent-leather shoes, and she held her parents' hands and walked into their house of worship with a bright and open face; she was taught the story of herself. The story of how she brought down the world. How she tempts men to do bad things. How she carries the blame in her body, in her very bones, in her womb. How she must leave her body, consider it base compared to holiness, for God was made in a manly image, not hers.

Didn't she see the pictures in their books? God is an old, old man with long white hair and a beard like an avalanche. He sits on His throne like a king. It's because of her that the world is full of suffering. If the first woman had only submitted to God, we'd all be living in a garden now instead of a world of pain.

Hasn't she learned that yet?

How bitter she feels about religion. How angry the pastor seems, flailing his arms about. Where is God's love, she wonders, where is God's compassion? Where are the feminine qualities that make God bearable? *Isn't God made in my image, too?*

They walk out of the country church and see a stand of graceful southern pines against a deep blue sky. "What the hell was that?" Frank says.

Sand shudders, a tremor that goes back to childhood. "I don't know. I call it the wife-beater god."

———

THAT SPRING THE newspaper writes of a mysterious scent that arrives after the murder of Dahlia Everston. For several weeks the surrounding hills are haunted by an airborne fragrance more elusive than honeysuckle, mock orange, or the lilac-scented breeze. Some think it's a manifestation of Dahlia lingering near the earth, but whatever it is, it's the scent of longing.

Sand crosses the river in her water shoes. Cold water ripples over her anklebones, her calves, her thighs, then folds around her hips. She sloshes over to a gravel bar. The strange, captivating fragrance hangs in pockets of scent, then inexplicably drains away. It seems to be drifting from beyond the river, from somewhere in the field that in summertime grows wild asters and Queen Anne's lace, or farther up the wooded hill. Almost the scent of lotus, she thinks, but that's impossible.

When she first caught a drift of the fragrance from the cabin deck, she was so taken, she simply followed it to the Seven Point River, which seemed to be its source. But down by the water the scent disappeared. Then she wondered if she was only imagining the fragrance, for ever since her honeymoon she's had a certain tendency.

Japanese honeysuckle has almost completely buried an old weathered fence, but those blooms seem cloyingly sweet compared with the fragrance that drew her from the house. She walks across the meadow to a stand of white oak before the smell returns, then follows the scent up the hill into deeper woods, where she loses it once more. She hikes through a grove of wild crab apples and presses her nose to the petals, but up close the blossoms have no scent at all. Farther up the hill, as she follows a trickling spring stream, she is enveloped by a delicious cloud of crab apple blossoms on the wind.

When she and Frank got married in South America, they decided to do something different for their honeymoon, so they took a bus from Caracas into the jungle interior. Chickens and goats choked the bus aisles. They took turns sleeping, one fanning away flies while the other dozed. They were traveling to a certain village in hopes of meeting a renowned shaman woman whom they'd heard discussed around campfires. Was it possible that the stories of her power were true? They wanted to experience a rite of passage that would mark the beginning of their new life, and if they were lucky, they might be invited to partake, or at least observe, a communal ayahuasca ceremony. Ayahuasca, a blend of psychotropic jungle plants, was used as a religious sacrament. Instead of the blood of Christ, the natives ingest a ceremonial drink that guides them to the spirit world, which is why ayahuasca is also called "the vine of the souls."

Sitting in the seat in front of them, a grandmother, with a gaggle of small, dirty children under her wings, was passing out tea. They accepted her humble offering and drank from a weathered Styrofoam cup that was probably picked from the city's garbage and saved for weeks of use. The woman told Sand the road was twisted like the anaconda. Frank said, "That is the way of knowledge."

"Where are you going?"

Frank said the name of the village, and in this way they were known, understood by all the travelers on that bus. There was something in the tea that made Sand's senses extremely alert, made the mountains stir in the distance like the anaconda snake sliding over a limb. The grandmother said, "No one goes to that village. The bus does not go to that village. My son can take you if you pay him well. He is not afraid." And so, with remarkable trust, they placed their lives in the hands of a peasant they met on a bus.

It was two days' walk through the jungle to reach their goal. Their guide was able enough, but by the time they reached the shaman woman's village, Frank came down with dysentery. He lay shivering in their tent, pallid and sweaty, taking metronidazole tablets and staggering with his bride's help back and forth to the pit they had dug, unable to keep anything inside. Sand placed cool wet cloths on his forehead and stroked his limp, damp hair.

"I knew this would be a good honeymoon," Frank whispered. "Full of passion and romance."

"Well, you'll never forget it," she said, and a half smile came to her lips.

"I had a friend in college who took a bus through Mexico on his honeymoon. When his wife came down with the drids, he just told her to take the bus home. Two months later he returned from the honeymoon, shocked as hell that she'd filed for divorce."

"I won't do that to you, Frank."

"I know," he said, and closed his eyes in exhaustion. "Besides, it's two days' walk to the nearest bus. I couldn't make it if I wanted to."

Sand brushed away a line of ants heading determinedly for her husband's prone body. "How many times has this guy been married?"

"Three times."

"I'm only going to marry once. I'm like the wolf, Frank. I mate for life."

"You know you are, you are a little like a wolf," he muttered, slightly delirious.

By afternoon Sand presented herself humbly to the shaman woman and begged that her husband be cured. The woman had standards, and curing Frank cost them their wedding bands, which they eagerly shed. The gold rings remained in the jungle that almost took Frank on the first week of their honeymoon and somehow were never replaced, for their sacrifice had been required. Besides, Sand regarded hand jewelry as bothersome and always thought it was enough to know that the slim gold rings of their love vows were having an interesting life down in the jungle, sparking on the hands of a marvelous shaman healer.

By day two of her ministrations, Frank was able to eat again. He felt like a wet dishrag, but this was such an improvement, he thought it would be all right for Sand to leave him and join the ayahuasca ceremony that was to take place that evening. All day long they could smell the elixir of plants brewing, and an air of excitement stirred in the village.

That night Sand sat among the villagers, her skin humming like the plucked string of a guitar. The air pulsed with drums, and whistles filled the night with eerie frequencies. The shaman woman they came so far to see wore a feathered headdress, bright beads around her neck. In one hand she held a long knife that she used to slice through the air about her as she circled round and round. She was severing her ties to life as the first step in the dance.

The villagers believed that when a woman wants to receive power, she must first symbolically cut all her connections to daily life, free herself, so that she may receive knowledge from the spirit plane. Later in the dance the shaman woman took the skin of a great anaconda snake and wrapped it around her belly, swaying and twirling in some kind of universal dance. By then Sand was utterly hypnotized. Floating in a world between worlds.

A gourd for purging was going round. As the ayahuasca invaded their consciousness, its first effect was to make everyone vomit. The villagers purged gaily and regarded this step as a cleansing, expelling bacterial infections and intestinal parasites that were a part of jungle life. It was best not to fight the purge, she'd been told, and when Sand took the bowl and saw the contents just deposited by the man next to her, she felt some great snake in her intestines suddenly rise up the tunnel of her throat and come shooting from her mouth, splattering her hands holding the gourd. A liquid mess of that day's cassava and rice spewed out like a fire hose. She gagged, tasted bile. Somebody handed her a rag to wipe her face; another chuckled and patted her on the back. Then, after this painful discomfort and a certain amount of civilized shame for publicly vomiting, a feeling of unearthly bliss invaded her limbs and heart. As Sand watched the shaman woman dance, the healer seemed to shape-shift before her eyes. At times it seemed that the dancer and the snakeskin were becoming one, and Sand had a communal feeling of connection with these people that she had never before experienced.

An hour after drinking ayahuasca, she found herself surrounded by two gigantic blue pythons who glowed in the dark and spoke to her, mind to mind. The one great python said to her: *"So, you think you monkeys are running things?"*

———

FRANK RECOVERED ON their honeymoon, and Sand was never quite the same. The "vine of the souls" had twined its pathways into her brain, and every once in a while an event or feeling would trigger those tracks burrowed deep inside her. Sometimes she sees things that are not there.

By the time she reaches a woodland spring, she's abandoned her search for the fragrance that drew her from the cabin deck, and there it is again. Near the base of a limestone outcropping water splashes from the rocks into the natural basin pool. The water is clear; the huge ancient boulders are moss-covered, dripping with cold springwater and improbably supporting a vertical garden of columbine, maidenhair, and walking fern. Watercress grows emerald at the water's edge. Sand stands perfectly still, and for several seconds before the lovely fragrance disappears, it appears to Sand as an egg of honeyed light, swirling in the air above the spring. She thinks it's like encountering a different frequency in the air. Like having a dream and yet she is awake.

Is it true what people are saying in the newspaper? Is this strange phenomenon somehow connected to Dahlia Everston? In the jungle where Sand drank ayahuasca, the villagers would have said that Dahlia's soul is still wandering about, lost between two worlds. She was unprepared for death. Ripped, as she was, so abruptly from life, her spirit remains in denial. She doesn't understand she's dead and remains attached to the world she knew.

Sand drops to her knees over the bank where watercress grows. She has a sudden yearning for the bitter greens, and her mouth begins to salivate.

That evening she and Frank eat watercress soup and chunks of homemade bread. They savor the cress's bite on their tongues, their senses enlivened by this simple pleasure. She notices a great blue heron winging slowly toward the river. And there is only the beautiful flight of the bird, this humble meal, this day ending quietly.

9

IN A DREAM Patti Callahan climbs the stairs of her big new house. Her hand glides along the polished banister up to the third floor, the floor with a ballroom for dancing. Tonight the floor is a black, boundless space paved like the Milky Way, and Patti feels inspired to dance. Deputy Callahan is dancing to a waltz, steps she vaguely remembers from Miss Arnett's dancing school. Her problem even then had been her inability to follow a boy's lead. The whole notion of trying to follow someone else's steps was perplexing to her and made her self-conscious. She had been clumsy and stepped on toes. But on the top floor of the house in her dreams, her three steps sway with a liquid grace as her toes flit among the stars.

As Patti wheels around, the light fabric of her dress caresses her hips like a breeze and her hips begin to roll. Then, in an unexpected turn of events, the Milky Way beneath her feet splits open and two electrical impulses shoot forward like flashes of blue lightning across the ballroom floor. The blue glowing, ropy lengths twist about each other and begin to weave and coil like big snakes. She is moving in a dance her body has never known before—something ancient and beyond her. Patti feels her own fearlessness, recognizes it as something she has always known about herself and forgot most of the time. But she never knew she could dance like this. Where do these steps come from? These undulating sensual moves that run like tremors through her body.

When the telephone ringing breaks into her sleep, Patti is drooling on her pillow. She lurches up, crashes into the day.

"Huh?" Patti gropes for the phone, and says, "Callahan."

"We got the luminol." She recognizes the gravelly voice of her boss, Sheriff Tom Gravette.

She swings her feet over the side of the bed. "Oh. God. Okay. I'll be there in forty minutes."

"Make it fifteen."

Patti stares at herself in the bathroom mirror, then shakes her sleepy head. *What the hell was that about?* She rubs her face, then runs her hands back through her tangled hair. *Something about that house.*

———

"YOU HAVEN'T SEEN him hang wallpaper," Patti says, "I have."

Her ex-husband, Deputy Reed, climbs down from the stepladder and hands her the roll of painter's tape. Before they can do the luminol test at the Everston house, they must first hang black plastic over all the windows and places where light can creep in. Spraying the whole house is a tremendous undertaking, so they will start in the bedroom hallway, Dahlia's room, the bathroom—locations where they suspect they will find traces of blood that can't be seen by the human eye. This preparatory work is almost domestic, so the men are happy to leave the blackout preparations to her. They go outside to the porch, where they can smoke and start mixing chemicals.

Lyman Everston stands in the doorway of his daughter's room

as Patti conceals the broken window with a sheet of thick black plastic, taping the edges to the wooden sill. Lyman is a tall, slender man whose skin is beginning to loosen enough about the face to fall into lines of laughter or sorrow. He has beautiful hair for a man, Patti thinks, not that she approves of long hair on a man. Lyman watches her tape the window until she is very aware of his eyes on her, until she wishes the Everstons had left the house, but Tom Gravette has allowed them to stay, so the sheriff must want the parents to see the results of the luminol test. Norah is in the kitchen making a pot of tea.

"Left side, a foot down from the top," Lyman says to her. "The tape came loose."

And so it has. The plastic is puckered and a ray of light peeks through. The bedroom section of the house is a long shotgun hallway off the living area—on the right side, Dahlia's bedroom, then Timothy's; on the left, the parents' master bedroom and the bath. Lyman Everston follows her to the window at the end of the hall. The window overlooks the woods.

"What exactly do you think you're going to find?" Lyman can reach the top of the windowsill and holds the plastic firmly as she tapes.

"Exactly? I don't know." She is not exactly sure what the sheriff has told the family. The bloodless state of the corpse . . . Tom might not have mentioned that. Surely Lyman could grasp the contradiction of his daughter being stabbed twenty times and the seemingly pristine state of the scene. "If there's latent blood . . . If blood was cleaned up—then we'll see that."

"It'll glow." His eyelids flutter as he takes in the meaning of his own words. His daughter's blood will glow in the dark.

"Any reaction will be obvious. Riley will take pictures. He's got a flash technique that'll pick up any luminescence while making the surrounding area identifiable."

"And a glow means there's blood?"

"Probably."

"What do you mean, 'probably'? It's not sure?"

"Luminol reacts to other things. Certain paints, metals, cleaning products. Even household bleach will cause luminol to glow. But the reaction is different. The luminescence fades more quickly than with blood. A reaction presents to us a likelihood. The likelihood of where the murder occurred, and how, and what likely happened afterward. If the luminol reacts, they'll do other tests to confirm it's blood and what type."

Lyman lowers his hand from the sill, and she sees the tremor.

"Like fireflies in the dark."

"Yes." Patti swallows a lump of emotion in her throat for Lyman, for this father. "Nothing vanishes without a trace."

For a moment he looks her in the eye. "That's something I want to believe."

Patti has never before witnessed a luminol test, although she's read about them and understands the principles involved. They are setting the stage for a light-producing reaction between several chemicals and the molecules of iron in hemoglobin, a protein in blood. If the luminol mixture encounters iron, a reaction is catalyzed and a dance of atoms begins. The original molecules have more energy than the ones subsequently produced, so they get rid of this extra energy in the form of visible light photons, a chemiluminescence caused by an excitation of molecules.

When they finish blacking out all the windows and doors, they turn off the lights to test their work. In the sudden inky darkness Patti feels an oceanic sense of a body without boundaries. She can feel Lyman's energy. It's as though the Patti Callahan she knows, her large, stable, plodding self—size sixteen, nine and a half wide shoe—no longer exists and is in fact a whirl of electrons moving through space, constantly coming together and breaking apart. She has a sense of being a consciousness, an intelligence, a cascade of energy. Her heart starts beating faster, because it is so very dark and Lyman Everston is standing close.

She finds herself whispering, "I think we got it."

In the hush that complete darkness brings, Lyman murmurs back, "No, not quite. This way."

"I can't see anything."

"I know the way. I know the way in the dark. You get up and pee three times in the night, every night, you know the way by heart." Reaching over, he fumbles, takes her by the forearm, his long fingered hand sliding down the soft flesh of her inner arm to the wrist, which he encircles with his calloused thumb and second finger, then leads her down the hall. Patti makes out the faintest ray of sunlight breaking through the blacked-out window at the end of the hall. Like the pinprick of an ancient camera, the tiniest green light of the forest is passing into the hall.

"There's a hole in the plastic," she says.

"You have the tape?"

"In my left hand."

His fingers slide away from her wrist and Patti is taping the tiny prick of light with a slightly unsteady hand. "There."

"We'll check the other rooms." He reaches to take her right hand without error and two of her fingers curl loosely around his own.

"Here's the bathroom," he says.

"All dark." Without sight, she feels the energy from his hand travel into her fingers and float on some invisible current up her right arm and into her chest. His energy travels in waves and subtle jolts that are as light as a feather. For a moment Deputy Callahan acknowledges within herself an excitation of molecules, which in other circumstances she would have described as sexual, but she has no sense that Lyman is flirting with her or she with him. Rather, their minds are so focused on their task that they have come together in a way that is natural. The feeling escapes definition, or maybe it is constantly changing, she thinks.

"What are you thinking about?"

"Hansel and Gretel," she says before censoring her thoughts. "Lost in the dark woods."

"So, you police are lost."

And she realizes he has turned the tables on her. He is trying to find things out. She does not blame him, but she has a certain role. "Deputies," she says. "It's a small point."

"Here's our bedroom. Norah's and mine."

They stand there studying the room for several seconds. "I think it's totally dark."

"Yes, absolutely dark. Do you think they'll find blood in here?"

"I doubt it. But we have to check."

They nip a pinch of light passing into Timothy's room. In Dahlia's bedroom the blackout is complete. Patti grips Lyman's fingers because his hand is quaking as they stand in his daughter's room.

"You think it happened in here, don't you? You think her room will light up."

"I don't know . . . that's what the test is for."

"You can feel it in here—like a huge rip in the atmosphere. Do you feel it?"

"We'll know very soon."

"This is the first time I've been in her room. Since. Norah comes in here. She doesn't tell me, but I know. It's because she can feel something, I'm sure. I didn't have the guts to enter my own daughter's room. Why do you think that is?"

Guilt, she thinks. Disbelief.

"Now I know why. It's because you can feel something terrible happened here. I can feel it now."

"Lyman. Steady."

"You're a good person," he says. "What is it they're not telling us?"

She wants to say, *I'm sorry. Please.* Then his hands are cupping her shoulders. She lurches back and he follows her until he is pressing her up against the wall.

"Tell me while there's no one around. Just tell me in the dark."

"Pull me from the wall—the evidence!"

Lyman clasps her shoulders, hugs her to his chest. She is shocked by his wiry strength, then remembers he is a carpenter, used to lifting and carrying—more than, say, a deputy, who rides around in a patrol car for eight hours at a stretch.

Patti whispers, "I'm not the weak link you think I am."

She hears his sharp intake of breath, and when he exhales, his mouth is close to hers, his warm breath grazing her lips.

"That's not what I thought."

"Yes, it is." She curls her right fist, raises it to his chest, and firmly shoves. "Let go of me now. I think we've finished everything that we can do."

Just then a shaft of light breaks over them like a wave. "How's it goin' back there?"

"Jesus, Tom, you're blinding us."

"You ready, or what?"

"Yeah, we're ready back here. Bring it on."

———

LATER SHE WOULD question Tom's wisdom in allowing Lyman and Norah to remain in the house. Was it worth what happened? Was he thinking the parents' denial would crack open like an egg? Was it fair for them to understand just how awful their daughter's last moments had been? What Patti witnessed shook her to the core, and she had never known Dahlia Everston as more than a corpse.

While Deputy Reed sprays down the walls and floor of Dahlia's room, even the bare mattress, the sheriff tells Norah and Lyman to remain in the living room. Patti has got used to working side by side with her ex-husband. Bob Reed has reddish hair, buzz-cut short, and a boyish face given to freckles in summertime. He no longer bothers her. It's as if she's grown a shell around some part of her heart, a thickened scar that his presence cannot touch. She feels only a sense of distance now. His blue eyes seem pale and wistful as he points the spray bottle of luminol and wets down the surface of the entire room.

When he's finally done, everyone is on edge, tense, waiting. Patti is thinking, *Thirty minutes ago I stood here in the dark.* Her cells are expecting that darkness again. Then Riley Gant, the photographer, flips off the light, and the walls of Dahlia's bedroom jump into a luminous blaze. "Oh, my God," someone says. Patti feels the shock of it. A blue phosphorescence in the rough shape of an egg radiates from Dahlia's mattress; the walls are glowing blue. The room is so bright, you can read a book.

"Wow," Riley says. Riley Gant is the sports photographer for the local newspaper. Forty-seven, lean as a split-rail fence and just as weathered. He has been taking crime photos for the sheriff's department for twenty-five years and is known for spotting details missed by the local coroner. Like the time the coroner determined Shelly Benoway's shooting death was a suicide. Riley Gant had noticed a second bullet hole in her head, and later the husband confessed. Riley flips off the lens cover and silently busies himself with his task, asking the deputies to step aside. They are all shouting directions to him, telling him all the places not to miss.

"We got a partial footprint—footprint over here!"

In a few minutes it's as though someone turns down a dimmer switch. The wattage in the room begins to dim.

"That's the first fade," Patti says. It is still light enough to perform ordinary tasks, but now they are able to see that lying behind the blue glowing smears—the cleaning solution layer that is fading out—are the first spatter patterns in their blue radiance.

AND SO HER story is told at a molecular level. From her body wounds and the pattern of blood on the walls, the deputies can tell that the first blow was to the neck, but this stab did not kill Dahlia. The angle of blood spurting upward onto the wall suggests she was standing for the first blow, but a struggle ensued on the bed. It is clear she wrestled with her assailant, that they fought from one corner of the room to the next.

"Reed, go spray down the hall while Riley photographs."

"Should I do the walls?"

"Just the floor. She was killed in here."

"Okay."

"And do the bathroom. Make sure you spray good in and around that tub. And over by the sink."

She was dragged from the room. A refulgent blue trail of her blood leads to the door. When Patti enters the hall she finds a path of blue streaks through the dark, and the present moment is ripped open as a flash of her early-morning dream darts through. She remembers two huge blue serpents dashing beneath her feet and gasps in recognition. These microscopic traces of hemoglobin that Dahlia left behind—the bits of protein that once carried oxygen throughout her body—suddenly gleam like phosphorescent blue snakes in the dark.

Patti takes a deep breath, then banishes the memory of her dream and follows the glowing blue trails of light down the hall. Dahlia's legs must have become tangled, her heels and calves flopping as her body was turned to be dragged into the bathroom on the left. Twin streaks trail across the floor to the claw-foot tub. The tub is like some glowing cauldron, or strange bright calyx. Patti emits a single gasp. The entire porcelain liner of the tub glows blue, the illumination growing ever brighter toward the drain.

Then Patti and the men hear noise from behind. A brief shaft of light momentarily lowers the bathroom luminescence and is followed by a woman's shriek. Patti is closest to the bathroom door, but Reed has already backed into the hall. When they reach Norah, she is standing in the blue light of her stepdaughter's room. Norah has brought tea for her guests. In one hand she holds a teapot, in the other a couple of empty cups. Her expression seems not quite human and yet utterly, awfully so. By the time they reach her, Norah is falling, fainting cold before she hits the floor, her fall partially broken by Deputy Reed. As her legs crumple beneath her weight, the hot tea scalds Reed on the thigh and the same hand where he was bit by a copperhead last spring when he opened a cooler and out shot this reptile with fangs bared and before he could even process this incredible sight, the snake was attached to the fleshy pad of his palm, below his thumb, fangs sunk into the meat, and the recognition of pain came afterward. The accident seemed as precipitous and unavoidable as being in the path of a scalding pot of tea dropped by a woman fainting.

Later, as Patti is dressing Reed's hand, the same fingers that once caressed her body, she says, "Is that the hand that got bit, or the other one?"

"That's the one."

"That's one unlucky hand."

When the teapot hits the wooden floor it shatters, and the rest of the hot black tea spills over the boards, smearing the glowing shoe print of Dahlia's murderer. The next set of feet that bolt into the room are Lyman Everston's. He is about to drop to his knees over his stricken wife when he is overcome by the luminous walls and floor of his daughter's room. "Oh, my God, oh God," he whispers, and Patti sees him swaying, like a stalk of corn in the wind.

She hears Tom Gravette's rasping voice. "Get them out of here!" And Patti follows the order of her superior in rank.

10

NORAH COMES TO see her on a Tuesday afternoon. Sand is sitting at the kitchen table, staring into space. In her mind she sees Dahlia ride down the lane on her new mountain bike, the sleek muscles of her legs pumping the wheels. The girl passes through the dappled sunlight on the lane as though she can still do these things. Then the doorbell rings, spilling its melodious chimes like water across the silent floors of the house.

"Norah."

"Can we talk?" she asks, and her hand shakes as she pushes back a lock of unruly hair from her temples. She looks exhausted, numb.

"Come in." Sand reaches for Norah's shoulder, gives a gentle squeeze. "I was just going to put on a cup of tea. Would you like some?"

"Do you have coffee?"

"Sure."

"I'm tired. I need a lift."

Norah follows her into the kitchen. Sand feels

guilty and ashamed in Norah's presence. She hardly knows what to say. It's all too awful, and she is a part of it.

Norah sits down at the table, her fingers absently brushing some toast crumbs left over from breakfast time. She combs them into a little pile before her.

"They came and sprayed our house down with their chemicals. We've all had nightmares ever since. They didn't tell us that when it got dark at night the whole back of the house would glow blue. From her blood. Can you imagine? I got up to go to the bathroom and there were still traces of her glowing on the floor, the tub. What's left of her, I mean. Well, it's faded now."

Sand busies herself with putting water on to boil, placing a filter in the Melitta holder, scooping out French roast. She can feel her stomach getting tighter just being in Norah's presence.

"Have you heard any news?"

"Oh, they don't tell us much. Every time they have a suspect, they seem to let him go. Last night I lay in bed and wondered if he'll come back to the house and finish us off. I keep hearing noises, you know. I almost wish he would. Just put us out of our misery. We'll never be the same."

Sand shuts her eyes for a moment. "I know."

"I keep thinking she's alive. That's how I wake up in the morning, thinking she's alive. And then I remember. She's never going off to school; she's not going to have a life. Some bastard made sure of that."

"Norah—I'm so sorry!"

"I keep thinking. If only we hadn't gone on that trip, she would be alive."

Sand places two cups before them and sits down. She wraps her hands around the coffee's heat. "You have no idea how awful I feel."

"Of course, no one blames you. You couldn't have known it was going to happen."

"No. I know that logically."

"Who could possibly have guessed a maniac would break into our home to kill our daughter?"

Sand begins to nibble at the inside of her lip, a nervous little habit, a habit of distress. She takes a deep breath, then exhales. "No one imagines that tragedy is going to happen to them."

"No, I don't suppose they do."

Norah's eyes begin to water, and Sand brings a box of tissues to the table as an offering.

"He's still out there, Sand." Norah looks up at the ceiling, and the wetness retreats from her eyes. "That's why we need your help now. We need you on TV. Tell people what happened that night."

"Oh—oh." Sand leans back in her chair. "I can't do that, Norah. I don't want to go on TV."

"Why not?"

"I just . . . don't want to be a part of that. I don't think it's appropriate."

"You don't think it's appropriate?"

"No. And to be perfectly honest, I'm a suspect, too. I was on the premises."

"You can tell people what you found."

"No. I'm sorry. . . ."

"I just don't see why you can't do anything the way I ask!"

Stunned, Sand whispers, "What do you mean?"

Norah looks away from her, and Sand feels her judgment as Norah stares at the kitchen window instead of meeting her gaze.

"I did what you asked. You asked me to check on them every few days, and I did. That's why I was there that night. You have no idea how responsible I feel."

"Then help us now. Please. Come on TV with me. Help us find her killer."

"I can't."

"What do you mean, you can't? Didn't you ever learn the meaning of that word? Just comb your hair and put on some lipstick and a decent dress. All you have to do is sit there and answer their questions. You have to do it. You were there! You saw the broken window—you can tell about that. How you and Timothy discovered the body. The missing jewelry, all of that."

Strange that she calls Dahlia "the body," as if she's distancing herself.

"We want your perspective," Norah says.

"No, you don't." Sand shakes her head.

"It's the least you can do—"

Sand's throat constricts and she says in an aching voice, "Because I didn't protect her."

"If you had kept an eye on them!"

"On them?"

Norah stares at her blankly, her fingers pinching the toast crumbs on the place mat and rubbing them into dust. "If an adult had been visible, he would have been scared off! He must have been watching her. He must have known we were out of town."

"If my presence would have frightened him, then why didn't Timothy's? He's a lot bigger than I am. Stronger, too."

"Leave him out of this! He's a victim here. He's been through enough. It's only by God's grace that he's alive."

"All right, Norah."

"I know what's going on."

"What?"

"Her ex-boyfriend! He doesn't have an alibi, but he's not sitting in jail, is he? Well, I've been doing a little investigating on my own. And guess who he's related to?"

"I don't know."

"That woman deputy. Deputy Callahan. She's protecting him. He's one of them, and we're not. As far as they're concerned, we're outsiders, even though we've been here for five years."

"Why do you call her a 'woman deputy'? You're a woman, too."

Norah sniffs. "Well, it's a very strange calling for a woman. The violence. The riffraff."

Even in the midst of her grief, Norah infuriates Sand. "Be glad she was there for your daughter. Be glad she was there to examine her body instead of a bunch of good ol' boys who might have made jokes about the size of her breasts, just because they were scared."

Norah says, "Why should you care about us? We're not from here."

"That's not what this is about."

"No? We'll see. We'll see about that."

———

SAND IS SO upset when Norah leaves, she wants to jump from her skin. She doesn't want to be inside herself. She wants to escape. There's a bottle of Maker's Mark on the bar, left over from her father's time. She thinks about slugging it down just to leave herself behind. It would be nice to be out of her head for a while. Passed out. That sounds nice. A good cry, despair, oblivion. But the afterward would be bad. She is old enough to know that now. Her father had never been old enough to figure that out. Or maybe he was just more desperate than she.

Sand picks up a trowel from the deck and heads out to the wreck the river has made of her garden. The flood has swamped the lettuce, the poles the Chinese pea pods were just starting up have collapsed and torn away. When the river receded, new dark topsoil remained, and a few leaves poke out of the muck. She tries to clean off some of the lettuce heads, salvage them from the mud. She is afraid to dig down into that wet earth, afraid she may pull out something that was hers—Dahlia's.

As Sand cleans the sludge from the lettuce, she imagines one of her fingers catching Dahlia's opal ring, or that under the low ridges of washed-up leaves and twigs she might pull out the filthy remnant of Dahlia's bloody gown. She may find the chain of an amethyst necklace wrapped around the slim bamboo poles half buried in the muck—something of Dahlia's might have been caught in the net of her land, for they are just downstream.

Then she understands she is searching for items from the Everston house as she cleans her garden bed. Heads of dead fish stick up through the muck; Sand buries them. They'll break down and fertilize her plants. What else may enrich her garden soil: the twin bedsheets, Dahlia's nightgown? She searches for sponges and rags. She pulls out a plastic flip-flop and what at first looks like the corner of a handkerchief, her heart thudding as she wrests the cloth from the hold of the earth.

I gave Norah my word, she thinks. My word. The concept is ancient. In the beginning there was the word and the word was God. Sand wonders, *What does my word mean?* What does a promise involve? Your word was your power, your integrity. If your word meant nothing, then you meant nothing, nothing at all. *You were a person who could not be counted on.*

She had failed to protect Dahlia, and she feels guilty about that. Norah can't make her feel any guilt that doesn't already lie inside her.

Keeping your word is an Ozark tradition. Without it, survival would have been impossible; and to the extent that Ozark culture still survives, it's because enough people still value the principle of keeping their word. What Sand loves about these people, who so shamed her when she was growing up, is that they are among those least touched by the grotesque materialism of American culture. They do not base their identity on the size of their house, a luxury car, or an array of clothes and possessions. They are a people who are traditionally not about making money at the expense of other human beings. Instead, like the plant refugia that came to this region with the last ice age, they are about finding a sustainable niche within a rugged natural world. Those conditions required a fierce individualism and the trust that when you needed help from your neighbors, your friends, your community, what you reached out for was real.

Yes, technically, she did what Norah asked of her. She checked up on Norah's kids, but as she kneels in the muddy wreckage of her garden, Sand admits that she's never really liked Norah. And now she wonders if her dislike of Norah affected the way she looked after Norah's kids. In her heart she fears that if she had really kept her word, Dahlia would be alive. And then there is this other ugly, furious part. She is angry with Norah for talking her into a promise she never wanted to make. Furious to be placed in a position of responsibility that turned out as badly as anything can. She doesn't want to be responsible for Norah and Lyman's kids. But she accepted that responsibility, without even really considering it, and now she is.

No one ever put it in so many words, but somehow growing up, Sand learned that if you do not keep your word, you destroy your own soul, your ability to bring forth something meaningful into the world, something good.

She goes to the shed and opens a coffee can where she's stored an old crumpled packet of Dunhill cigarettes. In London she told Frank she'd quit, and she *had* quit, for the most part. She fingers out a stale English cigarette and finds the stashed lighter. God, it's awful, but the nicotine steadies her nerves.

What does anything mean, what does marriage mean, if you hightail it when the relationship turns sour, awful, dull? If you just leave in all the various ways that a person leaves? Frank's right. Whenever she feels threatened she has the strong urge to flee. So she made a promise to Norah, thinking it was not a very important one. She promised to keep an eye on Norah's children, and one of them is dead. *What does keeping my word to Norah mean now?* She asks herself: *Is the pact over and done?*

Is she released from a promise she failed to keep? Oh, she knows what Norah wants of her now. Norah's asking her to make amends by helping what's left of her family stay together, intact. If Sand goes on TV and tells her story the way Norah wants it told, her words might affect the way people view the case, and public opinion can sway the path of an investigation. Everyone wants to believe that an outsider did this atrocity. To think such evil arises among us shakes our trust in one another, dislocates the bonds of a community. Causes everyone pain. But Sand will not lie about her own perceptions and feelings. She stubs out the butt and hides the evidence in her jeans pocket. She hopes her feelings are wrong, but she will not get on TV and lie in order to help Norah. That's one more betrayal of a girl named Dahlia Everston. And a betrayal of herself.

She's lugging a heavy old tire that has washed up over the kale and taken on sludge, when she once again smells a beautiful, mysterious fragrance drifting above the stench of river mud and dead fish. The lovely, ethereal smell compels Sand to stand up, go over to the spigot, and wash her hands. People are still calling the newspaper about the strange scent on the air. There's something beautiful on the wind. The elusive fragrance seems to be coming from the woods to the north of her land. She stands at the edge of her lawn, breathing in the scent that makes her forget about herself. There's no path, and traipsing through brush, entering a pathless woods, is no small decision. The ticks, the chiggers, the snakes. And what does she think she will find? Another pearly vision, an illusion, a flashback of some kind?

Like Dahlia, Sand had once owned a favorite piece of jewelry, an antique pendant that had been her great-grandmother's and was passed on to successive females in the family. Her mother had given the necklace to Sand before she died, and Sand lost it in Turkey. The necklace was stolen from her body one night as she lay in a tent, the thin gold chain snapped from her neck. An amethyst is supposed to protect you from illusions in this world, or so the folklore goes. Now Sand wonders if that pendant might not have saved her life. In a split-second decision, gaining a semiprecious stone had seemed more profitable than harming her.

When she told her father she had lost her mother's pendant, he had yelled at her for taking family jewelry abroad. Sand said she was sorry. Maybe she shouldn't have, but she had wanted some part of her mother with her, close to her heart. And maybe it had been a protection. Someone had wanted her mother's necklace more than he wanted her. She wishes that someone had felt that way about Dahlia Everston.

————

THESE ARE STRANGE days. Her inflamed emotions shift by the hour. When Frank walks in the door, Sand throws herself upon him and shoves her tongue into his mouth. People assume that death arrests the libido. But, in fact, death—so close—has the opposite effect. In the face of death you want to feel alive. You are an animal, and you are alive. So she fucks her husband and wails while she comes in his arms, then lies back, floating on a temporary sea of calm.

Her professional life has shrunk to a certain arrangement she has with an editor at one of those home-and-garden magazines back East. Every month Sand writes about life in these idyllic sticks, the simple pleasures of cooking without pressures or time limits, or gardening along the banks of a trout stream. In her last piece she described Frank fly-fishing from their backyard, grilling a couple of rainbows for supper, and searching for the accompaniments that might be found in their garden bed or among the roots of trees. This time Sand sits down at her desk and writes about searching for a dead girl's things in the mud of her garden. That nothing is what she thought it would be. There are no idylls. There is only life with its profound measures of pain and sorrow.

Her anger ranges about. She's incensed that a girl—another young woman—has been killed. As she writes, Sand is filled with rage, and her anger says that Dahlia was killed because she was a woman. If Dahlia had been male, she would be alive. She finds herself snapping at Frank.

"What are you mad at me for?"

"I'm not," she says, but she is. There are moments when she is furious at Frank simply because he's a man, and a man took Dahlia's life, Sand is sure of that. She cannot sleep at night. She tosses and turns. She dreams of a shadowy male figure chasing her with a knife. Sand dreams of Dahlia, of trying to reach her as she struggles against her murderer, and again and again she is too late. In bed she disturbs Frank with her restless legs, and that gives her an excuse to get up, slide a blanket from the closet, and take her agitated mind to the sofa in the living room. Sand wants to be alone. She is so angry that she needs those hours alone, untouched by anything male. Then she looks around herself, the paths of moonlight crossing the pine floor, the stone chimney built by her father's hands, and she knows the truth: she is still in her father's house.

She is surrounded by him, enveloped. She was his creation. Why else did she go into the field of journalism and reportage? To prove to him that she was good enough. She could meet his standards. Though she balked at the minor points, she's still playing by his rules.

Why is she here again in her father's house? Why has she returned?

Her anger connects the small scenes of her life: going to the doctor's in Greenville the day of the murder. Her doctor is male, and she's furious with him. Yes, her thyroid was swollen, he said, but the tests came back normal, so there was nothing wrong with her. Sand left his office in a state of mottled fury, then back in the car she burst into tears. *Don't tell me there's nothing wrong with me, you fucking dickhead.* She had never been a woman who cried, except when someone died. Now, in the two weeks before her period each month she gets so frustrated trying to open a stubborn jar, she dissolves into tears. The smallest obstacles throw her into outraged frustration. Two years ago she was hauling fifty-pound bags of rice over her shoulder for hours at a time. Now, most mornings, it's an effort to climb out of bed. Where is her strength, her energy? What happened to the person she has been up to now? Is she suddenly old?

Frank tells Sand she's beautiful, and inwardly she thinks: his eyes must be going now. She's like a car that dropped its shock absorbers one day, and every little bump in the road makes for a discomforting jolt. *Don't tell me there's nothing wrong with me,* she thinks.

II

THERE'S A QUARTER moon in the sky, a pearl boat floating on the dark waters of the night. Norah has the sensation she feels when riding in a canoe: She must remain very still, make no move to the right or left, hold everything inside. Her emotions seem dangerous, capable of throwing her overboard. At night the wind knocks branches against the house, and she waits for him to return. She just wants to look into his eyes and see for herself what kind of a beast lies there. She keeps her husband's fillet knife beneath her pillow. The floorboards creak in the house. If he comes, she will defend her family unless she is paralyzed by her own fear.

Since the murder, Norah feels she is the only one holding her family together. Lyman has lost any capacity for leadership. He has burrowed so far into himself that when she touches his skin she is no longer sure she's reaching him. So many times he remains unmoved by her concern, so unaware of her presence that she feels quite abandoned by him, left to take care of everything. In any practical matter he's no help at all, of no use in navigating their interactions with the law enforcement officers. Lyman doesn't even change his clothes, and when she last tried to embrace him she smelled that close chicken-soup odor of someone who's been ill and lying in fetid bedclothes for too many days. When he took a shower, she had to snatch his dirty clothes from the bathroom floor before he dried himself and stepped into them again.

Timothy, on the other hand, has stuck faithfully to his habits. Norah taught him to drop his dirty laundry into a clothes hamper in his room, and he continues to do so at the same rate as before. The hamper has wheels on the bottom, and this innovation makes it much easier for Norah to push her son's contributions to the laundry room.

Sometimes Dahlia folded clothes, sorted out the socks of four people and rolled the ribbed anklets into pairs, but Norah knows their clothes inside and out. She does not mind doing laundry, because this service to her family is also her power, her intelligence gathering, how she discovers the little secrets they might keep. It's Norah who noticed a small cigarette burn on the sleeve of Dahlia's white poplin shirt, and Dahlia swore it was her ex-boyfriend Dwayne's cigarette. Norah who found Timothy's blue T-shirt blotched by a chocolate stain that confessed he had used his milk money again for a candy bar at the school vending machine.

In the privacy of the small white cubicle of the laundry room, she sometimes sniffs the collars of Lyman's shirts, not the sweat-stiff work shirts but the ones he wears to go to town on Saturdays, the ones he wears for shopping and appointments he keeps. She goes through the pockets of his jeans and sports jackets, looking for phone numbers scribbled on small torn scraps of paper or matchbooks from restaurants, for Lyman has the habit of picking up a matchbook from the bowl the way others take a mint. She examines his collars for lipstick and sniffs his shirtfronts for traces of perfume, and each time she feels her power consolidated by the lack of evidence that he's doing anything but what he says. She has proved his truthfulness time and time again, and justifies this snooping as a necessary defense. She is protecting her family. She cannot again endure the humiliations her first husband put her through: washing the smell of other women from his clothes, the lies and her terror of confronting him.

She's sure there is no other woman in her second husband's life, and yet they are drifting apart. A few times he made overtures to do his own laundry, and that frightened her, made her wonder what was he trying to hide. Norah placed her hand over his and said, "I'll do it, Lyman. You do enough. This is what I do." Lyman shrugged and shook his head and said he was just trying to help.

Norah opens the dryer and pulls the hot jumble of clothes into the basket on the floor. She enjoys the ritual of folding clothes still warm from the dryer. She knows which jeans are new and which are growing threadbare at the knees. She reaches into the basket and grabs a pair of underpants. For the briefest moment Norah believes the panties are her own, but these are the slim underpants of a young woman printed with the days of the week. Wednesday. Her hand trembles, a stone lodges in her throat.

Dahlia's gone, but her clothes are still making their way into the family wash.

There's a blotch of faded brown on the cotton crotch. Blood. Oh God. The sight of blood makes her heart constrict. But this is the stain of old, faded menstrual blood. Norah sees the elastic is torn, leaving a two-inch gap, and actually thinks of repairing the rip, not that it matters now. Then she balls the panties into her fist and presses her hand to her mouth to stifle her cries through the wadded cloth. The basket brings forth one of Dahlia's bras and her teddy-bear nightgown. With a trembling hand, Norah lays the nightgown on top of the dryer and pulls the gathered fabric wide, examines the cloth with breath held tight in her lungs. She flips the nightie over and searches the back. There is nothing wrong with this gown, nothing wrong with it at all.

Norah carries the small pile of Dahlia's things to her stepdaughter's room, checking to be sure Lyman won't see what she's found, but he's holed up in his study. Timothy is quietly watching TV, and her passage does not cause his gaze to stray from the TV screen. She recognizes the sound track of one of his favorite shows. She slips by unnoticed and with a sense of wild escape, down the bedroom hall and into Dahlia's room, which makes her heart begin to beat violently, then she places Dahlia's clothes into their proper drawers. Her body shudders at the memory of how her stepdaughter's blood glowed blue on the walls and floor. Eventually she will have to take Dahlia's things to Goodwill or the church. She will have to face the recollections brought on by a skirt or a special dress that her daughter wore to a high school dance. But it is too soon, and besides, the sheriff told her she must keep everything for now.

Norah hauls a basket of Timothy's clothes to his room, lays the T-shirts into his drawers, the folded white Jockey briefs, the rolled-up socks. She feels the weight of the folded jeans in her arms as she stacks them on the shelves of his closet. She runs her palm over the rough cloth, fingering the metal studs at the waistbands and pockets. Her hand grazes the stack, then a small prick at the back of her mind alerts her to something out of place. She leans into the closet, pulls on the overhead light. Two Wranglers, one Levi's, and a pair of baggy skaters, which she doesn't approve of, because these are the kind of jeans that young gangsters wear, baggy pants that ride so low that when Timothy bends over, the obscene crack of his buttocks peeks over the waistband. Timothy saw the style worn on TV and by kids at school and bought a pair with his own allowance. Her heart begins to thud, and she reaches for the closet shelf to steady herself. Where are the second pair of Levi's? Maybe he's wearing them now. She closes her eyes and pictures her son: he's wearing a long-sleeved cotton shirt and a pair of baggy shorts with large, floppy pockets.

She checks the closet floor, the chest of bureau drawers, then begins to wonder if anything else is gone. How could whole items of her son's wardrobe disappear? She thumbs through the stacked T-shirts, slides clothes hangers across the closet rail, wondering: wasn't there a striped short sleeve? And when had she last seen him wear that shirt?

"Timothy?"

His eyes glance her way, then back to the TV screen. "Yeah?"

"I need to speak to you in your room."

"Okay, in a minute."

"Right now, son."

Timothy is leaning forward to catch the punch line of a joke. He never laughs out loud with the voices on the laugh track, and she wonders if he understands the jokes. It's just as well if he doesn't. Most of the jokes are about men secretly being homosexuals. Timothy frowns and chews his lip, and Norah has to admit that his slowness does annoy her sometimes. This is part of her guilt when it comes to her son, the fact that his disability does get on her nerves, that she tires of having to explain things over and over again. It took four years to toilet train the boy! It's a burden raising a child with subnormal intelligence, a burden that God has given her.

She keeps her voice low. "Right now, Timothy. I don't have time to wait."

A little whine rises from his throat, but he does stand up and follow her like a huge dog with his tail between his legs. Both of them step surreptitiously past the closed door to Lyman's study, and once inside her son's bedroom, Norah shuts the door for privacy.

"I can't find a pair of your jeans."

Timothy sits down on his bed and folds his hands together. Then he looks up at her expectantly, waiting for praise.

"I made my bed with the hospital corners. Just like you showed me how. There's not a wrinkle anywhere. I try to do everything right."

"Listen to me." She sits down beside him, takes hold of his wrist. It's been three years since she could encircle his wrist with her own fingers. "I can't find your Levi jeans. The ones with the flag emblem I sewed to the back pocket. Where are they, Timothy? Where are your jeans?"

"They're probably around somewhere."

"Somewhere's not good enough. Don't you understand?"

A baffled expression comes over his face. "Understand what?"

"Timothy." She takes a deep breath. "A shirt is missing, too. A striped button-down with short sleeves."

"So?"

"So? So? It doesn't look good. That's what. Right now it doesn't look good for you to be missing any clothes." Norah squeezes her forehead with one hand, trying to concentrate. "What did you tell the officers you were wearing that day—the day your sister was killed?"

"Mom, will you just stop?"

"Stop? No, I won't stop! Everything's left to me. I have to do everything. What did you tell them you wore?"

"I can't remember now."

"Well, they will. You can be sure that they'll remember what you said. These things can be checked. They've probably already talked to the students in your class, asked the kids what you were wearing that day."

Timothy frowned. "Why would they do that?"

"Because that's what they do. They ask all kinds of questions. You can't even know where they're going with some of their inquiries. Get down on the floor and look under your bed. See if the clothes got pushed under there."

"But I told them it was a burglar who did it, Mom. He took some of her things."

"They don't care what you tell them. They're going to ask their questions anyway."

Timothy's head and shoulders disappear under the bed, then he shimmies back out with nothing but a bit of lint on his fingertips. "There's nothing under there."

"Well, where are they, then?"

"I don't know! Maybe I lost them, I don't know."

"What do you mean, you don't know? This is an entire outfit. You don't just lose a pair of jeans and a button-down shirt. I trust you to take care of your things. You can't go losing your clothes like this."

"I'm sorry. I'll buy some new ones with my own money."

"That's not the point!"

"Well, what is it, then? What is it? Why does everyone expect that I understand when I don't understand?"

She has to take a breath to calm herself. She feels herself about to lose her temper with him. Good God, he's dense. He can be so frustrating, and Norah has to tell herself it isn't his fault. Because it's not his fault. Her voice comes out in a whisper. "I just need you to find those clothes."

"But what if I can't?"

"You need an explanation—a reason why they're gone."

"I don't see what the big deal is. They don't know how many jeans I have. Who's going to tell them?" He cocks his head and looks at her with the most serious eyes. "Are you going to tell Dad I lost some clothes?"

"Tell him? How can I tell him this?" She shudders at the thought, then says distractedly, "He has enough on his mind already."

"Mom, how long is this gonna go on? All these questions. Everything."

"Until they find him, Timothy. Until they find her murderer, it's going to be like this."

"He's probably gone by now. That's what Pastor John says. He's probably in a different state."

"Yes, he probably is. Oh God, I just don't know if I can pull us through. I question my strength. When I think about what it must have been like for her—the agony—" Norah flinches, and her son stares at her woefully. "If he touched her, Timothy—"

"What do you mean, 'if he touched her'?"

"You don't have any idea what I'm talking about, do you?" She places her hand on his head, smooths the soft flaxen hair.

"I want to go back to the way we used to be."

"If only we could!"

"It's weird without her. And Dad is so quiet. He hardly talks to me."

"Your father is deeply grieving. It'll be a long, long time before he's himself again."

"He acts like he's mad at me."

"He's not. He's just so torn up about her."

"I know it's bad. But he still has me. I am his son."

"Yes, you are."

"He shouldn't be mad at me."

"He's not. He's distraught. His daughter is dead."

"The glass is still half full. You have to look at life like that. That's what Pastor John says. When bad things happen. There's still water in the glass."

12

IN HER MIND it's still Harry's cabin, although his daughter lives there now. His daughter, Sand, has hung flower baskets under the eaves of the front porch, an embellishment Harry would have regarded as extravagant. As Patti Callahan and Tom Gravette drive by Harry's cabin, the sheriff sighs loudly. Tom glances at the cabin, then taps the steering wheel and turns to her. Patti stares him down. The cabin is lost to a green shivering veil of leaves.

Tom can't know, Patti thinks. Not for sure.

But maybe he does.

Maybe he knows, and it will always be this unspoken thing between them, the way the sheriff sometimes seems to be assessing her loyalty, sizing her up.

Tom returns his gaze to the gravel road, settles into an acceptance of their silent collusion. He won't ever ask. The world is always evolving beneath the surface of things.

They park in the Everstons' driveway, break the morning quiet with their car doors slamming shut.

"Here we go," the sheriff says.

Norah answers the doorbell with a frown of consternation. "I wasn't expecting you. You have news?"

"Well, there's something we have to talk about," the sheriff says, reaching up and lazily scratching his head. "Can we come in?"

Patti Callahan scans the furniture and picks a seat. The sofa is too soft and low, she knows from the night of the murder; you sink back into those cushions and lose all your authority. The two armchairs belong to the adults of the house. She chooses a large ottoman and sits with a straightened back, showing deference to the residents and also, she hopes, a certain edge. Norah calls Lyman into the room, tells him the law officers have something they want to say.

Lyman takes one of the armchairs across from them and leans forward, and Patti feels her heart quicken. How awkward to be around him. Something did happen, but what it was is hard to say. Lyman looks from the sheriff to her. Patti nods woodenly, then studies her knees. How strange. It's as if she has something to feel ashamed about, although she has looked at what happened in every way. When Lyman clutched her in the dark room where his daughter had been stabbed, it wasn't personal—he was simply desperate—surely it had nothing to do with her.

Except he wouldn't have done it to a man. A shuttered look comes down over Patti's eyes.

When they are all settled, Tom Gravette clears his throat. "There are a lot of things about our job that are difficult. In a situation like this—the murder of a young woman—"

"Would you like coffee?" Norah says.

"Oh—" Gravette turns to Norah with his sad, basset hound face. "Coffee? No, thanks. Like I was saying . . . the first thing we have to do is rule the family out."

"I beg your pardon?"

"Look, Lyman," the sheriff says. "May I call you that?"

"Yes, all right."

"When somebody's killed it's usually by a person they knew. That's a fact. Statistically speaking, I mean. If a wife is murdered, we have to rule out the husband first. It's standard investigative procedure."

"Why don't you come right out and say what you and the deputy have come to say."

Tom Gravette nods at him solemnly. "We need to talk to the boy. He was here. He's a family member. He has to be ruled out."

"Ruled out . . ."

"I don't understand this," Norah says. "What's this all about?"

Lyman says to Norah, "They need to talk to Timothy. They say they need to rule him out."

"They already talked to Timothy."

Gravette nods. "We took an initial statement, yes. But now we need to talk to him a little more in depth. Out of respect, we've waited—wanted to give you a little time."

"Ma'am, it's just what we have to do," Patti says.

"What you have to do? You had a suspect and you let him go! This is outrageous . . . to even suggest . . ."

The sheriff says, "We ain't suggesting nothin', ma'am. There's a procedure we have to follow, and looking at him is part of it. We'd be looking at the both of you, but you were out of town and you got an alibi that's been confirmed. So that leaves the boy we have to rule out."

"I won't have this," Norah says. "Timothy's a victim here—"

"Ma'am, it really would be easier on the lot of us if the family would cooperate." The sheriff turns to Lyman for support. "Is the boy at home?"

"He's in his room."

"You leave him alone! He's been through enough."

"Ma'am, no disrespect, but the boy was here. He was in the house. I don't see what the problem is, if he has nothing to hide."

"How dare you insinuate—"

"It ain't insinuation, ma'am. If you'd just ask the boy to come out here."

"Lyman, do something!"

"Norah, they're just trying to do their job." He turns to Patti then and looks her in the eye. "What exactly is it you want from Timothy?"

Patti clears her throat, where a queer thickness has lodged. "We want to question Timothy further about that day and evening. He was here in the house. We want to examine him and take a blood sample and hairs."

"What does that mean?" Lyman asks. "Have you got the results from the rape test yet?"

"No, no we don't."

Norah gestures in frustration. "How can you possibly think—"

"We don't think. We follow an investigative procedure, ma'am. Family always has to be ruled out."

"How dare you question my son. He's a good Christian boy, anyone can tell you that. He loved his sister. He loves his family!"

The sheriff leans in toward Lyman and speaks in a lowered voice. "Can you help us here? Ask the boy to come in."

Lyman finally rises from his chair and heads silently for the bedroom hallway.

"Damn you, Lyman! Stand up to them. Be a man!"

Patti exchanges a quick, sharp glance with her boss. When Lyman leads Timothy into the living room, Patti notices the boy is pale, his blue eyes wide with anxiety. He's wearing jeans and a long-sleeved cotton shirt. Outside in the sunshine it's seventy-eight degrees.

"Timothy, could you come down to the station with us for a little while?"

"I don't know." He watches them warily. "What for?"

"We just need to ask you a few more questions about that night."

Patti Callahan smiles at the boy. "Things you might not have remembered at first."

"Oh, and by the way," Tom Gravette says, "would you roll up your sleeves?"

Timothy flushes so deeply that two white spots appear on his cheeks. He stares at the sheriff and does not move.

"Roll up your sleeves."

"What for?"

"I just want to look at your arms."

Timothy stares coldly at Gravette, then something seems to settle in him and he looks down, unbuttons the cuff of one sleeve, and silently rolls it up. He unbuttons the other cuff, then stares defiantly at the sheriff as he rolls up the sleeve.

"Turn your arms over, son."

Timothy obeys. The smooth white undersides of his arms are raked with crusty scabs.

Lyman breathes heavily and says, "Where did you get those—those scratches?"

"I was pruning blackberries."

"That's good, son," the sheriff says. He goes over to Timothy and pats him on the back. "We'll be taking Timothy to the station now. We'll call you when we're done."

Norah follows them to the door. "Don't answer their questions. Don't say anything. I'm calling a lawyer right now!"

On the way back, Patti drives.

13

"WHAT ARE YOU doing to me?"

Patti says to the boy, "We're just hooking you up to a polygraph."

"A what?"

"A lie detector machine. They're just attaching these electrodes. It's not going to hurt."

"That's what they say at the doctor's office. But it isn't true. It does hurt, it does."

"Try to be calm, Timothy. It's just a little test."

"How can I be calm when you're stickin' electrodes in me?"

"We're not putting them in you. Tim, I'm just going to ask you the same questions I asked before."

"Ouch!"

"That's not hurting you."

"I don't want to be electrocuted!"

"I promise you, it's not going to hurt."

When they finish the hookup, they all take their place and Patti Callahan says, "Is your name Timothy Everston?"

Timothy takes a deep breath, then answers with confidence. "Yes!"

"Do you live on County Road 5683?"

"Yes!"

Patti feels a pang of despair as she watches Timothy jab his thumb into the wooden armrest of the chair, as if he's pressing a buzzer on *Jeopardy!* and these are quiz questions on some television show. "Are you eighteen years old?"

"Ye—" The boy pauses, then frowns. "No. I'm seventeen."

"That's good. Just answer yes or no. Is Dahlia Everston your stepsister?"

"Yes—no." Timothy shakes his head. "She's dead now. Is she my stepsister anymore?"

Patti continues in the same placid voice. "Did you kill Dahlia Everston?"

"What?" Timothy leans forward, whirls from Patti to the sheriff now, his chest heaving. "Why are you asking that question? A burglar or a maniac killed my sister. Why are you asking a stupid question like that?"

"We're testing your honesty. Just answer yes or no."

"But I thought you wanted to know what happened to her. I thought that was the reason for all these questions."

"I want to know if you're telling me the truth. Did you kill Dahlia?"

Timothy looks alarmed. "No! Why would I do that?"

"Did you argue with Dahlia the day she died?"

"What? Why do you keep asking things that have nothing to do with it?"

"Did you see the person who killed Dahlia Everston?"

"How could I see him? I was asleep!"

"Just answer the questions."

"No!" Timothy rips the attachments from his arms and leaps from his chair, trailing some wires from the polygraph machine. "I'm going home! I don't want to take your tests. I only have to take tests in school!"

They watch him flee the office, one electrode wire still dangling from his arm. Patti thinks how dangerous it is to bring children into this world. They could be killed, or they could become . . . and here her mind halts at some precipice.

The sheriff reaches into his shirt pocket and longingly fingers his packet of cigarettes. It's been two years since cigarette smoking was banned from the department building.

"How much you want to bet that was our last chance to question him?" He grunts and turns to Deputy Reed, who is the most expert at reading the polygraph. "How'd our boy do?"

This man, Bob Reed, who traveled the routes inside of her, who left his seed in her womb so many times, who occasionally slept with his head between her ample breasts. They might have had a child, but for some reason they did not. She is glad she and Reed did not have a child. It's simpler this way. She can look at Reed hunched over the polygraph, his round face scowling with attention, and remember the way his pale body shook and heaved, how his freckled, boyish face shuddered with release and trepidation when he came inside her. Like a hooked fish sailing through air. She can hold the memory at a distance now, the way she holds Reed.

Deputy Reed looks up from the polygraph into the eyes of his boss, and then into hers, and a brief moment of connection hits them, as if her eyes are telling him, *You bent me over the kitchen table and none of that matters now.*

"He's lying," Reed says huskily. "It's off the charts."

14

NORAH HAS ALWAYS hated Sand. She understands that now. Somehow that woman is tied to everything she has lost. Norah is speeding down the gravel lane, clenching the steering wheel in her fists, when her neighbor's figure looms into sight like some emanation of darkness casting a shadow on the road. Sand reaches into her mailbox to retrieve a bundle of envelopes, then raises a palm in greeting. But Norah will not give that woman the satisfaction of meeting her gaze, and a sputter of gravel leaves her behind.

She is stung with shame that her son failed the polygraph. Gravette had called and told her that Timothy had fled the office. Norah found him window-shopping on the square and brought him home, both of them too mortified to speak. As soon as they arrived, he slammed the car door in a fury of tears and headed for the kitchen. His huge awkward body paced back and forth across the kitchen floor. He had failed their test. He could not understand why. He tried to do everything right, and yet he failed. It was just like school, he complained, eyeing her sorrow-fully, for she alone understood how difficult school was on his pride.

Next, people will start gossiping. What if their allegiance be-gins to shift? Like Lyman. She's no longer sure even of him.

Instead of comforting their surviving child, Lyman stared coldly at the boy, watched her son with an objectivity that should never have come into his mind. "Something here isn't right."

Timothy whined, "Why won't they just leave me alone?"

Lyman's face went pale. "Because your sister is dead! It's not about what's convenient for you."

Her stomach went cold and hard. Norah felt slightly nauseated and had a sense of impending doom, as though the world, her world, were coming to an end and there was nothing, nothing she could do to stop what was unthinkable.

"Son, how could you sleep through it?"

"How do I know? I was asleep."

"Then put your hand on the Bible and tell me you know noth-ing about how she was killed."

"Hunh?" Timothy stepped back and gripped the countertop.

"Norah, get your Bible."

"We're not going to test our boy. You can't think—"

"I don't know what to think."

Norah pressed her palm to her stomach. Timothy opened the re-frigerator and hefted a liter Coke bottle from the door. He watched her from the corner of his eye as he rooted through the cupboard and brought down his favorite plastic glass that depicted scenes from a movie he liked. Soda pop was a special treat. He fended off her impending criticism by saying his stomach hurt. Her stomach hurt, too. Norah felt wretched—that was the only word that would do. She had to make sense of what was happening. It was all up to her.

"Go to your room. I want to talk to your father."

Silence pooled in the kitchen after Timothy left. The ticking of the oven clock, a heartbeat in the room.

"You are his father. You remember that?"

"But I don't know what you mean by that."

"You don't think . . ."

He shook his head. "Maybe he heard something or saw something, and he's too ashamed to say."

"Ashamed?"

"That he was afraid to help her, Norah. Afraid of being killed himself. Nothing else makes sense. And he failed the polygraph."

Sunlight filters through the sycamore trees along the river. The road that Norah travels winds along the riverbank. She approaches a pickup truck, and the driver lifts one finger from the steering wheel to greet a fellow traveler on a not-often-traveled road. Her heart reels back from Lyman's theory. There's a certain, awful logic to it, but it's just not possible. Timothy doesn't lie. She has always been able to count on his childish honesty, his naive innocence.

At the crossing her Buick rumbles over Old Faros Bridge. The river washes swiftly beneath her, and she remembers an argument her children had: Dahlia lording over Timothy what she had learned in philosophy her senior year—something about the river. What was it? The river is change. The water you see is not the same water you saw moments before. That water has rushed downstream. So you could never return to the same river. It was a concept that infuriated Timothy, for he got up every day and saw the same river outside the window, the same each day. They fought like two dogs over a bone, neither one giving in or conceding defeat. Norah had to end the argument, and it was true that she had taken Timothy's side, for it was all very well to talk about philosophy, but in the real world we all had eyes and saw the same river every day.

You always take his side. Halfway across the river, a memory of Dahlia floats into her mind, an angry morning before Dahlia went on the night shift at the hospital, and the girl, beating eggs for breakfast, complained that Norah always believed Timothy instead of her, that Timothy lied plenty if she cared to look. Norah has a sudden impulse to wrench the steering wheel to the left and swerve from the bridge. There's no railing. How easy it would be to die.

Why fight it, Norah? A throaty voice she calls the evil one rises into her heart. *It's all falling apart. There's nothing you can do.* She recognizes that voice: it's her neighbor—gloating. *You thought you were better than me, but you're not.*

I am better than you. You cross me, and you'll see what happens to you.

At the station Tom Gravette receives Norah with an uneasy solicitude and asks her to sit down on one of his hard wooden chairs. Has she come to hear the progress on the case? Norah sits very straight in the chair and tugs the hem of her skirt over her knees.

"I heard about your test. I know what you're doing. You're confusing the boy. Twisting what he says. Taking advantage. I believe you're trying to frame my son, and I'm not going to let you do that. The good people of this county are not going to let you do that."

"Mrs. Everston, I explained to you how we have to rule the family out. And we haven't been able to rule out Timothy. Now, your lawyer has made it very clear we are not to question the boy further, and we're gonna abide by that. We're not going to undermine our investigation by overriding your lawyer. The boy is off-limits to us—fine—but that doesn't change anything."

"I think you'd better start looking in some other directions, Sheriff. Starting with the most obvious person in all of this."

"And who is that, ma'am?"

Norah leans over the sheriff's desk and says, "You know very well who it is. My son wasn't the only one in the house. She was in the house. Our neighbor. There's no telling how long she could have been in the house." Norah can tell she's hit a nerve, for the sheriff's jowly face has taken on a new rigidity.

"She came to check on the children because of the storm."

"So she says."

"So does your son. He says that, too."

"Timothy was asleep. He doesn't know what she was doing in the house—"

"I see your point. She was at the scene."

"She had every means."

"And what would her motive be?"

"Who knows what goes on in her mind? She came into the

house, saw my son asleep, and went to Dahlia's room. When Dahlia fought her off, she stabbed her so the girl could never tell."

"That's a mighty big accusation, ma'am."

"Don't tell me it's not possible."

"Yes, well now, we'll be looking into all the possibilities."

"Then you had better start, because our son is a good Christian boy. He loved his sister. He loves his family. You think he's an easy target—well, you're wrong, Sheriff."

"Ma'am, I don't appreciate those kinds of remarks."

"That's what I'm talking about. Your bias. My son has proven his character—ask anyone at our church. But Sandra Mason—"

The sheriff's face reddens with some emotion she cannot pin down. "It's Williams, ma'am. Mason is the husband's name."

"You see? What kind of a woman is that? Why doesn't she take her husband's name?"

There are two other deputies in the room, sitting at desks, and Norah hears them go still, listening to her every word. They know what she's talking about. The kind of women she means. "She doesn't even wear a wedding band! Why is that? It seems very deceptive to me."

"Mrs. Everston . . ."

"Stay away from my son and start looking at the real suspects. She was in the house. She admitted it."

"I've known Sand Williams since she was a little girl. I know her more than, say, I know you."

Norah shakes her finger at him. "This is exactly what I'm talking about. This cronyism. You all protect each other. I'm going to report you to the state if you can't conduct an unbiased investigation. She's an obvious suspect. Start looking at her. Start ripping through her life and see what you find. You'll find something, believe me. Just walk into her house, and you can see she's not a normal woman. There's newspapers on the floor and dust everywhere. Books piled on the sofa—cups on the side tables with the dregs of yesterday's coffee. She doesn't even keep a clean house. What is she doing with her time?"

"You think she was plotting murder instead of cleaning her house."

"Don't get smart with me, Tom Gravette. I'm not going to let you or anyone destroy what is left of my family. You will have to deal with me, and I am a very righteous and angry woman. I'll get on TV. I'll make your life hell."

"I'm sure you will, ma'am." Tom Gravette sighs, then pulls out his cigarette pack and taps one out. He stares sadly at the NO SMOK-ING sign on the wall, then flicks his lighter and leans into the flame, closes his eyes as he deeply inhales. "Are you aware your daughter had strangle marks on her neck that were several days old?"

"That woman came over while we were gone. Maybe she put the marks of her hands on my daughter. Naturally Dahlia didn't tell anyone, so she came back and attacked Dahlia in her sleep."

Tom Gravette flicks some ash into his palm. "I do have one question, ma'am. Knowing how you feel about your neighbor, knowing how unnatural you feel she is, why did you leave her in charge of your kids when you went out of town?"

"I trusted her! With my child! Don't think an hour goes by that I don't wish I could take it back. Oh, I should have known! She's never even had a child of her own. She could have. There was no physical disability—I asked. What kind of woman refuses to be a mother? What kind of a woman is that?"

15

ON A WARM spring day in May, when dragonflies
float lazily on the air above the Seven Point River,
Norah accuses Sand of murder. In the morning
Norah drives hastily by the cabin but will not make
eye contact. Norah's expression remains fixed, her
eyes staring straight ahead. This Sand catalogs as
odd, and strangely disquieting, but she knows that
Norah is angry with her for not going on TV. When
Sand walks back into the cabin, she senses some mild
geological shift has occurred, an intimation received
without language but understood, the way cats and
dogs know an earthquake is on the way.

Sand is now one of them. One of the enemy.
One of the ones against Timothy, against Norah's
church and her God. But these thoughts come later
on. At the moment, she has only a sense of uneasi-
ness, and it's this very disturbance she wishes to escape. And so she does.

Because that's what she always does.

Frank wants to show her a cave he found on the
land across the river, the section of her father's land

that was once the old Hanover place. When Sand was a child, the old Hanover farmhouse was struck by lightning one night and burned to the ground. It was always hard to eke out a living from the thin layer of soil that covers the Ozark substrata of limestone and dolomite. After the house was lost, the family moved to Greenville. One son worked at the hardwood factory, the other went off to college and found the pleasures of urban life. The parents died and the sons sold the fifty acres to Harold Williams, owner of the newspaper.

Frank gets out of the truck and opens the creaky, gray-weathered gate held together mostly by wire. "Just wait." A lovely dimple sinks into the flesh above his jaw. He drives along the clay ruts through tall grass and weeds, their cave helmets rattling around the truck bed. At one point they splash across a wet-weather stream. The way is so overgrown that briars scrape the side panels of the truck.

"So much for the paint job."

Frank says, "Since when did you get practical? Live big."

"You call this living big?"

He turns to Sand and grins. "I do," he said, nodding his head. "I certainly do."

Frank carries their helmets and takes a path recently trampled through the woods. Sweat trickles down Sand's back in the spring heat. Frank's cave lies at the bottom of a ravine in a wall of dolomite, but at first she cannot see it, for its slim mouth is camouflaged by an elder bush. The entrance is nothing more than a narrow slit. She has never been here before, and Frank, a complete outsider, is showing her a cave that has been there all her life.

They have to turn sideways to fit through the opening, but once they're inside, the room is the size of the foyer in Sand's childhood home, the house in Greenville. Here in the foyer of the cave there are signs of black bear, scat piles, tracks in the mud that Frank points out with the flashlight beam.

"We're not going to run into the owners, are we?"

"Well, they're not hibernating," he says, which is not the same as no. "Look—over here." He points the light beam to a hole on the back wall.

"A fox den, maybe."

Frank laughs, a low, throaty chuckle that's somehow sensual and mischievous. He crouches before the hole, shining his beam into the pure darkness. Then he puts on his helmet, flicks its light, and crawls into the earth.

"Frank?"

Sand watches her husband's torso slip into the hole. Then the hole, like the mouth of a great snake, seems to swallow his hips and legs. She has a momentary sense of horror, seeing him be devoured like that.

She crouches to the hole and shouts after him, "You don't just crawl into an unexplored cave!"

"Too late! I already did that. I've been here before."

He moves forward into the cave. She shines her flashlight on the shadowy movement of legs. She has always found waiting back at the base camp somehow worse than being on the front line. She cannot stand being left behind. She calls into the hole, "Wait up! I'm coming in."

Then she is down on her hands and knees, crawling into the tunnel, and all she can see ahead is a small swatch of the cave floor highlighted by her helmet beam, Frank's shadowy haunches and the worn soles of his boots.

"I'm getting excited," Frank admits.

Sand's knees aren't quite what they used to be. She hears the faint sound of water trickling, and asks, "Is that water?"

"Oh, there's water in here," he says with a hushed sort of awe. "Right now, I think we're crawling on the bed of a losing stream."

As they crawl in farther, the sound of water becomes more pronounced. Sand has never been particularly good in small, confined areas—in fact, the word *claustrophobic* comes to mind—and her heart pounds in the utter darkness that smells of wet limestone.

She begins to have racing thoughts: How many tons of rock are on top of her now? Why on earth is she doing this? The sound of flowing water becomes so pronounced, it seems to be coming from inside her head, as if she's a part of this underground stream, or this underground stream is a part of her. She reaches forward and her hand sinks into cold water.

Frank says, "Here's a little narrow part where we're going to get wet." And with that they are crawling on their bellies through a shallow stream.

"My God, it's freezing."

"It's not freezing. It's fifty-four degrees. Now, right through here, you're gonna have to get down low—there's just about a foot and a half clearance."

"Frank, I'm not a kid anymore."

"That's true, kumquat. And yet we get to play."

"What if I have a panic attack?"

"Just crawl on your belly. Pretend you're a snake."

"You're starting to remind me of my father," Sand says bitterly.

Her chin trails through the cold water as she slithers forth on hands, forearms, and hips, over the hard chips of chert in the streambed. If she could turn around, she certainly would, but the shaft is so narrow, she simply has to follow him until they reach wherever the tunnel leads. There is no going back. What's behind her she has to leave. How easily a snake slides through the smallest holes in the earth. Think about that! Imagine the universe from a snake's point of view.

She feels she isn't getting enough oxygen, she can't possibly get enough oxygen in such a small space as this, so far from the cave entrance, so far from the daylight world.

"How much farther?" she gasps.

"I think I see something. Just about twenty feet."

"Goddamn it, Frank. Why did I let you talk me into this?"

"I didn't," he says. "You made up your mind, and once you make up your mind, there's no stopping you. Remember when we made love in India and you weren't on birth control? Remember that? Well, once you made the decision to suck my cock, you really, really did, and you swallowed everything. Remember that?"

"Will you fucking shut up?"

Sand ceases cursing him and simply concentrates on putting one forearm in front of the other and pulling her wet, shivering body forward. As she reaches to the right, her fingers sink into a cold, slippery goo. She examines her fingertips in the headlight beam. "What's this muck?"

"Guano."

"Bat shit?"

"Bat shit fuels this whole underground ecosystem, my dear."

"There are a lot of bats in this cave?"

"Oh, yeah."

"Oh . . ."

He is triggering all her subterranean fears. Bears, snakes, bats— a freaking colony of bats—and, last but not least, a fear of being buried under several tons of stone.

"How many is a lot?"

"Judging by the guano? Oh, several hundred, maybe a thousand. There's a lot of guano back here—there's a pile. The point is, we have to start being quiet now. We don't want to disturb them."

"No kidding!"

The truth is that for the time she crawls through that cave deep inside the earth, bruising elbows and knees, shivering from cold water and her own fear, she does not once think of Dahlia Everston. She completely forgets her life aboveground. It's as though she has crossed some boundary and truly left her life behind, shed her life like a skin. There's simply no room in this dark passage for the encasement of memories, good or bad. There's only room for dealing with her fears of the present moment and the moment after that. Each moment a strange, exhilarating pearl.

Suddenly Frank's boot soles and haunches disappear. Sand's headlamp finds his laced boots standing upright on the cave floor, and a flood of relief washes through her body. The end of the tunnel! She takes hold of his outstretched hand. As soon as her head is through the opening, the sound of water dripping echoes off the cavern walls, and she knows they have reached a large high-ceilinged room that feels like a cathedral inside the earth.

She wrings out the front of her shirt as Frank unfolds a couple of black trash bags fashioned with holes to be worn like wind-breakers for warmth. The chamber's ceiling soars twenty feet high or more. Sand swings her light across the walls and they glisten with a drapery of ochre and citrine crystals.

The stream they crawled through is fed by a spring pool bubbling up through the cave floor. Frank walks over and points his flashlight down into the water. There, caught in the beam of light, five or six small pale fish idle like two-inch koi.

Frank whispers, "You know what they are?"

Sand stares at them and nods. "The ghost fish. That's what the Native Americans called them."

The little fish are blind and almost transparent, for skin coloring and eyes have no use in a lightless world. As the species adapted over the eons, the Ozark cavefish lost their pigmentation. Their flesh is so translucent that crouching over the spring, Sand can see the pattern of their blood vessels gently pulsing, and the delicate tracing of their veins gives them a vaguely pinkish glow. They have no eyes. Just the faintest markings where eyes had once been. Instead of eyes, the fish have sensory organs on their heads and sides—tiny whiskery projections that allow them to feel their way through the watery darkness of their world, detect the minute vibrations of a future meal.

Frank kneels over the pool, his flashlight making no difference to the blindfish. "Do you realize what a treasure this is? Their ancestors have been living here since the last ice age."

"I've seen them once before," Sand says. "A long time ago. I was a girl. I was picking sassafras with my mother in the woods and it was hot. We went to a cave nearby and drank springwater. The little ghost fish were all around. You could drink the water then, when I was a girl."

Remembering that day so long ago evokes the heat of the sun

patches through the canopy of trees, the scent of pine needles and the spicy sassafras bark. Her mother was wearing pants, and most grown town women in those days didn't wear pants. Sand could feel the sweat trickling down her ribs. Standing close to her mother, Sand smelled her fragrance of Chanel No. 5 and her mother's own warm, comforting scent of perspiration. Sand lost her when she was young, and her memories of her mother are fleeting images and sensations that return from time to time, as they do now. She feels her heart connect to her mother, and tears spring to her eyes.

When her mother took her to the woodland cave, it seemed a magical world, and she was leading Sand on an adventure. They knelt over the cave spring, and there in the waters swam a dozen of the small blindfish. *Look, Sand. We're in luck.* The water was cold and ran down her chin and into the Peter Pan collar of her shirt. Her mother said, *People call them the spring-keepers. The well-keepers.* In those days people sometimes still found a cavefish in the bucket when they dipped for water in their wells. The little fish were regarded as good-luck charms, like finding a four-leaf clover, and everyone believed that the presence of cavefish meant the water was safe to drink.

Here in the springwater they hover, remnants of a nearly lost tribe. The little fish waver behind a blur of Sand's tears. The old childish questions return: *Why did Mother die so young? Why did she leave me? Why is my memory of her so vague, so piecemeal? Why do I still long for her? As if she's the piece I lack and without which I will never be whole.*

Sand sniffs and blots her eyes with the damp forearm of her shirt. "The water must be good."

"They're a pretty good barometer. Like canaries in a mineshaft. When they die off, it's a sign of what's going to happen to us. Do you know how rare they are anymore? These cavefish are some of the last of their kind. And they're still alive," he whispers, turning to Sand. "Alive on this land." His voice is tinged by a certain reverence that speaks of his passion. "Know what I'm thinking?"

"I've got an idea."

He takes her chin between his fingers. "One person can make a difference. Two are more than two."

"You still believe that?"

"I know it. It's always been that way. It's never been any other way. I can prove it to you."

"They're rosy because you can see the blood pumping through their bodies, Frank." This observation causes her to burst into tears. Her husband feels her shaking, wraps his arm around her, and asks if she's cold.

"I'm losing it," she says.

"Maybe you're supposed to lose it. Maybe it's just as well."

He kisses her forehead, then he invites her into his arms, and they hug each other until their wet chests are warmed beneath the plastic trash bags.

"Look, the first thing we have to do is photograph them, Sand. Document them, make them known to exist. Come over here," he says. "Very quietly."

They've been whispering over the pool, their voices a susurration that echoes off the walls. As Sand follows him to the back of the chamber, their flashlights pass over a glinting, crystalline drapery along the walls, and she notices a gentle draft of air across her face.

Frank whispers, "Don't scream or anything."

Then he raises the big flashlight and reveals a new tunnel. At first she thinks she's seeing some dark mineral excrescence from the cave itself. Then slowly she distinguishes the countless small furred heads and bodies. The ceiling and upper walls of the tunnel are carpeted with the hanging bodies of hundreds and hundreds of bats. A wave of revulsion spills over her, but she forces herself to study them. The disturbance of their boots on the cave floor, creates a ripple of movement among the sleeping bats. Their dark wings rustle, as though they are having a collective dream.

Frank places a finger to his lips. They step back from the new tunnel. "It's a big colony. The airflow suggests there's another entrance from the surface."

Sand kneels over the pool and casts her flashlight beam down into the water. "All right. I'll do it. The last time I photographed anyone, she was dead. I hated it. At least these fish are still alive. I'll do it because they remind me of myself. My lost pieces. And I feel as blind as they are." Then she dips her hands into the cave pool and lowers her face to drink.

"Hey, what are you doing?"

"I want to know if the old stories are true."

———

THE CAVE COMES back to her when they are making love. They have done it together so many times, and yet they can still return with delight. *I trust him,* Sand thinks. *I trust Frank.* This amazes her, but something about them is changing. They're no longer young. Their sexuality is taking on a different quality. They can rock together in a state of bliss or lie perfectly still, from time to time a ripple pulsing her vagina. They are together, sharing this wavelength that is trancelike and intensely pleasurable but no longer directly tied to sexual intercourse. In that place they are most themselves, without secrets, often unaware of anything called thought or fantasy—moving with the agility of fish through un-limited space.

Dusk is their time for making love. For those who are no longer young, the grainy light favors their beauty, makes them mysterious. Dusk hides the flaws of living beyond youth. Her wa-tery reflection in a mirror catches a certain fiery light in her eyes, and Sand recognizes in her face the child she once was and the middle-aged woman she is now. It's as though their true essences are coming out. When she holds Frank inside her, he says there's a whole new power and strength to her pelvic girdle—a rippling like a snake. *You are a goddess,* he says.

16

"MRS. EVERSTON? THE rape test came back from the state lab."

Norah is holding a big yellow bowl of cookie batter when she answers the phone and the sheriff tells her the news. The yellow bowl clatters to the kitchen table. She reaches for a chair to steady herself.

"No evidence of bruising or tearing was found. And no trace of semen. There's no evidence of rape." The sheriff gruffly clears his throat. "It appears the girl never had sexual intercourse."

Norah turns to the window over the sink, where a wedge of afternoon sunlight cascades into the room, almost blinding her for a second or two. "She never had . . . are you telling me, Sheriff, that Dahlia was a virgin?"

The sheriff's voice hesitates, embarrassed. "Uh, yes, ma'am. That would be accurate."

Norah lowers the phone to its cradle and bursts into tears. She wasn't raped. Oh, thank God, he didn't rape her. Thank you, God. She sits down at the table and cries. It is such a relief. They will not be cast out. She will not be shunned. She imagines walking down the aisle at church. She is embraced. The girl was clean. After all her worry. The girl was a virgin at eighteen. How many mothers can say that about their daughters?

A virgin still. Norah shakes her head giddily. She didn't really expect it. She always assumed Dahlia had given in to that boy, Dwayne. For isn't that the way of things? She never thought that the boy would have listened to Dahlia when she said no. A warm, rosy ball of pride rises in Norah's breast. Here is the proof that she is a good mother, that she raised her daughter right. She is so re-lieved, she doesn't hear Lyman walk in. He catches her wiping her face with a tissue. He goes to the cupboard and takes down the bottle of aspirin. "Who was that?"

"The sheriff. The test came back. It's good news. She wasn't raped, Lyman. With so much darkness, there's a bit of light."

Lyman sits down at the table. For a few moments he slumps there with his hand over his mouth, staring into space. A few stray gray and black hairs have escaped his ponytail.

"There was no sign of semen—nothing?"

"Nothing. She was clean."

"She was washed, Norah."

"There was no rape. They used their microscopes on her. Dahlia was a virgin. The test proved that."

"Ah." Slowly he turns to her. "You'll have to tell everyone at church."

She places her hand over his. "Lyman—this is good news."

"It means we have no evidence. The police found no finger-prints in her room that didn't belong to one of us. How is that good news?"

"At least he didn't rape her, Lyman. At least she was spared that."

"He didn't kill her for sex. It wasn't a sex crime, at least not in the usual sense. So there must have been another motive."

"Don't you see? So much has been lost, but no one can ever say that she was raped. Our daughter was a virgin when she died."

"Christ, you're like some Middle Eastern villager, holding the bloody bridal sheets over the balcony for all the town to see. She's dead, Norah!"

"You think I don't miss her? You think I didn't love her, too?"

"I don't think you miss her the way I do. I don't think you can love her the way I do. I'm her father. She was my blood."

"Lyman, please—don't do this. We always said we would love them both the same. We'll never see her again until we go to heaven—"

"Oh, stop with that. She's my daughter. He's your son."

"They're both ours. They're both the same."

"They're not the same. They were different. They were very, very different."

"He can't help that he's not as smart as she was."

Lyman gets up and starts pacing the kitchen. "Where is Timothy?"

"At church. I have to pick him up. There's something wrong with the engine of his truck."

"They fought, Norah."

She feels a streak of irritation and snaps at him. "Where are you going with this? All kids do."

"This was the first time we left them alone. Why is it we never left them alone before?"

"They were too young. You know that."

"It's because they fought. He's evasive. He knows more than he's told us so far."

"Stop it! Timothy's a victim here."

"No, he's not. My daughter was the victim. Timothy slept through her screams. Her dying agony did not disturb his sleep. A killer broke into our house, stabbed my daughter twenty times, scrubbed down the walls and floors, washed her, then laid her out in bed. And Timothy slept through it all!"

She cannot believe Lyman has stepped so far away from them.

"Finally I have something to feel good about, and you're . . . you're stealing it away."

He shakes his head in frustration. "His reactions to this—they don't seem right."

"There are no right reactions. Even the sheriff will tell you that. Everyone reacts differently. Some victims go through their lives as if nothing happened at all. That doesn't mean it didn't happen. I don't know if he really understands what death is. The finality."

"I'm not going to survive this."

She sees him drawing away from her like a receding tide. And what she feels for him is fury. He has to survive. He has to be strong. She speaks very evenly. "Lyman, we need you to be strong for us." It occurs to her that he may never be strong again. She says, "Time heals everything."

NORAH'S CHURCH IS out in the country, a well-made native-stone church with a wood-frame rectory where Pastor John lives with his family. Timothy's youth studies group meets in the pastor's living room. When Norah pulls up the drive, she sees that the parking lot is empty, so she must be late. A little trill of anxiety runs through her breast. She cannot tell if what she feels is anticipation or fear. Pastor John steps from the house, raises his hand in greeting. Norah returns the wave. He walks toward her with his limping gait, which he once confessed was the result of childhood polio. "How are you, Norah? I've been praying for you and your family." John Allen is wearing a short-sleeved white shirt and black pants, so well worn, they have a slightly green tinge like a grackle's neck feathers. His skinny arms and hollowed cheeks give him an emaciated look.

"I have something to tell you. Is there somewhere we can talk?"

He invites her into his office at the back of the church. The last time she saw his office it was very dusty, but now it is clean, the windows clear as water. The room smells strongly of Pine-Sol or Murphy's oil soap, the bracing odor of cleanliness. Norah settles into an old wooden office chair that swivels on its base, rests her purse on her lap, holding it firmly between her hands. "What is it?" he asks quietly. "Has there been a break in the case?"

"Yes."

How can she explain her excitement, the sense of anticipation she feels? Her story spills out like water breaking through a dam. How worried she's been. How fearful that everything about them will be known. But the rape test has come back and Dahlia was not raped. Her pastor's gray, watery eyes watch her not unkindly from behind his solid black-framed glasses. He takes off his glasses and begins to polish the lenses with a tissue he plucks from a box on his desk.

Does he understand? She died chaste.

The strangest thoughts come into Norah's head. *Maybe it was meant to be.* She almost envies the girl, for Dahlia escaped the humiliation, the despair, the sensation of being powerless. The wrenching pain of her head being raised by the hair, then slammed down upon the kitchen counter. No one will ever touch Dahlia that way. Norah recalls those nights as if they are happening still. Her first husband's intentions are focused and furtive. He is foiled by her waistband and curses her.

Norah's gaze falls to the pastor's inkwell on the desk. The inkwell is a kind of anachronism, like writing in blood. She blinks, feels the palpitations in her chest. That was long ago. Another life. *I never think about it.*

"Norah?" the pastor says. "You're staring into space."

Norah blinks. She was never that woman. How could she ever have been that woman? She reaches for her wedding band, twists the diamond ring on her finger. It's a good ring, an expensive ring, and proves she has a certain kind of life. She is cared for and cherished.

"I just . . . want people to know. My daughter wasn't raped. She was a virgin when she died. She was chaste."

Reverend John nods with a wistful smile. "That must give you great consolation."

"Oh, it does!" Norah leans in toward his praise. She is ready to receive the blessing he will give. How badly she needs his blessing.

"Dahlia was a good girl," she says, and waits for him to agree, but he hesitates, looks at the brass crucifix hanging on the wall, and slowly shakes his head before he weighs his words.

"Dahlia was a virgin. That counts in her favor, yes. A virgin is what an unmarried woman should be."

"Yes—"

"But she did not worship in His church, and so she broke His commands. Now Timothy—if, God forbid, he was struck down by lightning tonight, he would face his maker with a clean and honest face."

A gloomy pall spreads over her body. She feels her resistance waning, feels herself giving in to her pastor's greater moral authority. "Yes . . . I'm very proud of Timothy." She looks up to the reverend, for he is the leader of her church. He explains the Bible and who is a sinner and who is not.

"Timothy is one of the leaders of his youth studies group."

"Really?"

"Oh, not because he's the smartest one but because his heart is pure, and he loves God with all his heart. Timothy loves to serve our Lord."

"I know," she whispers. "It's true that Dahlia resisted God's path for her. She didn't accept the Bible and that she must obey." Tears spill over the rims of her eyes. "I tried. I tried to be a good mother. She was young, foolish. She simply didn't realize the unending horror of hell's fire. When I told her what she was risking, she would laugh at me."

"And you see what happened?"

Norah weeps openly. "But why? Why? I've tried to do everything right. I obeyed all of God's commands. Why has He not protected me? Why has He let this terrible thing happen to me?"

"Norah." The pastor reaches over and lays his hand upon her wrist. "You could have lost the boy, too."

"I know. When I think of how close he came to being slaughtered—"

"But God spared Timothy. Because God loves Timothy. Here,

come with me. I want to show you something. Something you need to understand."

Norah follows her limping pastor into the nave of the church. Again she catches the strong scent of oil soap warmed by splashes of yellow sunlight on the hardwood floor. There are few touches of adornment in Norah's church, no red or blue patches of stained glass—just sunlight spilling into the sanctuary like the pure, unadulterated light of God. They walk to the center aisle and gaze toward the plain altar at the front. Then she sees her son, down on the floor on his hands and knees. Norah takes a sharp, stunned breath. Timothy plunges a rag into the bucket beside him, then wrings it out with a single wrench of his fists and rubs at the floor, applying all the strength of his broad shoulders to the task.

"Look at him!" Pastor John smiles at her son with pride. "See how content he is serving God? It's his special offering."

The sight of her son cleaning is so disturbing, she feels a little breathless. Timothy has never given any inkling that he even knew what to do with a mop and rag. Norah pales. "I . . . had no idea he was . . . so . . . industrious."

The pastor beams. "Oh, I'm teaching him skills, skills he can later use in the marketplace."

Norah feels strangely faint, as though she were floating away from her body, only vaguely tethered to this wreck of herself. Her son has not yet noticed them. His healthy face is ruddy with exertion, and a lock of straight blond hair falls over one blue eye. He rubs at a scuff mark on the floor with his particular strain of determination. The black heel mark will come out. There is no question of that. Reverend John watches her son with the pure joy she always hoped to see on her husband's face, but Lyman has never been wholly won over by Timothy, never given his approval a hundred percent. That's all she had expected of him—to say that what she made in her womb is good enough. Was that too much to ask—that our lives have meaning?

Her pastor sighs and pats her shoulder before he withdraws his hand. "No, Timothy isn't like most adolescents, who have a tendency to be self-centered, I'm afraid. Our Timothy is above the temptations that consume so many teenagers."

She can describe her mood on the drive home only as queer, strange. She feels herself to be a step removed from her own actions and body and has to remind herself to halt at stop signs, look both ways. Her stomach is acting up again. The news she brought seems somehow pointless, her moment of triumph obscured. Instead, she feels encompassed by a cloud of free-floating anxiety. An attack of nerves. Timothy sits beside her on the passenger seat, tired from his labor, limbs sprawled, yawning. The special feeling of comfort she often feels in quiet moments when they are alone has evaporated like fog, and here is this big, gangly-limbed young man beside her whom she doesn't really know.

"Tired?"

"Yeah. And hungry. I'm starving, Mom."

"I didn't know you did all that cleaning over at church."

"Well," he says, stretching his back. She notices the thick cords of muscle in his neck, like some great tawny god. "I'm a good Christian young man," he says, pumped up with pride. "I love the Lord, and I want to serve Him."

Again she feels she's going to be sick. When she gets home, she will have to lie down. "You are, uh . . . very good at polishing."

"That's what Pastor John says. I'm the best."

She rubs the steering wheel with her thumb, glances furtively at her son. Her breath comes shallow and fast. Her head is pounding, or is it her heart? She can't tell the difference. "Did you do any cleaning at home while we were away?"

"At home? Mom, I'm not a girl."

"But since you do know how to clean. I just thought . . . well, at home . . ."

He holds up his fingers to count off his duties to her. "My chores are to mow the grass, carry out the garbage, prune around the house, and get the mail every day. Cleaning house—that was Dahlia's job."

"Yes, but dear, if you were living alone . . ."

His big head swivels her way in alarm. "Why would I live alone? I live at home. In my room."

"I, well, I just mean—someday."

"Why? You want me to leave?"

"No!" She squeezes the steering wheel. "Of course not."

"You want me to leave because Dahlia is gone?"

"Of course not, Timothy. You're all the more precious to us."

He turns forward again, brooding, thrusting out his lower lip. "That's a funny way of showing it."

"Son, how are you feeling?"

"What do you mean?"

"About Dahlia."

He shrugs. "All right, I guess. It's weird that she's not in the house anymore."

"It is."

"Sometimes I forget, and I think she will be there."

"That happens to me, too."

"But then I go look and she's not in her room and she's not in the kitchen or watching TV."

"No, she's in heaven."

"Well, I don't know about that, Mom."

"What do you mean?" She is shocked, a little appalled. The road sign tells her to slow down for the curve, and she pumps the brake several times, feels the tension of the wheels, frowns.

"I prayed for her soul with Pastor John. But she didn't come to church. She didn't believe like we do."

"I know."

"She wasn't right with God, Mom."

Norah understands he's parroting the minister, but she is suddenly unnerved by his patronizing tone of voice—as though he feels he is the more mature authority speaking to a simple child, and not the other way around.

"She was an eighteen-year-old virgin! What more do you want?" Her cheeks flush with heat. She tries to recover herself. "Excuse me, that's not something I should be talking about with you."

"She should have come to church and the Bible youth studies group, but she didn't do that. So her soul is in jeopardy. They're not going to open the gates of heaven to just anyone who comes along. You have to be a believer to get in. I thought you understood that, Mom."

"Yes, yes, I do."

Norah drives on silently. He has learned the word *jeopardy*. Norah stares straight ahead. Patchy sunlight glides over the windshield. She begins to steel herself for facing Lyman back at the house. That woman's voice rises into her heart: *everything falling apart*. Timothy stretches his arms, laces his fingers, then loudly cracks his knuckles. It's an awful sound that has always made her wince.

"Mom, I'd like to have a new Chevy truck. Built like a rock. God is the rock."

"Yes, He is the rock."

"Can I have a Chevy truck?"

She glances quickly. "No! And I wouldn't go asking for one right now."

"Why not?"

"It would look selfish! It would look like you didn't really miss your sister."

"I don't see what that has to do with it. I mean, you and Dad don't have to buy things for her anymore. So, if I'm that precious, why won't you buy me a truck?"

She feels her nerves breaking, her arms trembling. "How can you even think of yourself at a time like this? How can you be so selfish? Think of what your father's going through!"

"If I had a truck, then I can keep going to Bible school and cleaning the church for Pastor John and serving our Lord, Mom. I don't see what's selfish about that."

17

SPRING IS TAKEN from their hands, and summer unfurls the slow, hot days. Sand Williams is tired of always pushing, turning every effort into a fight. Norah has accused her of murder, and gossip trails her everywhere. In Meecham's Grocery, two women hurriedly whisper as they watch Sand push her cart down the aisle. Maybe they're parishioners from Norah's church. Sand wonders how they even know who she is, but that's a thought of a person who's been away from home for a long time.

Just before the Fourth of July she walks into Merlee's Café during the lunch hour and the raucous chatter dies. A wave of heat rises inside her, that paralyzing heat, a damn hot flash brought on by the shock that her very presence kills the easy atmosphere. She wants to turn on her heel and flee, but she can't do that, either. She hears her father's voice, and this time she's searching for his advice, the old lesson about the hungry dogs. *Look straight at them. Stand tall and calm, don't show them you're afraid. They'll rip your throat out if they see weakness now.* She meets every eye that will meet hers, one after another: farmers in overalls, timbermen, the courthouse staff, the women who work on the square. The air smells of chili. Merlee has decorated the place with little flags and streamers in red, white, and blue. The blackboard on the wall announces that chili con carne, meat loaf, and hot roast beef sandwich with mashed potatoes and greens are the blue plate specials of the day.

One of the counter stools is left vacant now in memory of Dahlia Everston—the red vinyl seat Dahlia sat upon and ate her last meal on earth. Sand hopes that breakfast was something Dahlia didn't often allow herself, like biscuits and sausage gravy and a mess of golden, runny eggs, the kind of breakfast that lasts with you all day. A farmer's breakfast, the kind they eat in here. She approaches another empty stool at the middle of the counter, and a wide-hipped matron sets her handbag on the seat. Quickly the next empty stool is covered by the *Greenville Clarion,* her father's newspaper, and she understands she is being shunned. Sand takes a seat at the end of the counter, the nearest human specimen a lanky individual with bristly hair and dirty bed slippers on his feet. He's carrying on an avid conversation with himself, and she pegs him for an inmate from the "nervous hospital."

Merlee flits about the room, hefting plates of food, but never seems to turn her way. Another wave of heat spills over her, and Sand decides she's too close to the grill, for she can feel the grease of hamburgers collecting on her face. By the time she's on her third hot flash, Merlee's old father shuffles out from the kitchen and asks his daughter in a querulous voice, "Merlee, have you seen my teef?" Merlee halts in her tracks, spins around, balancing four blue plate specials on her raised palms.

"What, Daddy?"

"My teef!" Her father reaches up and covers his mouth. "I wonnered if they're over at your house."

Once more the diner goes utterly quiet. Everyone is listening.

"Now, Daddy, what would your teeth be doin' at my house?"

He shakes his head in frustration, snaps his suspenders once. "I must'a left 'em somewere."

"You mean you lost your teeth? They aren't at my house," she says, and starts blushing then.

He stands there on feeble legs, bloodshot eyes scanning the room as if he might spot his false teeth on top of a napkin dispenser, perched among the condiments, or hanging from the pegs of the coatrack by the door. No one says a word. A few spoons are heard tinkling against the inside of a coffee cup or tapping a chili bowl like a blind man's cane to make sure no foreign object lies hidden there.

"Well, where could I uh lost 'em, then?"

"Oh, Daddy, how would I know?"

"I jus' wonnered. I sure would like to find 'em soon."

Sand walks out of the café, feeling superior to the farmer crowd. Isn't she educated? Didn't she leave and see the world? By the time she reaches her car, she's in tears.

She feels angry and betrayed by Norah, but how can she fight against Norah? *Who am I fighting anyway,* she thinks, *the aggrieved mother of a murdered girl?* What possible course of action might she take to defend herself? Begin a rumor campaign against Norah's son? No, no, she can't do that, and to accuse Norah's son feels like Norah's accusing her: a desperate stab at someone who feels like an enemy.

She's more lonely than she's ever been. She's not used to being "the outsider," not here where she was born and reared. At one point Frank says, "Let's pull up stakes and go," but leaving, she feels, would provide more evidence of her guilt. And besides, Weleda County is her home. She has a right to be here, and no one is going to drive her away. When she leaves, it'll be of her own accord and not because she's been run out by malicious gossiping. She refuses to leave under that shadow, for the shadow will remain attached to her name.

In the middle of July, Tom Gravette calls to inform Sand that her alibi fell through. Merlee is no longer sure when Sand left her café on the day of the murder. "You'd better stick around," he says. "Don't go traveling."

There is no escape. Norah has become this dreadful piece of furniture that Sand moves about in the rooms of her head. No matter the arrangement, Norah remains—like the antique chair Sand's mother inherited from Great-Aunt Pidge, part Victorian, part baroque. Every time she walks by the living room, Norah sits in the corner like some cold, judgmental pocket of air. But she can't throw Norah out the window. There's some rule about the chair. Something ancient and inarticulate. It's as if this old chair is carrying her ancestors' commands, their expectations that continue to thrive in the stuffed cushions. She can't throw Norah from the house, so she keeps moving her around. She shoves Norah into small dusty rooms she rarely enters, but that's where Norah is waiting for her, half hidden under a bag of out-of-season clothes, her damask seat a good place to set a sewing basket with its sharp scissors and tight cushions bristling with needles and pins. Sand lugs her to the basement and leaves Norah to the crickets and the damp. Puts her up on pallets so the occasional basement flooding won't leave white rings on her polished legs. She hauls Norah to the attic, where her intricately carved wooden arms will bake in summertime, become brittle as old bones, and hasten toward their eventual fate as dust, but every time Sand goes looking for some odd thing in the attic, there's Norah . . . waiting.

The house that Norah inhabits, the house that comes to mind, is not her father's cabin on the river but the house in Greenville where she grew up. One afternoon Sand drives by the house on Mellon Avenue. The wide lawns, the big old stately oaks. She parks and stares at the side porches with columns, the turret windows where her mother liked to read on Saturday afternoons and she would curl up on the window seat and watch the street like a cat. That large, spacious house on Mellon Avenue, the house of her childhood, is where she sees Norah when she envisions her as Great-Aunt Pidge's ugly chair.

LITTLE HEADWAY IS made that summer on the Everston case. The most significant change seems to be that the community, which was of one mind at the time of the murder, is now beginning to divide. The news that Timothy failed the polygraph leaks out, as these things always do. Some people begin to wonder. Maybe at odd times of the day, as they place a coffee cup into the dishwasher or comb their hair at the mirror, they see, for an instant, Timothy wielding a knife in his hand. The image unsettles them, and they don't know what to do with it, so they stuff it into some drawer, some crevice in their mind. But Timothy's teachers and classmates stand behind him solidly. Timothy is well behaved and follows all the rules at school. He's a model student in this special class. He's a good Christian boy. The parishioners of his church and Pastor Allen are loudly vocal on the subject of Timothy's innocence, which means the blame has to go somewhere else.

In the heat of the afternoon, Sand steps from the gravel bank into the river. The cool clear water swirls around her ankles, and she wades carefully over slick rocks until the water rides up to her waist. In the water lies the memory of glacial streams from the distant north and from deep inside the earth. When she turns upstream, the dappled splotches of dark green plant life along the river bottom make the stream look like the back of a mottled trout. Sand lies down, and the water carries her like a leaf. Blue sky moves overhead. She floats past a group of turtles sunning themselves on a fallen tree, and the current threads her on by.

Up ahead looms the Crossing Over Bridge, which still holds the memory of her father as a young boy running across the planks. What were his dreams on a day like this? It seems to her the river holds the memory of all of our lives; the knowledge of everything the water has touched is held within its molecules: our emotions, our thoughts, our souls, remembered by the water.

DEEP IN A stygian darkness, blindfish swim in black pools. It is a darkness beyond any experienced aboveground, so absolute, it carries with it a sense of otherworldliness. Down in this lightless world a marginal population survives: pigmentless crawfish, troglobites, salamanders that, as larva, have functioning eyes and brown skin. By adulthood evolution has taught them to lose their gills and breathe through their skin. Their eyes atrophy and lids fuse almost shut. The cavefish are rare, about two inches long. Pale, sightless, almost translucent, they hover in pools as if hoarding energy, but actually they are trying not to disturb the water, for their acute sense of vibration is what leads them to food. In darkness an entire food chain begins with the droppings of bats. Bats are not true cave creatures. Bats come and go. They live in both worlds and feed the dark.

Sand returns to the cave with Frank to photograph the cavefish. The coolness inside the cavern is a welcome relief during the season of white grass. She wonders if the blindfish are aware of this intrusion into their private world. Do the fish notice a minute rise in temperature from the heat of battery-powered lights, or the tremors of human feet on the cavern floor? How do they interpret the vibrations Sand and Frank make, or the peculiar click of her camera that's not the same as water dripping from the cave ceiling?

Do we register as the possibly edible, Sand thinks, *or something more ominous or profound?* She suspects that she and Frank are less substantial to the blindfish than the bat droppings that occasionally fall into their waters, or the small crustaceans and invertebrate animals they consume. No more real than ghosts. *Perhaps we don't even exist to the cavefish,* she thinks, *and yet our actions may alter the course of their species.*

Amblyopsis rosae. Status: threatened.

After the last ice age, the ghost fish survived along the inland shores of the Midwest. Did they once have sight and colored flesh and lose these sunlit traits with their evolution to cave life, or, when the ocean retreated, were they unprepared for ultraviolet radiation, and only those who found darkness survived?

What are they telling us?

They are so small. Why do they matter at all? People say adapting with nature is pointless now. So what if fish die, if birds die, if the water dies? Great dinosaurs once ruled the earth and *they* died. We're going to die, too. It's the natural course of things.

Her back aches as she rises from a crouching position over the cavern spring. She snaps on the lens cover of her camera and wonders how much time has elapsed. She no longer has any feeling in her fingers and toes. She senses the presence of bats along the back tunnel. Frank once told her a single bat could eat up to six hundred mosquitoes an hour. Every night they consume half their body weight. In a world where mosquito bites can make you sick, bats are a tremendous gift. They are feared and maligned because they're creatures of our shadow side, but if we can learn to appreciate them, they, in turn, will support our survival.

Frank gives Sand a nod. They silently pack their gear, and as they head for the tunnel, Frank whispers, "I love our life. I love our life together, Sand."

This time as they crawl out, Sand finds herself slowing down, and when she sees the first shafts of light breaking into the chamber ahead, she feels a great reluctance to leave the cave.

18

IN SUMMERTIME YOU can endure the heat of "the spirit room" only in the early-morning hours or after sundown, and even then you need the relief of an old caged office fan that whirls the heavy air about and dries the sweat on the back of your neck. The fan is plugged into the Weleda County Sheriff's Department by a long orange extension cord, for the old shed dangles like a wart from the main building. Once the shed housed a riding lawn mower that trimmed the moat of grass between the department and the street, retired patrol car keys, rat poison, Reed's bicycle, Tom Gravette's fishing gear, and, most recently, Patti Callahan's fifth-grade school desk, salvaged for purely sentimental reasons before the school building was torn down.

But over the years, as the department grew and strained the confines of the 1950s brick building, what could no longer be held inside the department was hauled out to the shed. Now all the deputies refer to the ugly appendage trailing off the backside of the department as "the spirit room," for here lie the remains of all the unsolved cases of Weleda County, cold case files that are removed from the department to make room for the new.

Final destination: two black metal cabinets gone rusty with the damp.

Patti Callahan sits hunched over her old school desk that does not easily accommodate her adult girth. She is thumbing through the dead cases, pulling every file from the past twenty-five years on the chance there's some connection to the Dahlia Everston murder. Tom Gravette told her they had to rule out anybody the defense could use for reasonable doubt.

Murders, unaccountable deaths, rapes, burglaries, stolen cattle, arson. Her fingers pause on the slight ridges of her name carved into the desktop so many years ago. "Patti loves Davey!" and the more risky prediction: "4 Ever." She has no idea what happened to Davey. The breeze of the fan lifts her bangs from her forehead. The skin between her brows is furled. Her mother always says, *Don't scowl, your face will stay that way,* and someday these lines will sink into Patti's face, the first age lines drawn by focus, concentration on her work.

She begins with the murders, of course, looking for any similarities and studying the lists of suspects once interviewed. The print of the oldest cases is beginning to fade, and Patti feels a certain wistfulness that eventually these crimes will literally disappear. She sets these files on top of the shelf beside a forgotten pair of garden gloves. To these she adds three deaths by unknown causes. Within minutes a large, brightly patterned wood spider begins stringing a silken web from the shelf to the half-rotten window frame, and after several tries, the spider snags the corner of the file folders. For a few minutes Patti watches the spider incorporate the unsolved murders into its web, before she reaches out and tears the threads away.

She moves on to the crimes of rape and burglary. Here are two touch points with the Everston case, for even though the rape test came back negative, Patti and the sheriff both agree a frenzied stabbing like that has a sexual component: it's close, it's personal, it's out of control, it's the puncturing of a woman's body with a long hard, sharp implement.

Just as she expects, there are very few rape cases from twenty years ago. Until recently the county sheriffs maintained that rape wasn't a problem in Weleda County; what they meant was, it wasn't a problem for them. Women were raped, but they didn't report the crime. If they did, they were in for another sort of violation, and before their ordeal was over, it wasn't the perpetrator's fault—it was something they had done.

When Patti came on the force seven years ago she was shocked by the department's callousness, but it was the kind of shock you have when you've buried some memory deep inside and discovered it again.

They fucked her in the barn. That's what she said! They took turns fucking her. The thirteen-year-old country girl interrogated by the deputies didn't know the proper word for what had happened to her. She used the word she knew, and the deputies thought the word proved she must have liked it, or they found her ignorance somehow ludicrous. Patti's husband, Deputy Reed, laughed with the rest of them, and that was it for him as far as Patti was concerned.

At that time Deputy Callahan was performing secretarial duties. The department files were in grand disorder. Her face burned with contained fury. She did her work. Very carefully. Then one night she went home, took a shower and changed her clothes, got back into her Crown Victoria with a thudding heart.

The night was soddened by a slow drizzling rain. She parked in front of the well-known river house of Harold Williams II, editor and owner of the local newspaper. Harry came to the door with a glass of bourbon in hand.

"Hey, Patti. What's a good-looking gal like you doin' in this neck of the woods?" He seemed glad for the interruption of his solitude. "How are the boys treating you?"

"About the same, Harry. You have anything to drink in there?"

"I think I can find a drop among the rations." He had a fire going in the fireplace and only a few lamps were lit. "Take a seat. What's your poison?"

"Beer, I guess." She sat down and studied the warm, dancing flames in the stone hearth.

"You gotta watch the beer, kiddo. I'm off the beer on account of my gout. Only touch distilled spirits now. But I still got a few beers stashed in the fridge, you know, for company. Oh, maybe now and then I'll have a beer after dinner for old times' sake."

He poured her beer into a glass stein, an act that seemed well mannered and elegant. The beer had a golden glow in the firelight, and as he handed it to her he said, "So I take it you're not on duty."

Patti shook her head. "I'm not here at all. Here's to courage," she said, raising her glass to him, and their two glasses made a clink.

"Courage is good." Harry took a seat in the armchair that was clearly his favorite.

Patti sipped her beer and once more studied the fire. He must have made the fire some hours ago, for a deep bed of red coals lay on the grate. One log crackled and broke, sending a shower of red sparks against the fire screen.

She remembered being small and hearing women relatives whisper the word *rape* in a way that made them shudder, as if it might happen to them just for saying it, for getting too near to the danger of the word.

"What's up, Patti?"

"Sexual assault," Patti said, feeling some refuge in the technical term. In that moment she became aware of Harry Williams as a man.

"Yes," he said, waiting for her to go on.

"Well . . ."

Harry Williams frowned, his eyes suddenly narrowing. "Patti, did something happen?"

"It's not that."

"What is it?"

"I have information. About the way things were done—are done—at the department. What happens afterward. When a woman is raped. I could lose my job, Harry."

Harry leaned forward, resting his elbows on his knees, his face a bilious red. "They wouldn't dare. Not while I run the newspaper."

"You know how they are. They can make it so you'll want to leave. I'll never get a promotion. Things like that."

"So you want me to leave you out of it."

"If you can."

"Which means you'll tell me anyway." He raised his empty glass. "Here's to courage," he said, and went to pour himself another drink.

She watched his lean back, his practiced hand moving over the shining copper of the bar. "Harry, you remember Doc Horgan, who moved to Columbia?"

"Sure. I know Doc Horgan."

"But did you know that until about fifteen, twenty years ago, he was the only doctor in Weleda County who would treat a rape victim?"

"What are you talking about?" Harry snapped, and she felt his renowned edge.

"I'm not lying. That's our very recent history. It explains why things are still so bad. I asked one of the older deputies and he said, 'Yes, that's how it was done. If you brought a beat-up woman to the emergency room, you had to assure them it wasn't rape before they'd take a look at her. If it was rape, they said, 'Take her to Doc Horgan. He takes care of that.' "

"Are you telling me that rape victims were turned away from our county hospitals?"

"That's exactly what I'm saying."

Harry slumped and rested his head upon one hand. He went a little pale. "Can you prove it?"

"I can help you prove it. I'm the only one who knows where anything is filed. And there's Doc Horgan in Columbia. And for-mer ER nurses."

"I can't believe this. . . ."

"You can't?" She stared at him so fiercely that he looked away. "You've lived here all your life. It is true, Harry. And you know it is. The problem is, what to do about it.

"We're talking about every law enforcement agency in the county and both the hospitals. Acting in collusion, engaged in illegal practices that denied civil rights. Victims were rejected from our hospitals. The doctors refused to touch them or go to court to testify."

"But why? I don't get it. The boys afraid they'd miss a round of golf?"

"I don't know, Harry. I can't explain it. No one can explain it. Maybe it's the taboo of the crime or that doctors were afraid they might know the perpetrator socially, or they just didn't want to be bothered testifying for some complaining woman! I don't know why. But they simply refused to get involved, and all the service agencies acted in complicity. This comes out, by the time the county gets through being sued, we'll have bankrupted our social services. Which are just barely surviving as it is."

"You protecting the blue, Patti?"

"Maybe. Maybe I just want a job."

Harry shook his head slowly and gazed into the firelight. "I can't let this pass."

"Neither can I."

"So," he whispered, "what are you suggesting, kiddo?"

Patti sighed deeply, then looked him in the eye. "Blackmail. Basically."

A month later Harold Williams II, publisher and owner of the *Greenville Clarion,* invited Sheriff Tom Gravette, the three chiefs of police, and the two hospital CEOs over to his river cabin for a friendly drink. Whatever transpired never made it into the newspaper.

After that, Patti was put in charge of sexual assault cases at the sheriff's department, female police officers were hired, and the hospitals drafted new protocols for treating victims of rape and domestic abuse. Patti declared the chaotic files were in order and took on her new responsibilities with a dispassionate, uncomplaining air. The deputies did not seem to know her part in things. Never suspected her. Sometimes she thinks Tom Gravette figured it out, but if he did, he never mentioned it. Just once in a while the way he looks at her, she thinks he's sizing her up.

Lately the crime of rape appears to be skyrocketing in Weleda County, but Patti knows it's only because women are starting to think there's a point in taking their grievance to the law. A small brownish stain curls up the corner of one of the old reports. She raises the paper and sniffs, wondering if she can still smell a faint whiff of bourbon from Harry tipping his glass while he read. No, it's gone. Only the smell of dust and faint mildew remain.

After sifting through the cold case files in the company of spiders and small armored pill bugs, and a couple of black and yellow garden snakes who have taken up residence on the shelves, Patti is haunted by the victims whose cases have not yet been put to rest. In the middle of the night she awakens to the vision of a strangled man, his tongue protruding blue-black. In her dreams Patti washes the defiled dress of a young woman who was stabbed to death in the 1980s. She hangs the shreds on the clothesline to flap in the breeze.

Three days of panning the turbulent details of the dead files does bring a couple of names to the surface, suggesting they are subjects who indeed "have to be ruled out." One is a known sex criminal named Howard Lampe, who Patti subsequently confirms was last seen in Weleda County during the week before the murder of Dahlia Everston.

19

THE SKY HAS gone a rosy mauve. Out in the yard a tiger-striped cat named Noodles slinks along the fence line. Patti stands at her kitchen sink and squeezes a lemon, using a knife to extract the juice into her glass. She tears open a packet of stevia, taps a little sweetener into the juice, then fills her glass with water and stirs, these healthy measures being part of her new resolve. She has begun to tally the pitiful story of what she eats in a day. One slow afternoon at the sheriff's department, Patti calculated how many doughnuts she was likely to consume over the course of her career in law enforcement and started to feel depressed.

Noodles lies down on a flagstone, rolls onto his back, and soaks up the sun's last heat. It is a beautiful time of day, and part of her resolve is to leave work behind when she comes home. It is sad to admit, but the victims in "the spirit room" made her hungry in the end, as did Dahlia Everston. The night of the murder at the Everston house, her stomach was tied in knots. Patti wanted to open her mouth and scream. Instead, she did her job as well as she could, but the stress made her ravenous. She ended up eating half a dozen sticky buns and was flying on sugar throughout that dreadful night. So part of her resolution is to come home from work and do quiet things like read or garden, or listen to music and thumb through magazines.

The front door is open to the latched screen door. Patti hears the screen door rattling against the jamb—someone knocking. Her slippers slap loudly against the hardwood floors of the house, and she longs for carpeting. A little cushioning would be nice. In Patti's dream house the floors are soft and her feet move through the rooms as silently as a cat's. She sees Lyman Everston faintly blurred behind the screen, his tall, lanky body, his thick gray-streaked hair pulled back into a ponytail, wire-rimmed glasses perched on his nose. He's standing with his arms stretched across the threshold of her house and seems to be looking into the dimness that dusk has put into the living room.

"I have to talk to you," he says.

Seeing Lyman Everston makes something catch in her chest. Patti unlatches the hook on the door.

Lyman pulls the door open. "He did it, didn't he?" His face collapses at the sound of his own words. "I need to know. I can't go on this way."

For a moment Patti feels adrift. "Look, we're in the middle of an investigation here. . . ."

"I'm living with the boy. I have to know if he killed my daughter."

Patti speaks very evenly. "Why do you think he killed your daughter?"

Lyman's eyes well up with tears; he rips his glasses from his face to wipe his eyes, and Patti knows she's been waiting for this, for the moment when the family suspects the person who destroyed them is no stranger at all.

"Can I come in?"

"Nope." Patti shakes her head. "I'll come out. Last time we

were alone you threw me up against a wall, and I'm the one who's supposed to do that." She gestures to the swaybacked sofa on the porch. "Sit down over there." An upholstered sofa outside on the front porch is recognizably "lower class," but a turbulent stream of citizens end up on Patti's outdoor sofa, pouring their hearts out to her, and all of them, she thinks, need a little cushioning. She sits down heavily beside Lyman and crosses her arms in front of herself.

Since Patti is a single woman, she is chaperoned by half the neighborhood. She glances over to Mrs. Yardley's house across the street to see if the curtains are pulled.

"What is it you want to tell me?"

Lyman wipes roughly at his eyes again, then puts his glasses on. "I don't trust him anymore. His reactions. There's just something that doesn't feel right."

"Like what?"

"For a while I thought he must have heard it happening, but he was afraid of being killed himself and he was too ashamed to say he heard Dahlia being murdered and he didn't do anything. But then I saw the scratches on his arms, the way he hid them from us, the way he just seems to be able to return to his life, and he's more popular now. Everyone's giving him all this sympathy—I think he's basking in it."

"It's human to be wanted, but it's not criminal."

"He flunked the polygraph."

"We can't use a polygraph in court, and your lawyer has blocked us from questioning Timothy again."

"He's not my lawyer. He's Norah's lawyer now—"

"If we question your stepson again, the lawyer will get it all thrown out."

"So what does that mean?"

Patti leans back against the sofa, stares up at the porch ceiling, which she painted sky blue to fool wasps and mud daubers into thinking this lovely nesting place was thin air.

"We need some evidence. Evidence directly linking a particular suspect with the crime. A knife or two, the stolen jewelry, the clothing the perpetrator was wearing at the time. Is Timothy missing any clothes?"

Lyman shakes his head in dismay. "I don't know. Norah would know."

"Would Norah tell you?"

"No. I don't think she would."

The little fountain on Patti's porch gurgles softly behind them. Tree frogs call with the onset of night and crickets set up their pulsing cadences. Lyman holds his head in his hands.

"What have I done? It's all my fault!"

"Your fault. How?"

"She—Dahlia—didn't want me to go on that trip."

The hardest part of her job, she thinks, is being around the victims. You can't help but absorb their pain, and you don't know what to do with that pain, but a lot of times you turn it into anger and use that rage. Patti feels moved to comfort this grieving father full of guilt, offer him the human embrace of two arms or a shoulder to cry on, but Deputy Callahan knows that by now Mrs. Yardley has spotted their two dark silhouettes, and it's clear there's a man sitting on Patti Callahan's porch. Deputy Callahan can never be seen embracing a man, especially the married father of a murder victim in an ongoing case. The restraint of her own impulses makes her shudder, and when Lyman drops his hands from his face, Patti takes his left hand in her own, gives his fingers a bracing squeeze before she lets him go. She is shocked by the strength of his hand clenching back.

"I didn't listen to her. I told her all the reasons why it was all right for Norah and me to leave."

"What exactly did she say?"

"Nothing specific. She just didn't want me to go. She kept complaining about her brother, the usual stuff. What was she trying to tell me? What was going on?"

"She had strangle marks on her neck. They weren't fresh. That suggests she had a violent relationship with her murderer. A boyfriend. A family member. Did you ever abuse your daughter?"

"Wha—" The air is sucked out of him. "No."

"Someone did."

"What are you saying?"

"Did you ever see Dahlia and her brother get into a physical fight?"

"Yes. Three years ago."

"That's not what you told Tom."

"I know. We lied. We had to tear them apart. We found them wrestling on the floor. Timothy had scratches down his face. Dahlia was kicking him, and his hands were clutching her neck. He was choking her."

"Would you testify to that?"

"Yes." The night sounds of frogs and crickets have grown more riotous. Lyman Everston has profoundly disturbed her equilibrium. For a moment Patti tries to collect herself and concentrates on the soothing splash of the little fountain on the floor.

Finally he says, "I left the house tonight. I can't be around them anymore."

"Where are you staying?"

"I don't know."

"Well, we want to know."

"We?"

"Yes, we need to know. We will want to keep close tabs on you."

"You think he did it, don't you?"

Patti glances across the street to Mrs. Yardley's window just in time to see the curtains twitch. She says more gently then, "It doesn't matter what I think. We're inside a process here. Anytime now the phone is going to ring. We have to go through a process, and there are rules. If I say things I shouldn't, it will harm the case against your daughter's murderer. If we can't get the evidence, then we need a confession. A freely made confession. Uncoerced. With his mental disabilities, any confession Timothy made would be strongly scrutinized, and a decent lawyer will try to get it thrown out. If there's been any coercion, any threats made to Timothy, anything that smells of manipulation—"

The telephone rings from the back of the house. For several seconds they sit there motionless, stunned, listening to the phone's banal, insistent beat.

"I have to answer it. How am I going to know you'll stay away from the boy? You understand the importance here?"

"Yes," he says, and looks down.

"Don't blow it, all right? You promise me? Do you promise?"

He shuts his eyes and nods.

"Stay here."

She looks over her shoulder at him before she walks into the house and feels something squeeze in her chest. The screen door yowls. Patti walks through the dark rooms back to the bright fluorescent light of the kitchen, where a vintage wall phone from the sixties rings. She picks up and is greeted by the smoke-stained voice of Sheriff Tom Gravette.

"Where the hell were you?"

"On the porch. He didn't come in."

"Well, you'd better wrap it up and call it a night, Patti-cakes. You need to get to bed, and, of course, I mean alone. You're gettin' up early in the morning. You're flyin' to California."

"What?"

"That suspect from the old Natalie Barson stabbing, Howard Lampe, our sex offender. They got him out in California on burglary."

"You want me to fly?"

"Well, maybe you'd like to drive and take a couple of weeks or so. See the country along the way."

Patti lowers her voice. "Lyman will testify he saw the boy strangle Dahlia once before."

"Lyman, huh? Oh, you're goin'. Unless you don't want to be the lead deputy on the case, and then, when I go to court, I got to explain why you dropped out."

"Tom, that's not it."

"No? That's good."

"I'm scared of flying, is all." She stares out at her side yard, where little yellow flames of fireflies are lighting up the dark. "I just haven't had any . . . experience."

"Well, you made the connection, Patti, and we got to follow the lead. Ol' Howard's sittin' in lockup right now. I thought you might like to have a little chat with him. Unless you're too chicken."

"Jesus, don't say that."

"Get some sleep. Come by before you leave."

She hangs up the phone and stands there feeling tiny dots of sweat break out along her hairline. Her heart already thumping. How can she explain to anyone that some part of her just doesn't believe in planes? Doesn't believe several tons of metal aren't going to fall from the sky. She touches the receiver, then turns and walks back through the house. She notices all the little angles and details of her objects sitting in the dark, and she feels a tremendous reluctance to leave these rooms, even for a few days. Who's going to feed the cat—Mrs. Yardley? No, she'd have to explain tonight. Maybe Reed. But Reed is so forgetful about important details, like feeding cats.

The screen door creaks. She steps back onto the porch. "Lyman?"

The porch is empty now. The slouching sofa looks vacant, pitiful. Patti feels strangely bereft. She walks down the porch steps, looks up and down the street. She sees the small whitewashed houses of the hamlet with their cottage gardens tumbling toward the street, or broken-down cars embellishing the most lowly abodes. Briefly she sees it all the way outsiders might view her home and feels she has to protect this humble place from their mocking gaze. She doesn't call out to Lyman. There's no one on the street. It's after ten, and the whole town has shut down for the night.

20

PATTI'S FRESHLY COIFFED hair bounces with her stride down the corridor as she follows signs for her gate. She's wearing a pale blue linen suit with white piping along the collar, white pumps, and in her hands a white straw purse and a small carry-on bag. She regards the cacophonous bustle of the St. Louis airport from behind the sleek, dark Ray-Bans she found in the Seven Point River. At the gate, as the time to board nears, Patti admits to herself that she wishes she had not found this suspect Howard Lampe's name in the dead files of "the spirit room." If only she'd been a little less diligent, she would be home gardening instead of sitting in this strange and awkward place.

The flight attendant calls for passengers with certain seat numbers, but Patti doesn't hear the numbers and is afraid she will miss her turn to board. It's all new to her: the lettered seat numbers, the overhead baggage compartment, the way everyone is so casual about the emergency instructions. She's glad she's wearing sunglasses, so her terror will go unnoticed.

She settles into her seat, five rows behind the wings, then studies the passengers positioned beside the emergency doors and decides they're poor choices for the grave responsibility they have concerning the lives of everyone on that plane. What if they can't get the doors open? They're not even reading the instructions, although the attendant has told them to do so in no uncertain terms. In her head she practices rushing an emergency door as the plane goes down, hopefully over water. If those frail, daydreaming passengers can't open the doors, she will have to do it. No one else is getting prepared. Patti reaches for the laminated emergency instructions and begins to study them with a furled brow.

Good thing she got an aisle seat. At least you've got a chance if you're sitting on the aisle. The man next to her says, "Nervous?"

"About what?" she says. Then she is undergoing liftoff, and every molecule in her sturdy body seems to be pressed inexorably down into the seat, into the fuselage. She has a memory of a certain roller coaster at the Greenville Fair that she never really liked, which means she laid her head back, closed her eyes, and turned white for the duration of that torture. The 747 lifts off from solid ground; Patti feels her breath heaving, shallow and fast. And everyone else is as bored as can be. She has read that takeoffs and landings are the most dangerous parts of the flight, but the others are all so complacent, they've turned their attention to *The Wall Street Journal, Vogue,* and *Golf Magazine.* The engine's roar is deafening, her heart thumping like a drum in the high school band.

Finally the strain of gravity lessens. The jet plateaus; the seat belt signs blink off. People get up and stroll. Patti stares at the deck of fluffy white cumulus clouds carpeting the sky below the jet. She watches that small square of window for much of the flight. The man beside her asks if she'd like to trade seats. Patti shakes her head; she's not giving up the aisle. "I'll just look from here," she says. Later on she orders a beer with her meal.

Before they land in San Francisco, Patti sees the ocean for the first time in her life. She gasps at that magnificent blue expanse dipping from the wing, feels her heart expand and tears welling in her eyes. Is this how everyone feels the first time? Better than the first time she had sex. Her mother told her on the phone this morning to be sure and take a handkerchief and dip it in the ocean, and someday that hankie will have been dipped in all the seven seas. At the time she thought, *Fat chance!* but now she's glad she's brought the white lace handkerchief.

She remembers her bag, then walks at a stiff clip into the throng of humanity. People look so different than they did at the St. Louis airport. They are all colors and from many countries, and several languages float on the air. Women wear saris, women wear burkas. Stylish, urbane women and men. *Their shoes must cost half my salary. And so thin!* There are hardly any fat people. Again she feels a blast of terror, but she follows the general flow of travelers until she finds her next obstacle: the taxi stand. Once again she is moving, sliding into the backseat and shutting the door. She requests the city jail.

"Where's that?" the driver asks.

From behind her dark glasses, Patti returns the driver's stare in the rearview mirror, then opens her purse, removes her ID, and flashes her badge. "If you don't know where it is, call your dispatcher and ask."

———

INSIDE THE CELLBLOCK something irregular occurs. The ugly clang of the barred door ramming into the locked position, and a mocking snatch of laughter as a guard walks away. In the silence that ensues, Patti understands she's locked in with the prisoner, Howard Lampe, sitting across the table from her. She reaches for the recorder and turns it on.

Before the Weleda County deputies decided that Patti was indispensable, she went through plenty of hazing, but she's caught off guard to find it repeated on the West Coast. When she met the tall, dark officer at the desk, she thought, *Man, are they good-looking out here,* then extended her hand, and said, "Deputy Callahan from Weleda County, Missouri." This simple statement of fact brought a taunt to his beautiful lips. "We got a redneck here! Red-state alert!"

She considers calling for help, then quashes the idea. *That's what they want me to do.* So she turns all of her attention to the suspect she's come to interview.

Howard Lampe: known sex offender, fifty-five years old. Lampe has a square face, a ruddy complexion with spider veins spread across his boyish cheeks.

"They're having their little fun with us, Howard. Fun with the hillbillies."

With a dip of his head, Howard Lampe smiles. "I guess we're all alone. . . ."

"You know what they asked me? If I wore shoes back home. Or had I just been shod for the trip. I told 'em these was the first shoes I ever owned. They sure was special to me. Then I asked if it was true that all of them out here were, you know . . ." Patti says, wagging a limp wrist. "They said they weren't, but if you ask me, any men that interested in shoes . . ."

Patti plants her elbows firmly on the table and leans forward. "And you want to know the truth? I don't much care for shoes. All these gay guys are right, Howard. I prefer to go barefoot, don't you? That's why we call summer the barefoot season. All this concrete out here—man, I don't know how you stand it."

Patti shoves her chair from the table, then turns her crotch away from Howard Lampe's view and removes her high-heeled pumps.

"Ahh, that's better," Patti says, rubbing her sore feet. Better to have two feet on solid ground if she has to make a run for it. She taps the heel of her pump speculatively against her palm, feels the firm punch of the leather-covered spike.

"Howard, is there really anything better than feeling the grass beneath your feet, or the cool, hard-packed mud after a summer rain?"

"Yes, ma'am," Howard says thoughtfully. "I can think of some." He tilts back on his chair and idly scratches his head. "Like shovin' my toes up your pussy after I slit your throat."

"Riii-ght." Patti nods, taking a slow, deep breath.

He comes at me, I'm taking out an eye.

"I know you can't help yourself, Howard. You sit there across from a female, and you can't stop yourself from having thoughts of how you'd like to butcher her. Funny you should mention knives. Is that how it was with Natalie?"

"What Natalie?"

"Natalie Barson, 1984. She was wearing a summer dress, and you stabbed her to death because you couldn't stop having the thoughts that you have. It's called a compulsion. I'm not judging you."

"That's a long time ago."

"Yeah, lot of water under that bridge," Patti says. "Things have changed since then. New technologies make all the difference. And you know what? That old Barson murder has gone and grabbed our attention again, 'cause we just had another girl stabbed to death, and it turns out you graced us with your presence in Weleda County around the time of her murder, too. We couldn't help but notice the similarities."

Patti shifts her wide hips against the plastic seat, then sets her shoes neatly on her lap. "Anyway, the reason I've come all the way out here is out of respect, a certain regard for a fellow hillbilly. We wanted you to hear it from one of us, instead of one of them," she says, nodding toward the locked door. "We've got you for the Natalie Barson murder, and we're going to indict. The good news is you can come do your time back home, instead of in a foreign land."

"You're crazy."

"No, not particularly, Howard. You see, you left a sample when you raped her first."

"I didn't leave no sample."

"Mmm, 'fraid you did. It doesn't take much, Howard, just a drop," Patti says, smiling. "Even you can leave a drop. And back then we were a little behind the times. DNA testing wasn't something Weleda County knew much about, but we kept the sample on file."

Now she's lying through her teeth, and there's a certain rhythm to it, a certain wild intensity. Patti recognizes it's something of the high that outlaws feel. Any DNA evidence from the old Barson case was destroyed long ago by summers of blistering heat and winter frost and damp out in "the spirit room."

But she's not obliged to tell the truth; she's obliged to get the truth.

"So this new case, the Dahlia Everston murder, has got us pretty interested in you. Turns out the DNA from the Barson murder in 'eighty-four matches the sample you left on that little molestation case you had in Weleda County a few years back. We just hadn't put two and two together. And now, here you are, back in the area, and another girl is stabbed. So let's talk about Dahlia Everston."

"I had nothin' to do with that."

"Howard, you know I hear that statement more than any other in the world? And ninety-five percent of the time that statement is a lie. Dahlia was also stabbed. A knife—that's your favorite weapon, isn't it?"

"This is bullshit."

"We have a witness ID'ed you at a convenience store close to where Dahlia lived, the very same week she was murdered. Stated you had stitches over your left eye, and I can see that scar's comin' along nice. We tracked you to the emergency room of the hospital where they stitched you up after you ran into a beer bottle at the Five Vikings. That's where you saw Dahlia Everston—at the hospital. She was working nights. You saw her there and began to follow her."

"You got a picture of her?"

Patti nods. She hopes her hand will be steady, imperative that her hand remain firm. She can feel part of her soul hanging below the ceiling of that miserable room, tethered to her like a balloon on a string, and a strange calmness pools around her physical body. She opens a folder on the table and slips out a photograph of

Dahlia Everston, a reproduction from her senior yearbook. "She was beautiful and you watched her, and you started having your thoughts. Is that how it happened with Natalie?"

"Nah."

"How was it different?"

"I don't have to talk to you."

"Well, we might as well talk. Better do it now before the indictment goes through on the Natalie Barson murder. It'll be out of our hands then. You tell us the truth about Dahlia and Natalie, we can cut a deal. Plea-bargain. Save the taxpayers the expense of a trial. We'll show our appreciation in return."

Howard Lampe purses his lips and blows her a mushy wet kiss.

"Maybe I've got a shank taped to my leg."

Patti shrugs. "Maybe you do. As you can see, they're pretty lax out here. If you get into trouble, you think one of these guards is gonna help you? So maybe you do have a shiv. I'd sure want one, if I was you."

"I can get you."

"I don't think they'll let that happen."

"Why not?"

Patti chuckles softly. "It would make 'em look bad. They're watching us right now. They're hoping for a laugh."

"By the time they come, it'll be over."

"Yeah, but if I survive, I'll sue their asses off. Then I'll retire to my dream house and never have to talk to a psychopath again."

Patti picks up one of her shoes, regards its length and breadth as though it's a remarkable object she gave short shrift to in the past, then gently taps the pointy heel against the tabletop, as a form of punctuation.

"Let's face it, Howard, they don't really respect people like us, who come from our part of the country. I'm offering you respect. This little hazing," she says, gesturing with her shoe, "is an insult, really, to both of us. Sure, you can do something bad, and our sheriff's department will suddenly get rich, thanks to you, and further disrupt the lives of your extended family and friends. Sure. But do you really want to do your time with all the gangs they've got out here? All the bad stuff that goes on in these California prisons—it's not your fight, but once you're inside you've got to pick a side. And then you're in a war, on top of doing time.

"If you just tell us the truth, we can save the Missouri taxpayers the price of a trial, and in return we'll show our appreciation for your cooperation, your honesty. We'd be willing to make you a deal. Really, Howard, we would make it worth your while. Otherwise you got to fight in a war out here, and then come do your time in Missouri. These gorgeous boys in blue are gonna get bored and come back here pretty soon. We can fix this up between the two of us. It's all on tape. You can hold me to the deal. Did you ask her out, and she rebuffed you, Howard?"

"There wasn't no rebuff."

"Sure there was."

"If you found my jism on ol' Natalie, it's 'cause she liked my jism. Liked it all inside and drippin' outta her."

A mask of calm slides down over her features, like a garage door, and she goes very still inside.

"So . . . how long were you lovers?"

"Long enough."

"But she wanted to break it off, didn't she? You were starting to frighten her. Because you were the kind of boyfriend she didn't tell anyone about. Natalie Barson was ashamed of you."

"That's a lie."

"Oh, come on, Howard!"

"Women don't break it off with me. I break it off with them."

"But you weren't Natalie Barson's only boyfriend, right?"

"Blah, blah, blah. You don't know a thing about it. You can't shut up anymore than she could. Raggin' me to meet her ol' grannie, meet her cousins, her parents—then force me into marryin' her."

"But that was your child inside of her."

"What child?"

"Oh, nobody ever told you? Sorry. Well, you didn't know Dahlia long enough to have a child with her."

"I've never even seen that bitch! Don't try to nail that shit on me."

"I just want you to tell me the truth, so I can help you."

"Sure." A bark of laughter rips from his mouth. "And why would you do that?"

"Oh, maybe to show up these hundred-dollar haircuts who think they're better than we are, Howard. Get a highlander out of their shitty gang-filled prisons and take him back home where he belongs. We take care of our own apples, Howard, even the bad ones. So Dahlia led you on. She smiled and let you think you had a chance. She was provocative. Or maybe it was just all those thoughts that come into your head. The tension built up. You had to get relief."

"I didn't do the blond girl. Get offa that."

"Are you telling me you only killed Natalie Barson?"

"That bitch—"

"Natalie?"

"Wouldn't shut up. Just like you don't shut up. She started it! I didn't want to do it—"

"What did Natalie Barson make you do?"

"Rag, rag, rag, I went off. I don't remember anything. Then it's over and there's a knife in my hand."

"You don't remember raping her?"

"I didn't rape the bitch. I fucked her afterwards. And she didn't complain!"

"She was dead, Howard."

"It was self-defense—"

"Killing Natalie Barson was self-defense?"

"She asked for it!"

"And Dahlia? Did she ask for it, too?"

"I never laid eyes on her—"

"You didn't kill Dahlia Everston?"

"No!"

"Howard, I believe you. I do."

ON HER WAY out, Patti thanks the officers for their support. She couldn't have done it without them, she says. The last thing she clearly remembers is tucking the cassette of Howard Lampe's confession into her brassiere, in case her purse gets stolen before she returns to the state of Missouri. A taxi drops her at a car rental agency near the airport where she rents a little red convertible. She removes her high heels and tosses them to the backseat. Then, because that freedom feels so marvelous, Patti lifts her hips and rolls down her panty hose, stuffs the filmy wad into the glove compartment. She follows the rental agent's directions for Highway 1, then turns south and drives barefoot along that fabled coastal highway, her toes curled over the accelerator, the wind whipping through her hair.

Near the cliffs of Davenport, she presses her fingertips to the outline of the cassette between her breasts to make sure the confession is still there. That's the last coherent reasoning Patti has before she reaches Santa Cruz, the space between her ears a ribbon of winding road above the blue Pacific.

This is as far west as you can go and still be in the country. She feels as if her life has been pitched into a higher intensity. Intermingled with the speechless beauty of the coastline she thought she'd never see are dreamy fragments of memories that had been lost to her but now return. Her mother shaking her shoulder early in the morning to awaken her, following her huge, lumbering grandmother across a field in search of burdock root, a red and yellow kite she'd flown with her father once. She lost hold and watched it rise until the kite disappeared into an endless sky. All these memories stored so deep inside are suddenly shaken loose, as startlingly fresh and alive as they were when experienced the first time.

At Santa Cruz she parks and heads for the beach, virtually ignoring the boardwalk, the colorful activity, the skaters, the vendors, the thongs. She heads for the water with the single-mindedness of a shark moving ever forward. The hot sand shifts beneath her bare feet. Her toenails, she notices, are the color of claret wine. The smell of the ocean fills her lungs. Patti bends over, plunges the white lace handkerchief into the surf. She feels the shock of the waves rolling against her calves, half stumbles, then notices there are tears rolling down her cheeks. She covers her eyes with the baptized handkerchief.

21

NORAH OPENS HER eyes: the same room. The same wallpaper border of lilies like a flowery garland crowning the walls. She touches his side of the bed. Empty, the covers hardly mussed. Yesterday she saw black birds on the periphery of her vision—crows winging above the trees—and their dark plumage seemed ominous. Today those dark bird wings have become more generalized, and when she turns she has a glimpse of being inside a black cloud or tunnel—a biblical sense of doom, this intuition that something will happen today. Something awful, some demise.

What is left? she thinks. She has been watching the river with an altered pair of eyes, and a certain fantasy unfolds. She attaches her son's hand weights to her belt and steps into the river. She fills her deep pockets with stones and walks into the water. No more problems, no more suffering. The river takes it away.

Everything that was has vanished. Lyman's a ghost that roams the house, but her husband isn't coming back. Sometimes she still sees Dahlia walking down the hall or through the living room, flipping her long blond hair or twisting that lovely hair into a knot at the nape of her neck. How Norah envied that luxuriant hair of youth, the firm, smooth texture of the girl's skin, the perfect legs that never knew the meaning of cellulite—all the attributes that were simply her daughter's by virtue of being young. The promise of a life ahead, adventures that would not include her family, passion—at some point passion would burst forth, followed by an implacable hunger to give birth. Gone. No husband. No grandchildren now. What girl could Timothy marry?

Norah sits up and leans over her knees. To expel her sense of dread, she releases a long, deep sigh. She presses a hand to her stomach and sees that her fingers are trembling. This sometimes happens before her period. She has a sudden urge to go to the bathroom. She hears herself sighing again as she walks down the hall that once lit up with blue trails in the dark. Sighing deeply gives her the slightest bit of relief, a sign that she's trying to take care of herself. The hall is normal today. Sun spills like honey over the pine floors. Norah's hand shakes as she grips the sink and sits down on the toilet; then her bowels shudder and move. The waste leaves her quickly, and when she's done she notices a little cold sweat beading along her hairline. *I must be getting sick*, she thinks.

She cannot eat breakfast. The smell of food makes her ill. She slips a sliver of ice into her mouth for the nausea, the way she did when she was pregnant and went through morning sickness. Her belly feels swollen and uncomfortable, as if she's full of gas. Norah sits across the table from Timothy and feels anxious watching her son eat his frosted cereal. The way his large head dips to the bowl like a horse over a trough of grain causes some nameless dread. Once in a while she sucks deeply at the air and sighs.

"Mom, you need to ask Dad to come home. That's what Pastor John says."

"Then maybe Pastor John should ask him to come home."

"Well, you just have to try." Timothy's mouth enfolds the spoon, his teeth begin to crunch, a little dribble of milk weeps from the corner of his lips. "We all have to try. Everything happens because of God's will."

Blood drains from her face. "You don't believe that God wanted your sister to be murdered."

"Maybe He didn't want that. Maybe it was . . . like an accident."

"Accident?"

"I'm just saying . . ."

"Saying what?"

Then her son gives her an appraising look, a look that seems almost capable of calculation. "That's what Pastor John says. God can see everything from heaven, and it's all happening the way He meant it to be. We just have to step back from things and see they are His will. People dying. It's His will. Everything, even the wars, they bring us closer to the Rapture, Mom. When the righteous ones will be taken up to heaven, and all the sinners are cast down. The believers from our church will have everlasting life; the rest will burn in hell. The flames of hell will lick their feet."

She reaches across the table and takes her son's large chin in her hand. "Timothy—look at me." She feels the light stubble of his beard, the hard thick bones of his jaw.

"What?" His blue eyes go as wide and innocent as the sky.

"Did you love her? Tell me. You loved her, didn't you?"

"You can love the sinner, Mom. But not the sin."

"Don't you feel anything—without being told what to feel?"

"I don't know what you're talkin' about." Timothy shakes his head disapprovingly. "The things you say sound kind of blasphemous."

Norah looks toward the kitchen window over the sink, and that black cloud billows into her day. Quickly she snaps her head, the illusion gone. Her car keys are hanging on a hook by the kitchen door.

"Where are you going?" he asks.

"I have to get something in town."

"I'd get it for you, but my truck is all broke down."

Now she feels that she is drowning; she can't possibly get enough air. She doesn't know where she's going. She simply has to move. She lowers the car windows, cranks up the air-conditioning. Already the day is hot.

If only he had kept his mouth shut! The night that Lyman left. She might have got them through that night, and then the next day and the next, but Timothy would not let go of a thing until he got his way. Whenever Timothy felt he was right, someone else was wrong, and halfway through that tension-filled dinner he asked his father for a new truck. He said that Lyman could afford one now. Lyman's fork clattered to his plate. The next sound was the hard shoving of his chair back from the table as he stood. Norah watched her husband walk from the kitchen, heard his feet against the floor of the bedroom hall.

Timothy was baffled. "What's wrong with him? Is he mad at me?"

"You idiot!"

Wounded, his face crumpled and Timothy thrust out his lower lip. "I don't see why I can't have a truck."

Norah found Lyman in their bedroom, lowering a short stack of his folded shirts into an open suitcase. He gave her a heated look, then went to the bureau and rummaged through a drawer for a handful of socks. "I'm leaving. I can't be around him anymore."

"What? Lyman, no—this is just a terrible misunderstanding. . . ."

"Is it?"

"He didn't mean it that way."

"He doesn't miss her."

"That's not true—he misses her. He told me so." She did not feel that she was lying then. Hadn't Timothy said that he wished things could return to the way they used to be? Wasn't that because he missed his sister terribly? "It's not his fault. You know, he's not like other boys. He doesn't really understand what death is. He loved Dahlia."

"Did he? How do we know he did?" Lyman flung some underwear into the suitcase. "Maybe he doesn't know what love is. Maybe that's one of the things he doesn't really understand. Maybe he doesn't even feel it."

"How dare you! My son *loves* me." She began to weep and she sat down on the bed. "He's a good Christian boy—"

"That's why he didn't kill her. . . ."

"Yes! Yes!"

Lyman leaned over her and said quietly, "Because good Christian boys don't kill their stepsisters."

"Don't do this to me! You can't leave. I've given you everything! I won't let you destroy our family."

"Our family is destroyed. We won't ever be the same. I will never forgive myself. I've seen him get angry. I've seen his face when he's enraged. I just can't be around him anymore."

"Well, I won't abandon him!" She grabbed an armful of her husband's folded clothes from the suitcase to return them to their proper drawers. "They're trying to frame our son for something he'd never do, and you're forsaking him!" She clutched Lyman's clothes to her breast: the pants she washed, the shirts she ironed, as if her efforts gave her dominion over his clothes, as if she could stop him from leaving simply by refusing to hand over his clothes.

"There's something wrong about his answers."

"Of course there's something wrong! God didn't give him the brains He gave Dahlia."

"And that isn't fair, is it?"

"God gave my son something more than brains!" Her mother pride sprang forth. "He gave him a pure heart! Why do you always criticize the boy? Oh, if you could only see him the way others do. The way others look up to him because of his faith."

"Norah—it's over."

"You can't leave! Don't you see how it will look if you desert us? People will start talking—"

Lyman seized his clothes from her arms. She tried to wrench them away, but he was stronger. His neatly stacked clothes spilled from her hands. She watched him lower the suitcase lid, zipper it shut. "Damn you!" She threw herself upon him. "I put my faith in you! I gave you everything. I thought you would save me!"

"From what?" He was shaking her by the shoulder. "Save you from what?"

She was raving, furious at him, bawling. "You son of a bitch! You're just like all the rest!"

"The rest of what?"

"Men! All you men! All you care about is yourselves!" And then his hand leaped out, and she felt the shameful sting on her cheek. Her eyes went wide with moral indignation. "You slapped me! You raised your hand to me! You're just like he was. You're no better at all. I thought you were different. I thought you would be my salvation—instead, you strike me in the face, you serpent. I let you into my heart. You lost your daughter, so now you're going to take my son from me. I hate you—I hate you!"

The sunshine through the woods casts a wavery light over her arms. Just past the curve in the lane Norah sees Sand Williams's mailbox, and that rusted post becomes a target for her fury. Briefly she allows herself to accelerate, to envision mowing down Sand Williams's mailbox, to envision Sand Williams standing there beside the mailbox and mowing her down, too. What a great pleasure that would be, what a sense of victory. Then that black cloud looms into her vision and Norah doesn't have time to ask if it's a cloud or a tunnel. *This is it,* a voice says deep inside her, and she knows she's lost control. Slams on the brakes. The car flies from the gravel road. Once again her first husband flings her like a rag against the flowered wallpaper of the living room. The old terror again.

This is what Dahlia felt—the sheer horror of not being able to make it stop.

The mailbox crumples over the hood. Norah's thrown back against the seat by the sudden release of the driver's air bag, which knocks the wind from her.

22

PEOPLE THINK OF the human skull as being solid bone, but it's not really solid; it moves. There are these long sutures over the top of the skull that create a gap, a tiny gap between the bones that allows the skull to shift. The movements are tiny but real. Sand massages the top of her head, nudging the skin along the suture line and feeling tension release from her jaw. Frank has returned to Wellington for the sewer project. Sand ovulated three days ago and has a slight headache. So she tends to her skull, that wonderful bowl of bone that holds her brain. The river looks cool, refreshing, and she thinks of going in. For some reason she remembers a Turkish villager holding the stewed head of a rabbit in his palm, scooping out the poached brain with a long index finger, then sucking the skull like a giant escargot. It was the simple way he ate the rabbit's brain. We are predators. We are food, all of us. What eats us is complicated, frequently invisible.

The crash breaks into these thoughts. An ugly, heavy metallic sound that says something has been damaged on this slow, sultry summer morning—an explosion of sound so piercing, she leaps from the deck chair and runs barefoot through the yard to the lane. The front end of Norah's Buick is smashed into a low stone wall. The mailbox has disappeared. Norah is peeking over the air bag in the front seat. Sand opens the driver's door and touches her arm. "Norah?" Norah is staring toward the river. "Norah, can you answer me?" Norah turns to her, her face a pale, sweaty moon. "Can you feel your feet?" Norah nods then. Instinctively, Sand places a hand on Norah's forehead, feels her cool, clammy flesh.

"I'm all right," Norah snaps. "Let go of me."

"How did this happen?"

"I thought I hit the brake. It must have been the accelerator. Just help me out of here. This damn bag," she says, huffing, "has got me pinned."

As Sand helps Norah out of the car, Norah's legs collapse.

"Are you all right?"

"I've got the flu or something." Norah sinks down to the grass and leans against the rear tire of her Buick.

"You seem short of breath."

"It's nothing. It's been this way all day."

"I'll get you a glass of water."

Sand rushes to the house, searches hurriedly for her purse, some shoes and underpants, some tincture of cayenne pepper, for it seems it might be that kind of emergency, the kind that requires the dilation of arteries. She brings Norah a glass of water, tells her to open her mouth, and squirts cayenne onto her tongue. "Hold it in your mouth as long as you can, then swallow."

Norah howls and spits. Sand gives her the water. Norah gulps, clutching the glass between her hands. Then Sand brings her Audi around and opens the passenger door. She crouches over Norah, takes Norah's shoulders in her hands. "Look at me. I'm taking you to the hospital. I think you're having a heart attack."

Norah stares at her bitterly. "You're ridiculous. You think I wouldn't know a heart attack?"

"No. I don't think you would."

"Leave me alone!" Norah protests, but she's weaker than she expects. Her arms slap ineffectually, and once Sand has her to her feet, Norah holds on because it's taking all her strength to breathe in and out. "Let go of me—I'll file charges!"

"You fucking bitch, shut up!"

"Oh," Norah wails, "I hate you most of all—"

"Just shut up! You're not dying on me now."

Sand pushes Norah into the passenger seat. Her skull falls back on the leather rest. She closes her eyes.

"You think I don't hate you, too?" Sand slams the car door shut. "You think I don't?"

Except for sighing deeply, Norah remains quiet for several minutes of the drive to town. She refuses more cayenne and asks if Sand is trying to kill her. They bump along over the potholed road. The shadow of a heron glides over the windshield. Halfway to the hospital Norah turns to her and yells, "There's no pain in my left arm!"

"That's a male symptom. Cold sweat, sighing. Look, your hand is trembling. These are signs. Do you, by any chance, feel a sense of doom?"

"My God, what else would I feel?"

"That's a sign—a sign for women—an intuition."

"Sandra, they've done studies."

"On men. They've done studies on men."

Norah sighs deeply, then mutters, "No one ever told me that."

"No kidding."

Norah is beginning to consider her neighbor's possible sincerity, but by the time they reach the emergency room, she comes to her senses and assures the nurse that there really isn't much wrong with her. "I'm just feeling a little off." She wrinkles her nose in distaste. "Having a bit of gas."

"Summer flu?"

"Listen to me, this woman is having a heart attack. She's under tremendous stress. She drove into a stone wall."

"I hit the wrong pedal is all."

"I want you to check it out," Sand says. "Run an EKG."

The nurse doesn't have time to coddle patients in the emergency room, and a look of irritation passes over her broad face. "There isn't any reason to do a test like that."

"She's got the symptoms of a female heart attack."

"Sandra, I think the nurse would know what she's talking about." Norah rolls her eyes at the nurse in sympathy. "We're sorry to have bothered you."

"Look, we're not going anywhere. You're going to have that test."

"Ma'am, we decide what tests are done."

"Well, you better start deciding to do this one, because we're not leaving until you do."

The nurse grows weary of them and decides to pass them off to a doctor, so Norah and Sand are led to an examination room, where they don't have to wait long, only about two hours. Norah has a sudden bowel movement and later on she throws up in a wastebasket. When the doctor arrives, Sand is told to wait in the lounge. After a little while Norah returns, wobbly on her feet. She looks pallid, sweaty, and is clutching some blister-pack pills in her hand. "They gave me some medicine for gas."

"What?" Sand grabs her arm and steadies her. "Where's that doctor?"

"Please." She closes her eyes in exhaustion. "Let's not make any more of a scene than we already have. Please take me home. I can't bear any more."

"Sit down."

Then Sand starts making a good deal more of a scene than she did before. Norah is so mortified, she just lowers her head to her hands, for she is too weak to shout Sand down. The nurse threatens to call security, and Sand Williams tells her to go ahead. Call Tom Gravette. Call in the whole goddamn sheriff's department. The doctor arrives and invites them to leave.

"Look, this is easy," Sand says, rummaging through her purse.

"If you're so sure she's not having a heart attack, then give her an EKG. I'll pay for it. I will personally pay for it."

"Ma'am, gastrointestinal distress does not warrant an EKG."

"A woman's symptoms can be different. You should know that. If this woman walks out of here and dies next week, I will personally ruin your life. Here's my MasterCard. Give her an EKG and we'll leave quietly. Otherwise I am going to ruin your day."

"Where are you from?" the doctor says indignantly.

"Here. I'm from here! My family ran the newspaper for seventy-five years, and I think I can still get their ear. I will make your life miserable!"

Norah murmurs, "She's good at that."

Sand is very good at that. After another half hour, Norah is finally given an EKG. Then there's a flurry of activity and Norah is flown to Springfield for bypass surgery, for she is indeed having a heart attack. The struggle to have Norah's symptoms taken seriously at the hospital leaves Sand feeling exhausted and hollow.

Of course, Norah isn't sure she wants to live. When Sand visits her at the Springfield hospital after her surgery, she lies there forlorn, pale, empty, hooked up to tubes and monitors.

"Where's Timothy?" Sand asks. "He isn't at home."

"He's staying with our pastor and his wife. They were here when I came to. Timothy was very upset . . . to see me . . . like this."

"I can imagine. . . ."

"No, you can't." She raises one limp arm with a needle and IV sticking into her flesh. "He thought I was being prepared for electrocution."

"Oh."

"We decided it's best he not visit me here. I'll be out in a week."

"So, that's good news."

"Good news?" Norah gives her a withering stare. "I suppose you expect me to thank you for keeping me alive. Well, you're nuts. I wish I was dead."

Sand feels close to tears. "I don't wish you were dead, Norah. I'm glad you're alive."

"What kind of a life do you think I'm going to have?"

"The one you make."

With great difficulty, Norah rolls over and turns her back to Sand. Sand arranges the flowers she brought in a vase and silently leaves the room.

23

BY THE END of summer Sand comes to understand that Norah is her shadow, the shadow side of herself she can no longer recognize. Why else does Norah annoy her so, even before their troubles began? What she hates about Norah are all the pieces of herself she thought she had cast out, those Norah parts buried deep inside. The more she hates Norah, the more divided she is from herself. If she could simply look at Norah without judgment, what would she find in herself that's screaming to be recognized, to be nurtured, cherished, held?

The little girl who was scared and always tried to do everything right?

Because if she was perfect, if she got all the good grades, if she met all his tests, her father would have no reason to be angry with her or, even worse, disappointed in what she was. The little girl who pushed down her fear until she could no longer attribute those feelings to herself.

In August, Sand is shopping at Meecham's Grocery when she looks up and sees Timothy Everston clutching a six-pack of Coke and a bag of chips. He quickly averts his gaze, then something inside of him solidifies and he turns and stares at Sand reproachfully. Her mouth feels parched, her voice halts in her throat. There he is, so . . . so absolutely normal—the big gangling boy she hired last autumn to rake leaves.

Again she is stunned by her own feelings and is filled with doubt. Is it really possible this childlike boy stabbed his sister over and over, that Dahlia's anguished cries did not stop his hand? Surely he's not capable of the grisly planning involved in the cleanup afterward. Why, she wondered, did Dahlia switch to the night shift? Was she afraid to be in the house with him when everyone was asleep?

"Hello, Timothy. How is your mother?"

"She doesn't want to see you."

"How is she doing?"

"My father's coming home soon. Everything will be all right."

Then he turns on his heels and heads for the checkout, clutching his purchases to his broad chest. Sand leans over the dairy case as a hot flash comes over her and leaves her breathless and weak. She sags against the cool air until she can move again. She feels like a vessel emptied of power, emptied of life.

But everything changes, nothing can remain fixed. No feeling can remain unaltered, not even unhappiness. We know that our happiness cannot last, that joy is a feeling we catch from time to time and savor. Yet somehow we're convinced our sorrow, our knowledge of loss, our sense of hopelessness, can remain, unlike anything else beneath the sun.

24

NORAH STARES OUT a bay window to her over-grown garden patch across the yard. She can see the head of Sand Williams, her tousled hair rising from the Johnson grass, then lowering until she almost disappears like a creature in the weeds. A fox, maybe, or a coyote. Norah wonders: *What on earth can that woman be thinking? I suppose she wants credit for saving my life. She probably thinks she deserves some award for that.*

In these moments a look of weary cynicism comes over Norah's face. Apparently her neighbor has taken on a strategy of engagement that would require Norah's speaking to Sand if Norah wants her to leave, and Norah doesn't want to talk to that woman.

For the past week her neighbor has been out there every couple of days. She never comes to the door. Usually she just appears in the garden about eight in the morning, sometimes earlier. By nine-thirty she is gone. She leaves produce from the garden on the porch steps—zucchini, okra, some dwarfed tomatoes.

Her neighbor has begun to fertilize, but God only knows with what. Possibly fish heads. There is a distinct possibility Norah saw the glistening scales of a fish in that woman's hand. Most of the time Sand Williams is on her knees, pulling weeds, for the Everstons' garden went to ruin this year. Weeding seemed pointless after Dahlia was murdered. Now there are only two of them in the house, and Norah can't do anything physical. Her days are organized around getting to the toilet and back, remembering to eat something, or standing before the bathroom mirror to witness the ugly scar running down between her pale breasts.

From her armchair Norah can observe Sand Williams trespassing on her property, notice when she comes and goes. This, she realizes, is a good part of how she organizes her day—by waiting to see if her neighbor has invaded the garden and needs to be watched.

Sometimes Norah falls asleep in the chair, and when she awakens, Sand Williams has left, and maybe there's a pile of zucchini on the porch stairs. The squash sit on the kitchen counter until once again the women from church arrive, as they did after Dahlia died. Then the squash are fried or shredded and baked into zucchini bread. Again the women bring plates of food, as they do for a funeral. *Maybe I've died,* Norah thinks, *and yet I'm still here watching it all. Watching them offer my son a cupcake with pink icing, watching them pat my hands and shake their heads over my husband's abandonment in my time of need. How pitiful I am. Not even a heart attack and bypass surgery can bring him home. The cut is complete. No matter what happens to me, he's not coming back.* They shake their heads and say, "Lyman strayed from God's will a long time ago. You see what comes of it."

In the hospital Norah believed she would lie to Timothy, tell him his father would soon return, for surely he would. But when she went home, she was too weak to put forth the effort of lying. And Lyman wasn't coming back. He called, he said he was sorry.

"It's over, Norah. I can't live with him."

When Timothy questions her, she considers protecting him from the truth, but she's so tired and she feels so much bitterness toward her son that she says, "He's not coming back. He doesn't love us anymore. All the love he had died when *she* died."

Timothy is so shaken, he has to sit down. "He doesn't love me? But I am his son. He's supposed to love me."

She closes her eyes in utter weariness. *He's wondering what I did, what I said to cause his father to leave.*

"Something in him died, and it was the part that loved us, too. I've lost everything. At least you have a life ahead of you. I'm saying you're going to have to plan that life without your dad. We've all suffered. We've all lost too much. That's just the way it is."

"But it isn't fair!"

"No," she says, shaking her head, and even this slight movement prompts an aching tug at the stitches below her throat. Her chest feels as if someone took an ax to her. She's been split open like a chicken. "None of it is fair."

"But it's supposed to be fair, Mom."

"Says who?"

"God. God says."

"God," Norah says, and in her mouth the word is a sound that strikes her ear somehow differently, with a quality of the unknown, her open mouth a cave where sound reverberates as if traveling up from deep inside the earth.

She begins to measure the days of what they are calling her recovery by watching the movements of Sand Williams's head above the tangled brush. Norah has come to expect her neighbor, and when she is late Norah fidgets and wonders why. If her neighbor fails to appear, Norah feels almost let down, for tracking Sand Williams's movements in the garden plot has become a major diversion for her.

"Mom, what's that woman doing out there?" Her large, hulking son stands behind her chair.

"She's taking care of the garden."

Timothy has stopped doing any chores since Norah returned from the hospital. He lies around the house, watching TV, giving every indication that he's waiting for her to get up and make them something to eat or do his laundry.

"You know, you might go out there and give her a hand," Norah says to needle him.

"No, I don't like her, Mom. Mrs. Mason took our Lord's name in vain. She is blasphemous."

"Well, if you went out there yourself and kept up with the weeding, she wouldn't come around."

"I have to clean over at the church and help Pastor John."

"What about here? Why don't you clean around here? Can't you see how weak I am? They operated on my heart. Don't you understand? I almost died."

"But," he says, flustered, "the weeding was never my job. You and Dad did the weeding, and sometimes Dahlia, too."

"They're not here anymore! It's just you and me, and I can't do anything physical."

"I guess we'll just have to put up with her, then," Timothy says with a sigh. "Do you know what there is to eat for lunch?"

"No, I don't. I have not ventured into the kitchen today. Just open the fridge and look for yourself. I think there's still food the ladies brought."

He starts for the kitchen with a loping gait, then hesitates at the door and turns back to her.

"I liked it better when you brought me my lunch on a plate, with a napkin and a glass of milk. I sure hope you get well soon, Mom. Maybe we should pray to God."

Her attention becomes fixed by a sunflower in the yard. Her life has come to a standstill. Her energy gone. Everything gone. At first she had simply been numb, any juice of her body sapped away. At the funeral she was stoic. She tried to hold them together, for Lyman was falling apart. And then, before she fully comprehended what had befallen them, the earth was yanked like a rug from beneath her feet, and the sheriff came for her son. At that point she became ferocious, a kind of warrior defending her mortally wounded family.

If she starts crying now, she'll never stop. Her brains, her heart, her bones, will simply liquefy and drain away. The night Lyman left brought her to her knees. Her heart gave out, and part of that muscle died. Norah understands that now from the way she looks at the world. She simply doesn't have as much stake in it all. And with Timothy there is this feeling of distance, too.

———

"GOOD GOD!" NORAH cries. The wooden floor reverberates against her bare feet. The whole room seems to be wobbling with the noise. "Turn it down! I'm trying to recover here!"

"But I like it this way," he shouts resentfully over the noise. "I like to be inside of it. I like TV to fill the room."

"What's gotten into you?"

Maybe she's losing her mind, but Norah has the impression that every day the television is getting louder. When she insists he lower the volume, Timothy watches her sullenly before finally rousing himself and picking up the remote, but the volume never returns to the serene levels of the past, before Lyman left. Timothy does obey, but it seems to take him longer every time, and he stares at her darkly as if calculating something about her, and Norah finds these looks quite shocking on the face of her son.

One afternoon when she is blasted from her nap by several buildings exploding on TV, Norah feels so frustrated and hurt that she simply gets up and walks out of the house. She can still hear the TV on the porch, so she teeters down the stairs, gripping the handrail, then shuffles across the yard in search of peace. The afternoon sun sears her pale, freckled forehead, and she heads for a forgotten chaise lounge under an oak at the edge of the garden plot. The effort to reach the lawn chair exhausts her, so Norah sinks down, closes her eyes, and falls asleep again to the lulling music of the river and the birds.

The shifting sun in the sky awakens her, for the lowering sun has shot a beam of light against her right eyelid. Norah's eyes flutter open and she rubs her face. "What time is it?" she says aloud.

"Five."

She sits up, startled by the answering voice, and sees the tawny head of her neighbor rise from behind a patch of weeds.

"You," Norah says.

"Yes, it's me."

"Why do you keep coming here?"

Sand leans back on her haunches, then tips the bill of her cap. "I'm not sure. Maybe I hate to see a garden go to waste. People starving, all of that. Isn't that what your mother told you when you were a kid?"

"If you think I'm going to thank you—"

"No, I don't think that," she says with a wan smile. "You don't have to talk to me. You can just sit there and observe. Critique the way I weed. Breathe the fresh air, that's good for you."

"Why does everyone think I care about recovering?"

"I don't think you do. But you might recover in any case."

"If you knew how many times I've wanted to throw myself in the river . . ."

Sand Williams rips out a tangle of bindweed, tosses the clump, then wipes her forehead with the back of her arm. "I highly recommend it. I do it several times a day."

"I mean with stones. I mean to drown myself."

"I'm just saying a little fresh air wouldn't hurt."

And so a kind of dance between the two of them begins. The strange truth is that Norah finds solace in watching her neighbor down on her hands and knees, doing the labor that Norah cannot do for herself. She starts taking her naps in the garden, away from the noise of the TV, where her son spends his afternoons inside whatever that world is for him. The timing of her neighbor's visits begins to shift, and often Sand Williams arrives while Norah is sleeping in the deep shade of the oak.

Usually the women do not speak. Norah lies in the lounge chair, looking up through the canopy of oak branches and leaves, her attention riveted by a young squirrel, scrambling in and out of a knothole in the tree. The coloration of his fur is so like the mottled bark that when the squirrel goes still he disappears against the tree and seems to become a part of the trunk itself. Norah dozes in and out, and when she gets up Sand Williams is gone, and Norah comes to find these interludes oddly refreshing; it's soothing to be in another woman's presence without having to say anything at all. The next time Norah seeks the solace of her forsaken garden, she sinks down gratefully into the chair webbing and says, "He likes the TV loud. I don't know when he started that."

Her neighbor glances at her, then continues pouring kelp water around the base of a tomato plant.

"That's how it was the night of the murder. When the lights came back on. The TV blasted us out of our skin."

Norah lays her head back. "He's been doing it since his father left."

Sand Williams sets down her trowel and looks at Norah, and Norah closes her eyes, begins to drift.

25

SHE'S BEEN DAYDREAMING and notices his shadow darken the grass before she hears his voice.

"You're not wanted here."

"Is that so?" Sand asks, kneeling beside the garden bed.

"Yes."

She turns to find Timothy holding a heavy ax in one of his stout fists. Her animal instinct advises her to stand, to appear larger than she seems when crouched low over the ground. She doesn't drop her trowel but keeps the small spade in hand.

Timothy frowns at her. "You shouldn't come around. You should go away."

"Well, Timothy, last I heard, there are still remnants of a free country here."

"You're on my land. I don't want you here. I'm the man now."

"Are you? Be that as it may, I think this is your mother's place. She'll have to ask me to leave."

"You are a disobedient woman."

"Yes. I am."

"Go away! You're bad."

"Tell, me," Sand says quietly. "Why am I bad?"

"Why? You worship the devil. You keep a dirty house. Maybe you killed my sister, I don't know."

She stares at him sharply. "Yes, you do."

"You sneak around here like a snake in the grass!" he says, flustered, brandishing the ax. "You don't wear a wedding ring, so you can go out with other men. You're a bad influence, a harlot."

"Watch it, young man."

"You're going to burn in hell."

"Timothy. Why are you holding an ax?"

He halts for a moment, stunned. "I came to chop the wood."

"Then go chop wood. Just don't do it behind my back."

He steps away from her but raises the ax once more to make his point. "Just stay away from us. We only want good Christians here."

Then, thankfully, he turns his back to her and begins to walk away, but she calls after him. "Timothy?"

He looks over his shoulder and regards her with a scowl. "Yes?"

"What if God is *bigger* than that?"

26

A PATH LEADS to a bluff above the river where Timothy sometimes liked to sit, but he has cared nothing for the grounds since the murder. He has not even gone swimming, so it seems strange to see him coming back from his secret place. Timothy walks in the side door while Norah stands at the kitchen sink, swallowing her afternoon pills.

"Oh. Hi, Mom."

"I had a thought. Why don't you drag a lawn chair down to the riverbank for me to sit, and you can take a swim."

"In the river?"

"Well, of course, silly. Where else?"

"I don't really want to, Mom."

"You don't? In this heat? It's been long enough. I think we can resume some of our activities."

"I'm going to Pastor John's later on."

"Why don't you like the river anymore?"

"I don't know. I just have other things."

"You used to love the river. That's where you

learned to swim. Taking a dip certainly would be better than watching TV."

"But my shows are on," he protests. "I came in to watch."

He turns on the TV, and the volume blossoms like some monstrous flower. Norah grips the lip of the sink. "For heaven's sakes, keep it down!" He's not even listening. My God, shouldn't she have some rights in this house, shouldn't some deference be shown? She feels her way toward the living room, touching the cabinets for balance, taking hold of the counter island and then the lintel of the door. Already his face has taken on that rapt, glazed look she finds so annoying. His lips part, he breathes through his mouth. "Timothy—" She's seen this look of rapture on his face in church. "Son!"

"Wha-at?" Reluctantly, with a trace of irritation, he turns away from the screen.

"Keep it down."

"It is down. It's not at the top."

"You are blasting me out of my noggin. Have you no concern for me at all? I almost died! Part of my heart died."

"Well, what about me? Why can't I have anything that I want?"

"Listen to yourself."

"Listen to yourself," he says, mouthing back at her. "You talk to Dad, and he goes away." Norah continues to inch her way across the living room. "I don't think you do a very good job, Mom."

In that moment her son so infuriates her that she drags herself to the sofa, leans over his supine figure, and raises her palm as though she is contemplating a blow to his head.

"Now, turn it down, like I asked you to!"

His eyes flash, then he sits up and thrusts his lower lip into a pout. He punches the volume down to eighteen, and Norah feels a heaving breathlessness, like a fish thrown up on the bank. Her body has turned into a sodden rag.

"I'm going to lie down."

She heads for her bedroom at the end of the hall. She does not ask for his aid. Instead, she feels along the walls to hold herself up.

By the time she reaches her bed, she's so exhaused, she collapses in fatigue. Her feelings about him are so bruised. She expected he would tend to her with at least the care he gave to the linoleum floor of their church, but instead Timothy resents her for failing to be his mother the way she was before. It doesn't occur to him to make a sandwich for her. She nearly died, and he wants to know what's for supper, just as he always has, but it's the church women who can answer such questions for him now.

She feels such a hollowness. When she thinks of her husband, she grieves more for the complete loss of her role in life than for the man himself. Even before Dahlia's murder the marriage was slowly souring, becoming something less than what she had expected it to be. Their children fought all the time—they didn't like the new arrangement. They didn't want this change. Norah even felt jealous of the hours that Lyman spent alone with his daughter. Some mornings when Lyman and Dahlia fished on the riverbank, Norah watched them resentfully while she stood at the sink and did the washing up from breakfast. She never showed her feelings, she is sure of that. She always tried to be helpful and would bring them glasses of lemonade, stand between them, engage one or the other in some discussion of minor details about the day ahead, instead of leaving them to what they were doing, which was being alone together.

Church sustained her, for here she discovered that any criticism she felt about the girl was justified. Dahlia would not even acknowledge the church's authority, while Timothy thrived within the structure of the church. Her son's faith was as good as anyone's. For years it was simply enough to feel superior to the other half of the family, but now everything Norah once felt is gone. She can't even look at her son in the same way. He irritates her now. She watches him basking in the attention of the visiting church women and understands that she has fallen in his eyes. She has failed to keep his father in the house. She wasn't enough, even a heart attack wasn't enough to bring Lyman back, and Timothy, she feels, blames her. This is the second father he has lost on account of her.

It must be something she has done or failed to do, for fathers' leaving just isn't right.

Later the TV awakens her in bed, and she thinks: *He wouldn't have dared do this when Lyman lived here.*

A tear of frustration leaks from one eye.

This is how Dahlia felt. Wanting to sleep and not being allowed to sleep.

She wasn't even a true believer. She wasn't one of us.

———

HER BEDROOM FLOOR is striped by moonlight falling through the slats of the blinds, as if night has left her behind bars. It occurs to Norah that if she doesn't leave the room right away, she soon won't be able to. The bars will cross the doorway, and there'll be no escaping then. Norah drags herself to the door, then looks down the hall to Timothy's room. He has left his door open, as usual, as if to say, *See, I have nothing to hide.*

He breathes evenly, with a slightly ragged snore, and in his arms he hugs a careworn, matted teddy bear whose ear he chewed on back in kindergarten. She takes hold of his shoulder, jostles Timothy until he moans and opens his eyes.

"We have to go over it. The night your sister was killed."

"Oh, what does it matter now?"

"It matters, because I have to make decisions."

He thrusts his teddy bear aside, then rubs sand from one eye like a little boy and stares up at her with the other eye. "Mom, it's still dark. It's not even breakfast yet."

His Bible is lying on the nightstand. Norah picks up the Bible and hefts its weight in her palm. "You just forget about eating right now. Give me your hand."

"Why?"

"I am your mother and you will do what I say."

Timothy watches the Bible in her hands; his eyes go wide with fear. "But what do you have that for?"

Norah clutches his large blunt fingers and forces them against the black leather of the Bible's cover. "You tell me what happened that night. The truth."

"Why are you doing this? I already told them it was a burglar or some maniac."

"But now you'll tell me, and you'll tell God, and if you lie, you'll go to hell and be consumed in hell's fire."

"Mom!"

She clasps his palm to the holy book. "Where are the clothes you lost on the day she died?"

"I don't think I want to answer any of your questions, Mom. I've already answered their questions again and again. This is all in the past, and I have to put the past behind me. Pastor John says I'm a model young man. I do not have temptations like the other boys."

"What on earth are you talking about?"

"Some girls give you impure thoughts. A model young man has to be strong, or they'll make you sin."

"Timothy, either you will answer me with your hand on the Bible or you will not be my son anymore. I will cast you out. You came home after school. Then what?"

Timothy stares at her, aghast, and Norah realizes that finally she has frightened him.

"Tell me."

"I–I came home from school. I turned on the TV. Then I made cookies. That's all."

"The TV woke her, didn't it? Just the way it wakes me up. She yelled at you to turn the volume down."

"She called me names—bad names! Then she turned off the TV, and that just made me mad."

"So you turned it back on, didn't you? And made it even louder."

"Why does she get to tell me when I can watch TV? She's always telling me what to do, and I don't want to do what she says. I made it louder, because that's the way I like to watch. Then Dahlia yanked the TV cord from the wall. She started it. You don't pull it by the cord. You have to take hold of the plug, or you can ruin a TV cord. She was yelling and screaming, and all I was doing was watching TV!

"She kicked me in the leg. She cursed and blasphemed our Lord's name. She said I was stupid! I just wanted to teach her a lesson. So I went to the kitchen and I got the bread knife. That's not even a serious knife. It's only any good for cutting bread—that shows I didn't mean anything bad. I was just so mad, I ran to her bedroom. I jumped on her and she fell back against the bed and I . . . just cut her once. Here," he says, touching his own throat. "Just a little cut, but it was bleeding everywhere."

"Oh, Jesus . . ." Norah takes hold of the bedpost to steady herself.

"I didn't know what to do! I couldn't let her suffer. I wouldn't even let a squirrel suffer. I tried stabbing her in the ribs, but that bread knife's not a very good knife, so I had to go and get a better knife with a sharper blade."

"But why?" Norah whispers in a strangled voice.

"Because that's what you do. When you shoot a squirrel in the woods and it doesn't die right away, you have to put it out of its misery. She was suffering, Mom. I was trying to help her out, but she kept fighting me.

"We fell on the floor. She shrieked and made this awful glug-glug noise, and her blood was flying everywhere. So I sat on her and I kept using the knife until she stopped fighting me and she kind of fell asleep. Then I cleaned up everything. I didn't want you and Dad to see her that way. I made her nice again, because she was all dirty."

This is her son, her little boy. A boy who likes to make figures out of macaroni on his plate. "What have you done?" She grabs his large hand and squeezes tight. How is it possible that he has done this thing?

"It was a terrible mess. I thought about it, and then I took her to the tub. I made her nice. As nice as I could."

Norah says, choking, "You drained her—you drained her in the tub?"

Timothy blushes, then hesitates as if he's searching for a delicate way to put the facts to her.

"Everybody knows you have to drain a carcass, Mom. That's one of the first things you learn in hunting. If you shoot a deer, you have to hang it by a rope to do it right, and I couldn't do that. So I used the tub. That's the biggest drain in the house. I just sort of drained her in the tub. I didn't want to leave a mess. I cleaned up everything. I made the house spotless, like nothing happened at all, and she was just sleeping in her bed, all clean and in fresh pajamas. I got rid of all the bad things. I made her nice again."

"You hid the rags, the knives, all the evidence!"

"Well, I threw them in the river. I didn't want to get in trouble, Mom. I made the one mistake, but after that I tried to do everything right, the way you'd want me to."

Norah takes hold of his collar and yanks him close, staring into his baffled eyes. "You stabbed her twenty times!"

"But it isn't my fault! She wasn't dead. She was bleeding everywhere. I'm a good Christian young man. I wouldn't even let a squirrel suffer!"

"Oh, Jesus. Save me!" Norah calls out in a swoon. She lays her head upon his pillow, breathes in the sweet sour scent of her boy.

Finally he says in the gloom, "What are you going to do, Mom?"

"I don't know. I have to think."

What should she do with this issue of her womb? She's responsible, she brought him into the world. She has to take care of him.

"If you tell the police, it's just going to make more trouble, and people will be mad at me. You don't have to tell anyone."

"I know," she says, whispering in a blur of tears. "I know. I'll think about what's best. You told me the truth, and you're still my son. I have to decide what to do." Norah feels the softness of his hair beneath her palm. She strokes his head. God, she has loved this head. "Why don't you go back to sleep or watch a little TV. I'll call you when it's time for breakfast. I need to think. We'll have something special, like pancakes or waffles. What do you say? I believe I'm up to it."

"That would be good, Mom," and she sees the relish in his eyes, like the eyes of a faithful dog.

———

THE DECISION COMES to Norah in the potting shed. She doesn't really remember how she got to the shed, but she must have wandered out in search of solitude and ended up inside, her fingers tracing over the powdery dust on the shelves. She finds herself scanning the boxes of poison and thinking she must protect him somehow. Protect him from the world. A little hill of Sevin dust is spilled beside the bag, and some unfortunate spider lies like a dried-up husk on the white powder. Rust and scale killer. Diazin for spreading on the ground for the ticks and chiggers. Rose spray. They didn't use any of it this year.

Does she have any pills? She could use pills; she doesn't want him to suffer. There's still some Valium that was prescribed for Lyman. Once Timothy fell asleep, she could decide what to do next. Or her heart medication—perhaps if she ground up enough of that . . . but she wants to go with him, be at his side through whatever it would be, and if they take the Valium, it might not be enough to kill them both. Whatever it is has to work. And fast. But won't poison be painful? Oh, she cannot do this thing, but she can't turn him over to the state. What would happen to a boy like Timothy? Prison. How would he survive?

A little later she is stirring a pan of blackberry syrup on the stove. The blackberries were frozen, and the chunks slowly melt in the pan. She dumps in two cups of sugar, thinking: *Even if it tastes a little strange, as long as it is very sweet, he will eat it happily.* Pancakes are sizzling on the grill, making little sinkholes in the dough to signal the cakes are ready to be turned. Norah flips the pancakes shakily but admires their perfectly golden brown skins and feels a silly sense of pride in her cooking. She hasn't made pancakes in . . . well, not since. Before.

She turns off the burner under the saucepan and makes sure

he's fully occupied watching TV, then she spills the white powder into the syrup and rapidly whisks with a wooden spoon. Norah dips her finger into dark purple syrup, notes how nicely it coats her fingertip. She slips her finger between her lips and sucks. The acrid bitterness makes her wince. Now what? More sugar and vanilla.

"I sure like it when you make things special for me, Mom."

"Oh, there you are," she calls. "I'm making my special syrup with our own blackberries." Timothy starts to reach for the pan and she swats his hand away. "Don't spoil your appetite. I want you to be hungry when you get your meal."

The warm sweetness of pancakes fills the kitchen like sunshine. She tells her son they'll eat breakfast and then they'll decide what to do. It's hard to think on an empty stomach. Timothy sits at the table waiting to be fed. He tells her that he's planning to go to the church today, to polish the hallway for Pastor John, and then in the after-noon there's his youth studies group. He's no longer as frightened as he was earlier. He feels she's going to protect him somehow.

"You know what you did was wrong. What you did to your sister was a terrible, terrible crime."

Timothy's thick eyebrows furl and a little whine escapes from his pouting lips. "I just made the one mistake," he whispers, trying to placate her. "The first time I stabbed her, that was a mistake, but the other times were to make up for that mistake."

"If you had just stopped—" Norah whirls away from her son. She looks out the kitchen window over the sink, and it is then she sees her neighbor in the garden, the crown of her head rising above the ruff of grass. That mop of auburn hair hits her like a blow to the gut. Somehow the last thing she expected was for her neighbor to be out there now, at this critical moment in time, but there she is, kneeling over the bed, weeding with a small hand trowel. Norah takes a breath and piles hot pancakes onto her son's plate. She is not even aware that she has stopped breathing, only that she is remaining in control, doing the things that she must do. As she hands her son the plate, he looks up to her with big, soulful eyes, and her heart is wrenched. "I love you so much," she whispers shakily. "I've always loved you. You're my golden boy."

Timothy begins to butter each cake individually. He is thorough and detailed at the butter work and likes to spread the softened butter all the way to the rim of each pancake so everything is equal. The work is very orderly, and Norah wonders: if he is so neat about buttering hotcakes, why is he so sloppy at carpentry or whittling a cross with a knife? You'd think if the instinct for neatness was there in him, it would come out in all his activities—equally. The way he butters his pancakes. The way he cleaned . . .

"I knew you would understand, Mom."

Norah leans against the kitchen sink, feeling the cool porcelain against her belly, her gaze rising to Sand Williams's head above the long grass. She has gotten used to her neighbor being there and not having to say anything. Just watching her and not having to speak. No defenses. No explanations. Just her silent presence nearby.

"I'm ready for the syrup now. I'm hungry like a horse!"

The morning sun hits Sand Williams's tousled hair in a corona of golden light that steals Norah's breath away.

Timothy says, "Dahlia wasn't really like us, Mom. She didn't believe in God like we do."

Norah shudders, her fingers lose all feeling, and the pitcher slides from her hand, cascades as if in slow motion to the floor, then shatters and seems to explode upward, splattering her legs, her dress. Like a vision sent to her to show the way, that bright head of hair above the weeds draws her from the house. Dazed, she steps through the pool of berry syrup and the broken shards of white pottery. Her shoes leave dark blue prints across the pine floor of the living room. Out the door she goes, without thinking, traversing the yard as rapidly as her legs will carry her. She aims for that corona of bronzed light above her garden patch, her hand clutching her chest as if holding the seams of herself together like the edges of a bathrobe that falls open when she moves.

SAND WILLIAMS IS weeping as she drives. Norah cries in the backseat of her Buick, her arms wrapped tightly around her son. Norah doesn't think Timothy realizes the horror of what he's done, but he does understand he's going to be punished, and he's crying over that. *I'm a good boy,* he says, and now they're going to punish him for something he never meant to do.

He never meant to hurt Dahlia. He only wanted to teach her a lesson.

The road wobbles behind Norah's tears; a liquid light streams down through the trees. Dahlia had fought for her life. Furious that she was going to die and had lived so little, really. What did she know? Nothing. Nothing. She weighed 120 pounds, he weighed 190. Unfair . . . that he was so much bigger. She screamed and fought, and the rain consumed her wails of agony. It must have seemed there was no God except the one who had forsaken her, and there it would end in death, while the drama of life carried on in her wake.

Norah moans in the backseat, holding Timothy's head to her breast. Once, she looks up and meets Sand's eyes in the rearview mirror, and they exchange a glance that neither one can name.

Norah feels that all she has left in the world will be gone at the end of this ride.

After that. She cannot imagine what life will be after that.

When they reach the sheriff's department, Norah cannot move. *When people die, is this what it's like? This terror of the threshold between life and death?* She and Timothy wail at the sight of the old brick building. Norah's awash in tears. She has always feared that once she started bawling, she wouldn't be able to stop. All the life inside her would drain from her body, and she'd be left a dry husk. Then the sheriff steps out the front door and stands there, waiting.

Sand turns around, leans over the front seat. "Do you want me to come in?"

"No," she says coldly.

An hour later Norah returns to the backseat and slams the door. "Take me home. I'll stay here. I don't want to talk."

SAND PULLS INTO Norah's drive, turns off the ignition, and sits there quietly. Norah watches a blue heron glide along the river, its shadow moving downstream.

Finally Norah says, "I was going to kill him. Kill both of us."

"Norah . . ."

"If he had just stopped!"

Norah stares at her hands in her lap. She has taken off her wedding ring, but a white band of flesh remains on her finger. In another season this reminder will also fade. Why does she feel she can tell Sand Williams what is most awful in her, all the things she has tried to hide from other people?

"He begged me not to tell, and I didn't *want* to tell! Then I saw your head above the weeds—the way the sunlight caught your hair—it looked like flames. I was so shocked that the pitcher dropped from my hand, and I started running. I told you."

27

ONE DAY IN late October Patti pulls up to her bungalow and sees a truck parked in front of her house. She turns into her driveway as Lyman Everston steps down from her porch, and something quickens in her chest. She closes the car door quietly. They meet on the flagstones crossing the grass like a stream. Lyman doesn't look quite as gaunt as he did at the courthouse, but emptied out. More gray streaks in his hair than when she saw him last.

At Timothy's arraignment the bereaved father and Deputy Callahan exchanged a solemn nod. Patti noticed that Norah and Lyman sat on opposite sides of the courtroom. Afterward, the parents spoke together in the lobby, but neither showed up for the sentencing, when Timothy made his allocution of guilt to the judge. Timothy craned his head around the courtroom, looking for his parents, and found he was alone.

"How are you doing?" Patti says. "Are you all right?"

"I came to thank you. For everything you did. You and the sheriff, getting him to confess."

"It was Norah who brought him in."

Lyman nods slowly, taking this in, then burrows his hands into his jeans pockets and shifts his weight from one leg to the other.

"I see."

Patti and Tom Gravette both heard Timothy confess that he stabbed his sister to death, but when they came out of the interrogation room, they didn't agree on what had been said. The sheriff shook his head sadly. "His being slow and all. Almost makes you feel sorry for him."

"Yeah. I saw. You got a little misty there."

"An argument gone bad. Sure got out of hand, didn't it? I don't believe he would hurt a squirrel."

"But she wasn't a squirrel, Tom. That's the point."

"Jesus, you're testy. What is it, your time of month? You should be happy. This case is done."

"What makes him so different from that psycho Howard Lampe? He drained his sister like a deer carcass!"

"Timothy ain't no Howard Lampe! He's just a retarded kid. We've never had any trouble with Timothy Everston. Dahlia and him had a combustible relationship—they fought and it got out of hand. I'm damn sure he'd never kill anyone again."

"I'm not. You really think he wasn't in a frenzy every time that knife sank into her?"

"He just wanted the girl to stop bleeding."

"That's not what you said before—you said it had to be sexual."

"Well, I heard his story and I changed my mind. What's the matter with you?"

Patti clears her throat.

Lyman has dark circles under his eyes. Grief's gauntness hangs over him like a shroud. "Does it help?" Patti says.

"I don't know," he says with a shrug. "But it had to be. Judge gave him seven years. He'll be out in three. Not sure how I feel about that."

Patti nods in agreement. Her cat, Noodles, has spotted them from the fence line and is slinking across the grass. Noodles pads over, leans up against her leg, then rubs his wet snout across her calf.

"I just wanted to thank you and the sheriff for taking care of this. You don't have anything to do with the sentencing."

"No," Patti says. "We don't."

Noodles winds back and forth between her legs, and finally Lyman glances down at Patti's feet. "Who's this?"

"This is Noodles."

"Well . . ." he says, letting his voice trail off. He gazes at his truck parked on the curb. "Well . . ."

A few leaves fall with a gentle gust of air. Golden brown, they make the sound of dry husks as they tumble across the drive.

"You want to come inside? Have a glass of iced tea?"

"You asking me in?"

"It's daylight," Patti says.

He takes a long, deep breath and slowly nods. "Okay. I could drink some tea."

Patti leads Lyman through the living room of her house, and he admires the craftsman bungalow. He calls her house a gem. And everything is in its place. The wood gleams; dust does not mar any surface in her house. "Take a seat," she says, nodding at the two rocking chairs pulled up to the kitchen table. He sits down and the rockers squeak beneath his weight. She hefts a pitcher of tea from the fridge. "Stevia okay with you? I'm kind of on a diet here."

Lyman nods absently, then runs his fingers back through his gray-streaked hair. A long strand falls from the rubber band fastening his hair to the base of his skull. He watches her over the rims of his glasses and sighs. "This is pretty awkward, isn't it?"

"Yeah. That's the way things are sometimes. It's okay with me."

"If I ever did anything I shouldn't have . . . With you, I mean. I want to apologize."

"Oh, that."

Patti blushes, and the most beautiful roseate glow suffuses her porcelain skin. She has a lovely bone structure, a clean-lined jaw, and her flush seeps down her smooth, pale throat and into the V collar of her white shirt. "You were under a lot of stress. People do all kinds of things we have to deal with. It's just part of our job. It wasn't personal." Lyman gazes into her eyes. His green eyes, flecked with amber and gray, are rimmed with dark eyelashes, and there's something sensual about his mouth. She feels as if the molecules inside her are beginning to shift about, and she has to admit she's attracted to this long-haired carpenter from a "foreign land." There's really nothing she can do about that now. But she knew that when she asked him in. "It's not, is it?"

Staring at her, he slowly sets his glass of tea on a woven place mat. "Not what?" he says, as if he's coming back from being lost in thought.

"Personal."

"Of course it's personal."

"Oh."

This exchange causes her to flush again.

"It felt personal," he says, lowering his eyes. "It shouldn't have been. But it felt personal. As if we knew each other very well. But we don't. I know that."

"No. We don't know each other at all," Patti says, wrapping her hands around the soothing coldness of the sweating glass.

"Did it feel personal to you?"

"It was very unusual. It would be hard to explain. Like I wasn't really solid, and, as you can see, I am."

"I think you're beautiful."

She pushes the glass away, wipes off her damp hands on her jeans. "It was hard to be around you after that."

"And you know I do. You know it."

She can think of nothing to say to this. In the silence that pools about them she notices the ticking of the oven clock. Sometimes she regards that ticking as a low, pestering noise, an insistent message that she's losing out, time's running out, not enough time, and this external reminder that her reproductive years are running down makes her anxious and annoyed. But now that simple rhythm seems to bloom, and she thinks maybe it's slowing down, or she has stepped into it and is inhabiting the sound; she's deep inside of it. What she's hearing is the sound of her own heart beating, the quiet percussion of her blood pulsing in her veins. And there's nothing to question, nothing beyond this slow, delicious stretching out of time in which she is fully present. And knowing this can't last. That whatever is now will become something else.

"Have I offended you?"

"Not really," Patti says, and another petal of rose salmon spreads across a spot on the upper right side of her throat and seems to beat of its own accord. Lyman's gaze falls to that throbbing spot. He lifts one hand and she knows he wants to touch her there, to feel her pulse lightly beating under his fingertips. His hand moves slowly upward; two fingers touch his lips. He tilts back in his chair.

"Rocking chairs at the table. I like that. It's unusual."

"Not if you're from the hills."

"A table's not just for eating at?"

"No," Patti says. "I mean, people always end up at the kitchen table."

"They do."

Now there is nothing more to say. She can think of nothing to advance this conversation further. She feels ground down to speechlessness. A temporary stupidity, a kind of paralysis. The oven clock is ticking very loudly now, and she can't make it stop. It feels so intimate, the ticking of that infernal clock.

Lyman takes a long drink of her tea, then wipes his lips with two fingers of a contemplative hand.

"I read in the newspaper. How you broke that old murder case."

"Natalie Barson."

"Yes," he says. "A girl named Natalie Barson."

"She died in 1984."

"I think I know what it meant to that girl's family."

Patti nods. She remembers the clang of a cell door, the brittle laughter of the guard walking away, leaving her locked in with a maniac who likes to kill women. Patti raises the cold glass to her forehead, holds it there, and briefly shuts her eyes. "I got lucky. He was ready to confess, and I showed up."

"Well," Lyman says, "you showed up. That case was long forgot. By everybody but the Barson family. They were still waiting to know what happened to their girl. Well, I can tell you, Patti, that knowing is awful. But not knowing is even worse."

"Maybe now—you and Norah . . ."

Lyman slowly shakes his head.

They sit without speaking. Noodles pads into the kitchen, then sits at the base of Lyman's rocker and peers up at the guest. Noodles crouches, then leaps onto the table, strolls over, and rubs his snout against Lyman's glass.

Patti says, "You can throw him off the table, but he'll jump back up again."

Lyman begins to stroke Noodles' back. Patti watches his fingers wrap over the cat's spine. He makes long, even strokes from Noodles' large head to his tail. The cat purrs and slowly the tight lines on Lyman's face begin to soften. Patti feels a quiet peacefulness suffusing through her chest. It's the strangest, lovely feeling, and she wonders if she just sits quietly, whether he will feel it, too.

"I won't be a decent man for a long, long time."

"You're already a decent man," she says.

"You know what I mean."

He looks into her eyes, and she does know what he means. They rest on this plateau where time seems to slow down and whatever will happen between them hasn't quite begun. Some sturdy wall in her chest is dissolving back to sand and water. And what will be most difficult between them lies in the future yet. No one can say they are cowards, and she feels that she might be able to trust in his gentleness.

One day she knows she will open to him. She will be like water; he will plow her warm seas. His sad, insistent seed will swim into the furthest crannies of her, seek out every part of her to know, and she will hold him with a silken gratitude. Maybe it has already begun. That warm loosening of her limbs.

"Patti?"

"Yes?"

"I feel like I know you—it's strange."

"You don't know anything about me," Patti says in a husky voice.

"Yes, I do. I know some things."

"Maybe," she says.

He leans forward over the table. "Tell me something I don't know."

She feels strangely comfortable sitting in the kitchen with this man. Patti remembers parking her red convertible on the beach at Santa Cruz and walking barefoot over the hot sand.

"I saw the ocean out there—for the first time."

Lyman watches her, a half smile rising to his lips. "How was it?"

"It was beautiful," Patti says. "It was big."

28

I TOLD HER things I didn't tell other people, Norah thinks. How odd, this friendship that has bloomed. They are nothing alike. The things that bothered Norah about her neighbor have not changed, and yet they don't seem to bother her so much. What does she care about how Sand Williams keeps her house? Can cleanliness protect us from anything but the common cold? *If a great flood comes, my house will go the same as hers. I found her so annoying, and yet it was only to her that I could speak. Why is that?* Norah wonders.

After Timothy confessed, Norah went to stay with her pastor and his wife. They opened their house to her, and for a couple of weeks she slept on one of the twin beds in the guest room, where a cross of Jesus bleeding to death was tacked to the wall above her head. She sat on the plaid spread and felt she had a greater understanding of His suffering.

Norah's pastor was undergoing such shock, such disbelief, that Norah felt she should look after him.

"Are you all right?" she asked Pastor John.

He sat at the kitchen table, his fingertips resting upon his eyelids. "I'm having a hard time understanding this. A boy like that . . . It must have been self-defense."

Norah thought to herself: *How do you go on from here? Everyone else will go on. And I'll either be here or I won't.*

The church ladies came and went, but their kindness seemed too polite, stilted by unease. *They don't know how to behave around me anymore,* Norah thought. *They're fighting their own revulsion, for I am his mother. I brought a killer into this world.* She felt the women were trying not to hate her, not to think of her as unclean, for she shaped the boy who picked up the knife and stabbed his stepsister twenty times.

He wasn't free of temptation or greed. Pastor John was wrong about that.

She knew she would have to leave her church. Her pastor would come to resent her for letting the boy confess.

One of the ladies touched her arm. "Norah, dear? You need to eat. Would you like some cake? It's red velvet cake."

Norah shook her head no. She felt like an alien among them. She had no desire for food, and there was something awful about a red velvet cake—as if the cake itself had been soaked in blood.

But Sand Williams would understand. Though they cannot agree on much of anything, Norah knows her neighbor understands her horror at the sight of a red velvet cake. And she won't tell Norah not to be silly, that it is only red dye number forty. No, they meet in a place inside them where they can feel compassion for the other one who seems so strange and yet somehow oddly familiar. So familiar, they know each other's heart.

I tell her things I don't tell other people, Norah thinks, *because she understands my disgust for red velvet cake.*

Norah knows this is true because one day when they are sitting by the river, Sand Williams says, "I swam in her blood. Last summer, I must have. I think about that sometimes, how she is remembered by the water. That's why you wanted to kill yourself in the river. You've always been drawn to the truth. The way you were drawn to her room."

Sand sits on her haunches over the gravel bar, her hands sifting through the river stones. She picks out a flat stone the size of a tea saucer and sends it across the river so it skips against the water's surface three times before it sinks. Idly Norah lets her hand drop from the aluminum armrest of her camping chair and feel among the stones. She picks one and flings her arm back to skip it, but the stone plops heavily into the stream.

"It wasn't flat," Sand says quietly, then leans forward, her knees pressing onto the river stones. "We'll find one for you."

"I was never good at these things. I always threw like a girl."

Strangely, this causes her neighbor to laugh, and Norah feels her own mood lighten. Sand searches among the stones for a flat rock for Norah Everston.

"Here, woman. Throw like a woman."

Norah flings the stone, and it flies on a curve above the river, hits a tree trunk on the far bank, then bounces back over the stream with remarkable force, skips twice, and drops into the water with a splash.

"That's not bad," Sand Williams says.

"I wonder how long it takes a pebble to be ground to sand."

"A long time. These rocks will be here longer than we are."

All through the winter she stood on the cold riverbank when the water ran dark and clear. She could look into the water and not fantasize about hooking her son's hand weights to her belt. This, too, seems strange, for nothing is better. There is no going back to the way things were before. Dahlia's gone, and she will always be gone. Norah and Lyman are finished. Their divorce will be finalized in a few months' time. Timothy is in a correctional facility, perhaps for as long as seven years. Sometimes she feels guilty about what may be happening to her son. Most of all, she feels guilty that she can't face seeing him.

In the spring Norah begins attending another church in town, but some days she walks to the river's edge and talks to her soul.

"It's not listening," Norah tells Sand one afternoon.

They are weeding her neighbor's garden, which is in great need of weeding. A family of bunnies nibbles contentedly on her neighbor's lawn, just feet away from the garden bed. Norah finds her gaze resting on the rabbits without judging them for wanting to eat.

"It will," Sand says. "That part of you isn't used to being loved."

Norah tosses her spade to the dirt. "I can't go visit him. I haven't gone yet. Not once! I'm so ashamed. I feel full of loathing and hate."

Norah's new pastor says that anger is a part of grief, but she does not know how to go on.

Sand says, "Wait. One day it'll feel right to see him again."

"And what if it doesn't?"

"Then one day you will accept that and be able to let go."

That spring Norah looks older, and Sand does, too. They take a walk in the woods across the river and come upon a grove of bloodroot flowers. The beautiful white flowers each have one leaf curled around their stem. The white petals seem to be floating above last year's dead leaves on the forest floor. Sand kneels down and breaks a stem. Red sap beads from the end and drips upon her fingertips. At the sight of blood staining her neighbor's hands, Norah sinks to the ground and begins to weep. She weeps for a girl she never quite liked, and then she weeps for Sand.

"I never thought about what it was like for you."

Norah drags herself up on her elbows, sniffling, and looks at the white flowers of the bloodroot moving gently on the breeze.

"Look," Sand whispers. "Do you see?"

"Yes."

It's as though the individual petals are dancing on the air. Behind the blur of Norah's tears the white bloodroot flowers gently sway, as if this is their way of speaking to the wind. As if nature itself longs to comfort her. Distract her from sorrow, comfort Norah with the passion of what is beautiful.

A Note to the Reader

THE SEEDS OF this novel were first planted in me several years ago by news reports recounting the killing of a teenage girl in her home in a nearby county. The girl was found lying dead in her bed by her younger teenage brother, who had been watching TV. Their parents were out of town. There were no signs of forcible entry or sexual assault, and robbery was ruled out as a motive. After an extended investigation the brother was indicted for voluntary manslaughter. According to authorities, the girl's death occurred in the course of a fight between the siblings and was not intentional.

This novel takes the bare-bone outlines of that incident as the jumping-off point for a work of fiction. All of the names, characters, and surrounding events portrayed, including the character Dahlia, her family members, neighbors, and officials involved in the criminal investigation, are products of my imagination. They do not, and are not intended to, portray real persons or events.